HOOK'S REVENGE

THE PIRATE CODE

W9-COI-980

Also by Heidi Schulz

Hook's Revenge

THE PIRATE CODE

by **HEIDI SCHULZ**

with illustrations by **JOHN HENDRIX**

Disney • HYPERION

LOS ANGELES   NEW YORK

If you purchased this book without a cover, you should be aware that this book is stolen property. It was reported as "unsold and destroyed" to the publisher, and neither the author nor the publisher has received any payment for this "stripped" book.

Text copyright © 2015 by Heidi Schulz
Illustrations copyright © 2015 by John Hendrix

All rights reserved. Published by Disney•Hyperion, an imprint of Disney Book Group. No part of this book may be reproduced or transmitted in any form or by any means, electronic or mechanical, including photocopying, recording, or by any information storage and retrieval system, without written permission from the publisher. For information address Disney•Hyperion, 125 West End Avenue, New York, New York 10023-6387.

Printed in the United States of America
First Hardcover Edition, September 2015
First Paperback Edition, September 2016
10 9 8 7 6 5 4 3 2 1
FAC-025438-16211

Library of Congress Control Number for Hardcover: 2014049766
ISBN 978-1-4847-2369-2
Visit www.DisneyBooks.com

SUSTAINABLE
FORESTRY
INITIATIVE

Certified Chain of Custody
Promoting Sustainable Forestry

www.sfiprogram.org
SFI-01054
The SFI label applies to the text stock

To my mom and dad,
and the children they once were

CONTENTS

Secret Burdens

Secrets are tricky things. For many years, I was one of the few who knew about Captain Hook's daughter, Jocelyn, and the way she succeeded in avenging him upon the Neverland's monstrous crocodile. I held that knowledge close to my chest, gripping it tight as a new puppy, though at times the story wriggled and nipped, desperate to be put down.

There came a point where the burden grew too heavy. I thought that telling the world about the girl and her heroic victory would allow me some measure of relief, but it would not do. I have merely exchanged one affliction for another. Since I last had the misfortune of speaking to you, I am followed by throngs of children wherever I go. They reach for me with sticky hands, plead with lips stained by sweets, and constantly fill my ears with their unceasing, high-pitched refrain: "What happened next? Did Jocelyn find Hook's treasure?"

Even now, here you sit with your scabbed-over knees and insipid smile, waiting for me to tell you the tale. Without any effort, I can think of a dozen more pleasant ways to rid myself of your presence—ways that reduce you to nothing more than a stain and a memory—but still the remaining secrets I carry would demand to be released. And so, for my own sake, I must continue down this path and see it through to the bitter end.

It is true that Jocelyn's adventures did not end with the killing of the crocodile, nor with the return of her lost boy. There is more to be told. Much more.

Let's get this over with.

CHAPTER ONE

*In Which Our Heroine Asks,
"What Could Go Wrong?"*

There are many wonderful things about gold. The way it shines, the cool feel of it in one's hands, the sweet cries of those from whom you have stolen it... As far as I am concerned, there is only one undesirable thing about gold: not having enough of it.

Jocelyn was sorely feeling that one bad thing as she counted the remaining pieces of eight her father had left her. There were pitifully few, especially compared to the long list of needed supplies Mr. Smee had given her that morning.

She brushed the coins back into their bag with an irritated swipe of her hand. If only she could go after her father's treasure! It had been weeks since she killed the

Neverland's crocodile and found her father's iron hook in its remains. A hollow section of the hook had held a key to a locked box Captain Hook left in her possession—and within that box had lain a map to his vast treasure hoard.

It was rumored to be the greatest cache of treasure known to man, and Jocelyn felt anxious to find it. With even a portion of that gold, the girl would be captain of her own destiny. She wished that Mr. Smee, loyal bo'sun to both herself and her father before her, knew more about it, but Hook had never shown him the site of the treasure. Indeed, he had rarely even spoken of it to Smee—other than to tell the man that it was none of his business.

Jocelyn set aside the bag of coins and turned her attention to the map spread out before her on the writing desk. She brought her nose close to the paper and squinted but it did no good. The map would share none of its secrets.

A knock at her cabin door startled her. "Who is it?" the girl called, rather more gruffly than she intended.

"Roger Redbeard! Terror of the seven seas!"

Jocelyn flung open her door. Standing on the deck outside was a brown-skinned, curly-haired boy, who in just the last few weeks seemed to have passed her in height—though certainly not by much.

"Roger Redbeard, indeed? You look more like Roger

One-Whisker to me!" Her face broke into a grin, and she admitted the boy into her cabin.

"Really? I have a whisker?" Roger exclaimed, crossing to examine his face in the mirror.

"No. Not really." She giggled, feeling much happier than she had a few moments before. Roger always seemed to have that effect on her. She peeked over his shoulder, looking at his reflection. "I think that may be a bit of breakfast on your chin."

"No matter. One day it will be a full beard. You can't very well stop time." He turned to face her, pretending to stroke an impressively long beard. "I'll have more whiskers than Gerta!"

Jocelyn pictured the ruddy, stubbled face of the maidservant she had been inflicted with at finishing school, before they came to the Neverland. "It is good to have ambitions," she said with a wink.

Roger gave a gentle tug to one of her curls. "Speaking of which"—he motioned to the map, unfolded on her desk—"still trying to make it spill its secrets?"

Jocelyn became very interested in a loose thread on her sleeve. "No," she mumbled. "Maybe."

The boy stepped toward the map, bending over to take a closer look. Jocelyn followed the movement of his eyes, knowing exactly what they would see. One large corner contained the edge of a landmass bordered by ocean.

The rest was a mess of squiggles and symbols, presumably coordinates and instructions, written in some kind of code. A code *without* a key. Roger, Jocelyn, and all the crew—with the obvious exception of Blind Bart—had each tried to crack it, to no avail.

Even though she knew it was of no use, the girl couldn't help but continue to stare at the map, hoping to find a clue she might have missed. There was something familiar about the bit of ragged coastline and the small river—or was it a creek?—penned on the page, but she couldn't place it. The Neverland changed so much and so often that even if she were to recognize the place, it certainly wouldn't look the same now. Without instructions, the adventure was over before it could properly begin.

"Any word from Smee's mapmaker acquaintance?" Roger asked.

"Not yet. I sent Meriwether again this morning to see if he has come back."

The pirate village boasted a single mapmaker. Mr. Smee had suggested that the former Captain Hook might have employed him in the creation of the treasure map. If that was the case, the mapmaker was almost certain to know how to break the code. Jocelyn and Roger, with the help of a generous sprinkling of fairy dust, had flown into the pirate village under cover of darkness. Unfortunately, the pair had found his shop dark and shuttered, a sign on the door stating that the man was off on his annual kraken hunt and pillaging trip. There was no indication as to when he might return. Every few days Jocelyn sent Meriwether off to see if the mapmaker had come back, but as of yet, luck was against them.

Without any hope of breaking the code, Jocelyn's dreams of hunting for her father's treasure were becalmed as surely as a ship without wind. She had tried to take her mind off her frustrations by practicing her flying and exploring the island with Roger. They spent days in daring Neverland pursuits: hunting for bluecaps in an abandoned diamond mine, saying increasingly bad words in an attempt to summon Bloody Bones, and forcing an eyeless ghost to tell their futures. (Which was less exciting than it might sound. Their futures, as told, were rather mundane. To Roger: "Tomorrow you will spill juice in your lap." To Jocelyn: "You will fall asleep reading two nights this week.") Amusing as they were, those diversions were no longer helping. She wanted—no, *needed*—to go after the treasure.

A ringing bell interrupted her thoughts. Meriwether was back!

Jocelyn and Roger dashed out to the deck to greet the little blue fairy. He stuck out his tongue and gave Roger a pinch on the ear before settling onto Jocelyn's shoulder.

"Meri," she scolded, "leave Roger alone."

The fairy prince gnashed his teeth at the boy.

Knowing from experience that it would be unlikely

to do much good, Jocelyn didn't waste time on further reprimands. "What did you learn?" she asked. "Is the mapmaker in?"

Fairy language is very different from that of humans. To the untrained ear, it sounds like nothing more than the tinkling of bells. However, the more time Jocelyn spent with the little creature, the more easily she understood him. She thought it might have been because she had nearly been a fairy herself, if only for one night.

Meriwether nodded and jingled affirmatively, indicating that he had seen the mapmaker.

"Really? Are you sure?" Roger asked.

The fairy ignored the boy's questions and began polishing the buttons on his autumn-leaf jacket.

Jocelyn shrugged, making the tiny man bob on her shoulders. "I'm sorry, Roger. It is really quite silly of him to be jealous. Meriwether"—she turned her head to face him—"are you quite certain?"

Again his bells rang in the affirmative.

"Mr. Smee!" Jocelyn called out. "Tell the crew to prepare the ship! We enter the pirate village tonight!"

There are times when the wisest course of action is to throw caution to the wind and follow your own counsel. Those were the only times Jocelyn cared about. She sat in the galley polishing her sword in preparation for the night's adventure.

Mr. Smee joined her. "Beggin' your pardon, Captain, but if you'd like to steer us into port yourself, you may want to take the wheel. Blind Bart says he can hear cussing and spitting about three miles off. We're nearly there."

Blind Bart was Jocelyn's lookout, but since he chose to cover both eyes with patches (as a way to avoid seeing the ocean he so greatly feared), he relied on his unusually honed sense of hearing.

"Thank you, Smee," Jocelyn replied. She stood.

"Miss?" he said, before she left. "I know we've been over this a time or two, but I wouldn't feel right if I didn't say it once more."

Jocelyn sighed. She knew what was coming.

From the moment she'd found the map, Mr. Smee had been as nervous as a lobster in a pot, waiting for Captain Krueger to attack.

In case your memory is as short as your stubby, child-size legs, I'll remind you about Krueger: The man was a dark and ruthless pirate, cursed with an insatiable desire for gold. He would do anything and harm anyone to collect it. He had even gone so far as to pull his own teeth for their gold fillings, replacing them with razor-sharp points plucked from the mouths of baby sharks.

"I don't think the men should be set loose on the village on their own." Smee said. "They aren't ready. And with that black-hearted rogue Krueger thirsting for blood and treasure, and seeing that you have an abundance of one and a map to the other, I . . . that is, Johnny Corkscrew and me"—he gave a loving pat to the sword strapped to his side—"we think it wise for you to keep your distance as well. I could nip down to the mapmaker's real quick-like and even have time to pick up some supplies. You an' the crew could wait here for me to return."

If Jocelyn were being honest, she would admit she wasn't quite eager to meet Krueger again. She had already had one run-in with him, and it had been more than enough. The man had viciously attacked her ship under the mere suspicion the girl might have information about Hook's gold. Jocelyn had only escaped his sword when she fell overboard.

However, abject honesty aboard a pirate ship—particularly about one's feelings—is about as useful as woolen socks for a wooden leg. Jocelyn gave Mr. Smee's suggestion the tiniest bit of consideration before tossing it over the railing.

"Thank you for your concern . . ." she began. Mr. Smee gave her a hurt look. How it pained him when she was polite. She softened her speech with a "You filthy dog!" and continued: ". . . but the crew will be fine. *I* will be fine. We'll be careful. What could go wrong?"

What indeed?

The girl stood proud at the wheel of the *Hook's Revenge*, executing an almost-perfect docking just outside the pirate village. (She was certain no one would miss the last six feet or so of dock, as it had been, in her opinion, far too long to begin with.) Before disembarking, she took a moment to survey the village spread out before her in the early evening light.

Little had changed since she first set eyes on it. The beach was still crowded with row upon row of weathered docking. The gulls still screamed their shrill screams. The air was still ripe with the scents of brine, unwashed men, blood, and rotgut grog. The pirate village was still a veritable bouillabaisse of piratical atmosphere, full to the brim and running over. The only difference, really, was Jocelyn herself.

The last time she had visited, she had been a child on the brink of her first adventure and, like most children, so frightfully ignorant that she hadn't even known what to be afraid of. Since that time she had plunged into the depths of terror, been tested over and over, and in the end emerged victorious. I hardly blame her for squaring her shoulders and standing tall. I suppose she had earned a bit of posturing.

Get ready, pirate village, she thought. *Captain Jocelyn Hook has returned.*

Jocelyn strolled down the gangplank, her fairy on her shoulder, Roger at her side, and her crew close behind, looking every inch the captain she was. Even clad in the same ragged, threadbare dress she had been wearing so many weeks before on the night she came to the Neverland, she exuded an air of authority and confidence. The island itself seemed to notice the young captain, hailing her triumphant return and framing her face with a sunset painted in pink and orange and blue.

Jocelyn stuck her tongue out at the pink.

The harbormaster waited at the bottom of the gang-plank, ready to interrogate all new visitors to the pirate village. He held his lead pencil and ledger book at the ready, but the girl merely scowled at him. "I've no time for your questions just now; I've important business this evening."

He didn't argue, but stepped aside and tipped his hat. "Yes, miss, young Captain Hook. If I can be of assistance to you, please don't hesitate to call upon me."

She brushed past him without reply, eager to find the mapmaker and begin her next adventure. Roger gave a polite nod, but stuck close to Jocelyn in order to keep from being ensnarled in the man's bureaucratic red tape.

I've said it before and I'll say it again: That boy was a wee bit smarter than most. It's not saying much, but it's something.

At the end of the dock, Jocelyn turned to her crew. "All right, you dogs," she growled with a smile, "go show this town what you're made of. You've earned it. We'll meet back aboard the ship by first light."

"Tie the colors to the mast, boys! There'll be no surrender tonight!" Dirty Bob called, and with many an *"Arrrrr!"* the men set off to celebrate their victories.

Mr. Smee stayed behind. He patted Jocelyn on the shoulder. "Do be careful, miss," he said, then set off toward his own tailor shop, turning just once to give a fretful look back.

Jocelyn grabbed Roger by the arm, pulling him in the opposite direction. "Come on," she said with a grin, "let's get this adventure under way."

CHAPTER TWO

The Mapmaker's Magic

Jocelyn and Roger zigzagged through a maze of narrow streets, brushing past women in heavy makeup and men in heavy weaponry. Presently, and without much difficulty, they found the mapmaker's shop. A bell above the door announced their arrival. "I'll be out in a minute," someone growled from a back room.

While they waited, the pair took in their surroundings. The shop was small, crowded with dark corners and the scent of paper and ink. A maze of lidless casks and barrels crammed with scrolls littered the shop's floor space. In one corner, under a hanging lantern, a large writing desk held an impossibly high stack of parchments, teetering so that the slightest breath might send them careening over.

Opposite the door they had entered, and also buried in piles of papers, a short wooden counter ran the length of the room. Behind it a myriad of jars and bottles, containing inks of all colors, were arrayed haphazardly on floor-to-ceiling shelving. Quill pens and boar-hair brushes clustered in clay pots, ceramic mugs, and bourbon glasses stood at attention. Jocelyn instantly felt at home in the cozy chaos. It reminded her a bit of the carriage house, her favorite place at the otherwise dreary finishing school she had attended before escaping to the Neverland.

Roger also seemed enamored with the cluttered shop. His eyes sparkled as he took it all in. He reached out to touch a detailed map lying unfurled on top of a barrel. The phrase *Catacombs, Holy Order of the Newt* was written out in what might have been blood across the bottom edge.

From another room came a shouted "No touching, ye young scalawags!" causing Roger to snatch his hand back.

Meriwether seemed unperturbed by the scolding. He flitted about, sticking his face into jars and wriggling under papers, trying to see everything at once.

"Meri, get back here!" Jocelyn called, motioning to her shoulder. "Sit down and try not to get into trouble!" He obeyed, but not happily. The fairy began pulling loose threads from her collar and throwing them to the floor, a petulant look etched on his tiny face.

"And I'll thank you to stop making a mess of things!" The voice was large and gruff, not entirely matching the man who followed it through the door behind the counter. He would have been fierce, even terrifying, if he had been more than three and a half feet tall. Thin, white hair defied the laws of gravity, reason, and sense, sticking out every which way upon his bulbous head. His bloodshot eyes were wild, magnified behind thick lenses. "I know just where everything is catalogued, and I won't have the likes of you coming in here and disrupting things. Or"— he scowled at the few threads on the floor—"adding your own, unauthorized leavings." He pulled a paper from his inside jacket pocket, unfolded it, and waved it around in the air. "Just take a look at this!" he demanded.

Jocelyn and Roger carefully made their way through the labyrinth of papers to stand before the man, but his frantic waving made it impossible to determine what he hoped to show them.

Jocelyn matched his scowl with one of her own. "If you want us to know what that is, you'll have to stop flapping it around."

The man gripped the paper in both hands and held it above his head. The parchment appeared to be a perfect map of the cluttered shop, right down to the last bottle and brush on the shelves. MAPMAKER'S SHOP was clearly labeled in the upper left-hand corner. He slapped it down on the counter and, using a toothpick-size pen and miniscule bottle of ink, added a few tiny lines, so fine Jocelyn could scarcely see them.

"Now that the chart has been amended to reflect the changes you wrought"—he scowled again at the threads Meri had dropped—"we can get down to business. Move closer to the counter here, you miscreants, and let's have a look at ye." He blinked at the pair for several long moments before speaking. "What can I do for you?"

The girl pulled her own map from her pocket, but before she unfolded it, she drew herself up to her full height. "I'm here because my bo'sun, Mr. Smee, says you are talented"—she pulled a gold coin from her pouch and slid it across the counter—"and discreet."

I've found that if gold isn't enough to ensure discretion, cold, hard steel often will. Pity that in this case, it appeared the coin would do.

The man licked his wrinkled lips, scooped up the coin, and bit down on it. Apparently satisfied it was genuine, he slipped it into his waistcoat pocket and nodded. "Discreet I am. Let's have a look at what you've got there."

Jocelyn unfolded the map and held it out. "Did you make this?"

He barely glanced at it. "Certainly not! The paper thickness is all off. I'd never use something so flimsy."

Jocelyn tried to swallow her disappointment. "No matter. You still may be of use. Take a closer look. Can you tell me where it leads?"

"I'm a very busy man." He didn't seem busy. He stood there, looking as if he had all the time in the world.

Jocelyn pulled another gold piece from her dwindling supply and slapped it on the counter. It disappeared into his pocket.

"Let me see that map."

Jocelyn gave it to the mapmaker and held her breath. Next to her, Roger fiddled nervously with a button on his shirt. It came off in his fingers, and he jiggled it in his palm.

The man leaned close to the paper, assuming much the same pose that Jocelyn had that morning. "Interesting," he mumbled, sweeping his unblinking eyes from side to side.

"What's interesting? Do you know that shoreline?" Roger asked.

"I know many places in and out of the Neverland, but no, I don't know this. Might be an old section of the island that changed before I got here. Might be someplace else entirely. Now if you'll keep your porthole closed, I'll examine it more fully."

Jocelyn smirked at her friend. He grinned back and shook his head.

After several more minutes, the mapmaker lifted his head and spoke. "It appears that you have a map to Captain Hook's treasure."

"We know that part," Jocelyn snapped. "It's written right across the top. We want to know what else it may say."

"It doesn't say anything else at all—"

Jocelyn huffed in frustration. Meriwether mimicked the action from his perch on her shoulder.

"—not that I can make sense of, that is, on account of it being in code."

"Yes sir," Roger said, "but we hoped you might know how to break the code."

The old man bent his head to the map again. "Break the code? Break the code! Break the code . . . no. I cannot do that. Not without its key."

Jocelyn's heart sank. "So there is no hope, then?" she asked.

The mapmaker peered at the girl over the top of his glasses. "I didn't say there was no hope, now, did I? I said there was no *key*. Leastwise not one that we can see. Likely there are instructions here, and lots of them. We just need to wheedle them out. Many a pirate likes to use trickery and invisible ink in order to keep his secrets hidden. I use it some myself. All you have to do to make it reappear is apply the right substance and coax those words to the surface, real easylike." He looked up again, his eyes wildly roving the room. They settled on Meriwether. "That ought to do it," he whispered.

Jocelyn didn't like the crazed look on the old man's face. She took a half step back. "Do what?"

In a flash he shot out his hand and plucked the fairy from her shoulder.

"Don't hurt him!" Jocelyn cried.

The mapmaker turned Meriwether upside down and shook him like a saltshaker over the map. "Aw, it won't hurt him none. I just need a bit of his dust. If there are any words there, it should lift them right up." He finished his vigorous shaking and placed the fairy on the counter.

Meriwether stood and flew tipsily to Jocelyn's outstretched hand. He jangled a few choice insults, climbed up her sleeve, and remained hidden from sight.

The girl hardly noticed, so intent was she on the map. Glowing words began to appear, floating to the surface of the page from some unseen depths. Before they were clear enough to read, Jocelyn snatched up the map, holding it away from the eyes of the mapmaker. Ignorance would help to ensure his discretion even better than more coins.

She and Roger silently read together:

You will not find the treasure lying safe within its place
Until you find the key that lies behind my face.

After a short time, the words faded and disappeared. Jocelyn folded the map and placed it back in her pocket.

"Did you find what you needed, then?" the mapmaker asked.

"Not entirely, but we have a clue. That's a start, I suppose." She tried, but Jocelyn couldn't keep the disappointment from her voice.

Roger nudged her. "I know it feels impossible, but so did defeating the Neverland's crocodile, and look how that turned out. Your entire crew is now wearing crocodile-skin boots!"

The mapmaker gave the girl a shrewd look. "So you're the one that did in the beast, eh? Wait here a minute, if you don't mind." He came out from behind the counter and made his way to a barrel filled with scrolls.

As he riffled through it, Roger tapped Jocelyn's locket and whispered, "Isn't there a painting of your father's face in there? He *did* send it to you. Maybe it holds the key."

Jocelyn looked over at the mapmaker. He had his head so far down inside the barrel that his feet barely touched the floor. She flipped open the locket and looked at her father's portrait.

"Is there anything behind it?" Roger asked.

Jocelyn tried to pry the painting up, but it didn't budge. "I suppose that would have been too easy." She turned the locket over. "And the back has nothing but the engraving: 'To E. H. on our wedding day.' I don't see how that could help break the code."

They were interrupted by the mapmaker's shouted plea for help. He had found what he needed but was having trouble extricating himself from the barrel. Roger rushed to assist him and pulled the little man out. He smoothed his jacket—and his dignity—before handing

Jocelyn a tightly rolled paper. "This might aid you in your search."

She unrolled it and saw a map of the Neverland itself. Under her gaze, a section of coastline bulged outward, blooming into a peninsula.

She gasped. "The drawing changed!"

"It certainly did." The mapmaker seemed to grow with pride. "I crafted that there map from the paper-thin bark of a Neverland dragonmaple, harvested under a blue moon. It holds a bit of the magic of the island, changing as she does. Hard as the dickens to get it right. I've only ever succeeded with a few. Take it and get off with ye."

"But..." Happy as she was with the map, Jocelyn couldn't understand why he would just give it to her. Discretion and information had cost her two gold coins. What would he want in exchange for this?

The mapmaker cleared his throat. "My cat was eaten by the Neverland crocodile. Consider this a token of my gratitude to ye for ridding the island of the monster." He sniffed loudly and pointed to the door. "Now go." Jocelyn turned to leave, her face still buried in the map.

"Thank you, sir," Roger said, "and my condolences for the loss of your cat."

If you were to ask me, I'd say *congratulations* would be more fitting. The crocodile did the mapmaker—and us all—a favor.

Cats are only slightly better creatures than children.

CHAPTER THREE

A Rough Patch in the Black Spot

Outside the shop, Roger paused and took Jocelyn by the arm. "Can I see it, Jocelyn? The Neverland map, I mean? Just for a minute?"

Her first impulse was to say no, for it was hers, wasn't it? The mapmaker hadn't given it to Roger, and even if he had, *she* was the captain. Why shouldn't she get to study it first?

She opened her mouth to say so, but when she glanced up at Roger, his eyes filled with excitement, she remembered how it had felt to have him look at her without any recognition at all. When Roger had come to the Neverland with Peter Pan and become a lost boy, he'd forgotten, for a time, nearly everything about his life before—including his friendship with Jocelyn. She had thought he was lost to her forever, but in the end, he'd come back to her. A sudden surge of gratitude filled her heart. What would she do without him?

She tapped the boy on his nose with the rolled-up map. "I'll do you one better. Why don't you keep it? You have a head for directions, the ability to navigate by stars, and that most excellent brass compass. All you need is this map and you can be my navigator."

"Aye, aye, Captain!" the boy called out. "I accept this commission and will serve loyally to keep us on track." He gave a smart salute, making Jocelyn giggle. There was no one she liked half as much as Roger.

The same could not be said for Meriwether, who, now recovered from his shaking, pulled a second button from Roger's shirt, tossed it to the gutter, and flew off alone in a huff.

The boy simply shrugged, unperturbed by the fairy's antics. Roger offered his arm to Jocelyn, and, as they had several hours before needing to return to the ship, they set off with no real plans. The pair ambled along under buildings cobbled together from old ship parts, through an outdoor market lit by oil lamps and starlight. Jocelyn was sorely tempted to buy a tempest in a teapot, in case she ever needed a decent storm or a nice cup of Earl Grey at sea, but she held back, telling herself that once she had the treasure she would be able to buy the entire tempestuous tea set, right down to the last tornado in a teacup and tsunami on a saucer.

"Roger," she asked, "what will you do with your share of the gold when we find it?"

"First thing, I think I'll buy some new clothes." Roger still wore the thick bearskin pants he had been given as a lost boy, paired with a threadbare tunic. "Thanks to Meriwether, this shirt is barely holding together." He sniffed the air. "And you may not have noticed, but these trousers are beginning to smell."

Jocelyn wrinkled her nose. "I hate to be the bearer of bad news, but I think we are well past the beginning."

Roger grinned and nudged her with his elbow.

She nudged back, just a smidge harder. "What else do you want? Bigger than a tea set or new clothes, I mean."

"Don't laugh, all right?" he said.

Jocelyn made her face very serious. "I won't. I promise."

"To tell the truth, the thing I want most out of the gold isn't a thing at all. More than anything I want to travel the world, finding new lands and learning about..."

"Go on," Jocelyn prodded, slowing her steps to look over at the boy.

His next words came out all in a rush. "I want to learn about the different kinds of plants that grow throughout the world." He patted the pocket containing his map and compass absentmindedly. "I suppose that is rather dull."

Jocelyn shook her head. "Not at all. I think plants could be very exciting. If you found the right kind."

Roger flashed his special just-for-Jocelyn smile. "Not to most people, but thank you for saying so. What about you? What will you do with the treasure?"

They stopped in front of a stall selling manacles, shackles, and saltwater taffy. Jocelyn trailed her fingers over an iron chain. "If I have money of my own, no one will be able to tell me what to do. My grandfather will give up his ridiculous idea of having me marry into a wealthy family. I'll be able to live whatever life I choose, either here or back on the mainland. Perhaps I will even captain the ship that takes you to all your exotic plants."

Roger's eyes sparkled. "I'd like that. Here's to finding the treasure, and making our own futures."

He held up an imaginary glass. Jocelyn lifted her own to his. Their pretend toast was punctuated by the sound of real breaking glass. The girl stared in puzzlement at their still-raised hands for a moment. More sounds—crashes and bangs, screams and yells—filled the air. Just up the street from where they stood, a flying bar stool came crashing through a window and out into the gutter. More shouting followed, louder now that the window glass was gone.

One man's voice was perfectly distinguishable, even if the words themselves were not. They sounded somewhat like English, but only if it had been chopped up, heavily seasoned, and stuffed into a sausage. Only one person Jocelyn knew spoke with such a heavy Scottish accent, and he happened to be one of her crew.

"That's Jim McCraig with a Wooden Leg!" Jocelyn cried. She took Roger by the hand and ran with him to the source of the commotion: a seedy-looking establishment with a crooked sign over the door. It read THE BLACK SPOT.

In my younger years, the Black Spot was a particularly favorite haunt of mine. Nearly all my most important milestones happened within its hallowed walls, from the first time I was rightfully accused of cheating at cards—after being wrongfully discovered—to the first time a woman tried to steal my heart. I've still got the scar to prove it.

Jocelyn hurried up the steps, pushed through the door, and walked right into the middle of a brawl, with her crew members at the heart of it. Jim McCraig grappled with two enemies: a small man and a large woman, both entirely covered in tattoos. The man stomped on Jim's "wooden leg" (a mighty sliver protruding from his big toe), while the woman squeezed his head in her beefy hands. Jim's eyes popped, and a string of what would likely have been judged to be profanity—if anyone could have understood it—poured from his gaping mouth. This strange scene was made stranger by a brightly colored parrot circling the air above Jim's head, screaming words every bit as impassioned, and every bit as unintelligible.

Off to Jim's right, One-Armed Jack was locked in battle with a foe of his own. Somewhere in the course of the evening, Jack must have procured a new prosthetic arm. Like the man himself, it was somewhat unconventional: a long wooden stick with some kind of flexible red bowl at the end. The bowl reminded Jocelyn of the sucker on an octopus tentacle—mainly because it was suctioned to a table, trapping Jack in place while an elderly pirate slapped him about the head and neck with a rolled-up newspaper.

Blind Bart and Jocelyn's crew cook, Nubbins, were similarly engaged, each doing his best to hold his own in the melee, each falling fathoms short of adequate.

In the middle of the brawl, Dirty Bob stood on a table. In one hand he held the jagged neck of a broken bottle, in the other his sword. His eyes darted this way and that, nearly filmed over with a crazed excitement. Spit flew from his mouth as he roared, "Get up, you filthy yellow dogs! Fight like men! You're pirates under Hook's flag— let no man dishonor that!"

"Bob, get down from there this instant!" Jocelyn called, but her voice was lost in the sound of curses and crashing fists. "Roger, we have to stop this!"

"Aye, Captain. I have an idea!" He stepped to a battered

piano in a darkened corner, sat, and began to play. His notes rose above the brawling cacophony, and the fighting men paused and looked around.

Roger began to sing:

Oh, hi derry, hey derry, ho derry down,
Give sailors their grog and there's nothing goes wrong.

It was like magic. The pirates stopped fighting immediately, even as their fists still hung in midair. Nearly everyone joined in for the next lines:

So merry, so merry, so merry are we,
No matter who's laughing at sailors at sea!

When the last note died down, Dirty Bob threw his broken bottle to the floor in disgust. "What the devil did I just witness? None of you are real pirates! Yer just a bunch of ladies in the church choir!"

Before he could start up the fighting again, Jocelyn pulled a tattered scrap of sail, serving as a tablecloth, out from under him, sending the man tumbling to the ground. "That's enough of that!" the girl commanded. "My crew, get back to the ship. Your furlough has been canceled."

"Wait just a minute there, missy." A bearded giant of a man in a stained apron came around from the other side of the bar. He narrowed his eyes under a single bushy brow. "Take a look at this place."

There wasn't a table left standing other than the one Dirty Bob was lying next to. Most of the chairs had been reduced to sticks and splinters. Broken glass and broken teeth littered the floor like confetti left over from the world's worst birthday party. (Mine. Age seven.)

Jocelyn nodded. "I see. But why should it be my concern?"

"Because yer men started the affair." He pointed a meaty finger at Bob. "Especially that one. Coming in here talking about how Cap'n Hook's flag had been raised again and he and his mates were the only ones tough enough to sail under it. I warned him to take that kind of talk outside, but he just kept at it, challenging anyone who'd have him and his shipmates to a fight. We get a lot of rough talk in here, and most paid him no mind, but then he . . ."

"What did he do?" Jocelyn turned to Bob. "What did you do?"

No one answered for a moment; then a tremulous voice at the back of the crowd called out, "He insulted our mothers. We just couldn't let that stand!"

Jocelyn sighed. She would never understand the silly preoccupation with mothers that was so prevalent on the Neverland. On the other hand, she had once flown into a rage at Prissy Edgeworth, a horrible girl at school, for insulting *her* mother, so she could hardly blame the men for their reaction.

The bartender continued, "Aye, insult 'em he did. It's clear he's responsible for this mess." The man tilted his head, cracking the joints in his neck. If she hadn't been there herself, Jocelyn would have never believed such menace could be packed into a little popping sound. "And you," he went on, "are responsible for him. Make it right."

Jocelyn felt the dwindling pouch of gold at her waist. "I'm a bit light of doubloons at the moment—"

"I'll take what you have." The bartender held out his hand, and Jocelyn dropped her remaining coins into it.

Nubbins pushed a broken table off his chest, picking himself up from where he had fallen to the floor. He clapped the girl on the back and smiled with lips swollen and bruised. "Don't worry, Captain, there'll be enough gold to buy this place a hundred times over—and put in a shiny new kitchen—once we find Hook's treasure! How did it go with the map?"

She glared at him. "Stow that talk, Nubbins!" she whispered, her eyes darting around to see who might have overheard.

In the back of the room, she caught a glimpse of a familiar, warty face. When Krueger had attacked her ship, a man that looked suspiciously like this one had nearly thrown her overboard. What was his name? Benito? Could they be one and the same?

The girl wiped her palms on her skirt, heart thumping. "Let's go, men. Back to the ship, now. Heave to!"

They followed behind in sheepish silence.

CHAPTER FOUR

*Wherein What Could
Go Wrong, Does*

The thing about friends is, you never know when you might need them. It's always best to keep them imprisoned nearby.

Jocelyn had foolishly let her crew govern themselves, and look how that ended up. At least Meriwether didn't let her down. He came darting out of the night practically the instant the girl called.

"Meri," she commanded, "fly on ahead and watch for trouble. If you see Captain Krueger, flash your light. You'll know him by a hideous scar down the side of his face, a mouthful of pointy teeth, and a general air of spite surrounding him."

Meriwether chimed an emphatic (and somewhat saucy) *yes, dear* and flew into the night.

Jocelyn's stomach was full of knots—the really snarly kind Jim McCraig tied. If Krueger knew she had a map to her father's treasure . . . She didn't like to think of what he would do to take it from her.

Still, she *was* the captain. And she *had* defeated the Neverland's crocodile. Even her father hadn't been able to do that. The girl squared her shoulders, stood tall, and turned to address her crew. She caught Roger's eye. He nodded, giving her encouragement.

The rest of the men stood in a subdued mob, nursing their wounds. She noticed that the parrot had accompanied them. It was settled on Jim McCraig's shoulder and, at the moment, mercifully silent. "Men," she said, "get your arms out—"

"Aye, Captain! I may only possess one good arm—and I didn't think it respectful to take on a hook of my own for the other—but I do have *this* standing at the ready!" Jack waved his suction cup on a stick.

The strange appendage momentarily distracted Jocelyn from her commands. "But what is it?"

"The man at the shop called it a 'plunger.' Don't they have them in your When?"

Since visitors to the Neverland came from many different times, the island was positively crowded with strange and wonderful artifacts that Jocelyn had never encountered at home. She regarded the "plunger." "No. What's it for?"

Jack growled and thrust it forward, as if warding off a potential threat. "I think you plunge it into your enemies."

Mention of enemies reminded Jocelyn that she and her crew might be in danger. "All right then, Jack. Be ready with it, and everyone, be watchful."

There wasn't much to see. The streets, fairly bustling with activity before, were deserted; the shop windows, shuttered.

"I don't like this, Jocelyn," Roger said. "Where is everyone?" As he spoke, the gas lamps all blew out. The only light came from the cool, thin crescent moon, a clipped toenail in the sky. Ahead, Meriwether zigged and bobbed, too far away to offer any illumination.

Gooseflesh erupted on Jocelyn's arms. She gripped her sword tight in her fist. "Let's get back to the ship."

They reached the dock at the edge of the village. Too late, Meriwether flashed his light. A man stepped from the shadows cast by the last of the village's buildings. The knots in Jocelyn's stomach tightened.

The man pointed a crooked finger at them and shattered the silence with his voice. "There you lot are. Johnny and me, we was beginning to wonder where you had got to."

Jocelyn lowered her sword with relief, grateful to see Mr. Smee.

He continued speaking, oblivious to the scare he had caused. "We've been seeing to the loading of the goods you men had delivered. On our own, I might add." He stepped closer, catching sight of scrapes and bloodstains that even the pale light couldn't hide. "Dear me! What the devil kind of mischief have you stirred up?"

"Not now, Smee. We need to get back to the *Hook's Revenge*. I think one of Krueger's men has spotted us. And"—she gave Nubbins a pointed look—"he may have overheard something about the treasure."

"That he did," a voice called from the deep shadows, "and I thank you and your bumbling crew for it." A shiver crawled up Jocelyn's spine and curled around the base of her neck. She knew that voice.

Krueger.

He stepped from the darkness, though it clung to him like a dirty smell. "I'll be taking that map from you now, girlie." The sliver of a moon illuminated the long, white scar disfiguring his face, the razor-sharp points of his teeth, and something Jocelyn hadn't noticed before: his eyes, two dark tar pits, so black that not even the pupil was visible. The girl got the sense that terrible things hid in their depths.

Roger stepped in front of Jocelyn. "There are eight of us, nine counting Meriwether"—the fairy clanged a series of curses—"and only one of you. We'll fight to protect our captain."

Jocelyn pushed him gently aside and stepped next to

him. "I'll fight to protect myself, my crew, and the treasure. I defeated the Neverland crocodile on my own. You shouldn't be much trouble."

Krueger whistled, and more men separated themselves from the shadows. He was now flanked by at least a dozen big pirates, Benito included. "Give me the map, child," Krueger snarled.

Jocelyn drew her sword. "Never!" She tried to sound confident, but judging from the brawl she had just witnessed, her men were no match for his. Still, she couldn't—she *wouldn't*—simply hand over the map and go home. Her father had intended that treasure for her! Her future depended on it.

The girl rushed Krueger, the clang of her steel against his echoing through the night. She had the blind enthusiasm of youth on her side, but he was bigger, stronger, and meaner. In an instant he had disarmed her. He placed the tip of his sword on her chest. "The map."

The sound of Meriwether's reed pipe rang through the night, and the once-dark sky blazed with a furious swirl of lights. Fairy soldiers darted in, stinging Krueger and his men with their holly-leaf lancets. The rival pirates fell back. Jocelyn scooped up her sword and commanded her men, "Run! To the *Hook's Revenge*, quickly!"

Her crew followed her, pounding down the dock and up the gangplank. Mr. Smee set everyone to work preparing to cast off. Jocelyn climbed to the poop deck to see what was happening onshore. Meriwether left his soldiers and settled into his favorite place on her shoulder.

The remaining fairies gave light to the scene. Krueger and his men were on the ground, faces and hands distorted with angry-looking boils where they had been stung.

The foul pirate turned his head and peered at her over the distance with hateful, slitted eyes. Jocelyn felt fear, cold and sharp, in her stomach. She hadn't felt such dread since before she defeated the crocodile. The emotion's reappearance both surprised and angered her. She stuck her tongue out at the man to make herself feel better, but, as is the way of most empty gestures, it didn't much help.

Perhaps you have heard it said that there is more than one way to skin a cat. There are, in fact, thirty-seven and a half ways. Likewise, there is more than one way to react to the threat of a deadly pirate—one you know will not stop until he has drained you of your hopes, your future, and, more likely than not, your last drops of blood. Jocelyn, to her extreme frustration, chose the option she thought best.

"Roger," she called to her friend, "use that map of yours and find us somewhere we can hide."

CHAPTER FIVE

Breaking the Code

It did not take long for Roger and his fantastic Neverland map to find a safe place for the *Hook's Revenge* to lie low. While en route, Jocelyn sat atop the poop deck at the aft of the ship, her legs dangling through the railing, heels drumming the rear timbers. The starry sky was spread out above her, the cold, dark sea beneath. She might have felt lost in all that vastness, had Roger not been nearby, taking a turn at the wheel. The rest of the crew were scattered below on the main deck, too keyed up from the evening's dangers to think of sleep.

Jocelyn pulled her spyglass from the pouch at her waist where she kept it, along with a few other important things: flint and steel, a claw from the Neverland crocodile, two unusually pretty rocks, and a phoenix tail feather she had found on the island. The girl scanned the waters behind them, searching for any sign of Krueger's ship, *Calypso's Nightmare*.

"How far are we from that hidden cove you found, Mr. Navigator?" she asked Roger.

The boy consulted his map, holding it up to one of the ship's lanterns. He checked what he saw against his pocket compass. "Not far now, Captain. We should be there within the hour—provided the Neverland doesn't decide to turn it into a cape or peninsula." He grinned at Jocelyn, clearly caught up in the adventure of it all.

She felt the same spark of excitement for a moment, but it fizzled. "I hate that we are hiding from Krueger like a pack of cowards."

"I know." Roger took another look at his map and compass, and, apparently satisfied that the ship was on course, abandoned the helm to come sit next to her. "But maybe you are looking at it the wrong way. We're not hiding; we're exercising stealth. Once we are settled in a secure place, away from any distraction Krueger may provide, we'll be free to solve that clue your father left on the map."

His words cheered the girl. That's right—she was no coward! She was simply focusing on getting what she wanted. Jocelyn thought back to the advice she had received from her mother—or at least the spirit of her mother—before she fought the crocodile: *Decide what you want. Believe you can have it. Don't let anything get in your way.*

The girl wanted her father's treasure. It was the key to the future she planned for herself and, since she was Hook's only heir, it was her birthright—not only the treasure itself, but the getting of it. This was *her* adventure. She wouldn't let Krueger, or anything, keep it from her.

She bumped Roger with her shoulder. "Thanks. I can always count on you to help me feel better."

He winked at her. "That's what best friends do. Now, have you given any more thought to what that clue might mean?"

She repeated the words they had seen float to the surface of the map: "'You will not find the treasure lying safe within its place until you find the key that lies behind my face. . . .'" She shook her head and frowned. "I have no idea, but I'm going to ask Smee his opinion."

Mr. Smee had sailed with Jocelyn's father for years and was still deeply mourning his loss. Better than anyone Jocelyn had met on the Neverland, he knew Captain Hook.

Roger tapped her locket. "Maybe he has a portrait like yours hidden under his shirt."

She giggled. "Either that or under his pillow. Since we don't appear to be in mortal danger at the moment, perhaps I'll ask him now."

Roger resumed his place at the wheel as the girl got up to call Smee to the poop deck, but before she could, another pirate climbed the ladder and stood before her. The scowl on Dirty Bob's face could have curdled milk, if his ugliness hadn't already done the job.

He removed his sterling-silver double cigar holder—a gift from Jocelyn to apologize for smashing his pocket watch—from the corner of his mouth and tapped the ash to the deck. "I've a thing or two to say, Cap'n."

She placed her hands on her hips and glared up at the pirate. "I have some things to say to you as well, Bob, but I'm busy just now."

Jocelyn tried to step around him, but he blocked her. "This won't take more'n a minute," he said. "I don't like what we're doing here. Real pirates don't turn tail and run at the first sign of trouble. And they don't hide, neither."

The girl stood a little straighter and glared a little harder. "We aren't hiding. We are using stealth!"

Roger nodded in agreement.

"Besides that," Jocelyn went on, "I had to protect the map, not that I asked your opinion on the matter."

"Oh, yes, the map. The map that you can't read." He softened his voice a bit. "Unless yer visit to the mapmaker proved to be successful?"

Jocelyn caught Roger's eye and gave an almost imperceptible shake of her head. Between Dirty Bob's surliness and Nubbins's earlier blabbing, she didn't feel it was wise to share what they'd learned with the entire crew. "Not just yet," she said, "but we've made some progress."

Bob's voice resumed its surliness. "Progress!" he scoffed. "In the meantime, you've not a sliver of gold left to line your purse."

"She has you to thank for that!" Roger spoke up.

"That's right!" Jocelyn agreed. "What were you thinking, Bob, goading those men into attacking the crew?"

"Goating? I did no such thing! There wasn't a single goat there." He spat on the deck, next to his growing pile of ashes. "And as for the fighting, your men need the experience. It's not good for them to be so weak. It goes against the Pirate Code."

Jocelyn's hand strayed toward the map in her pocket. "The code? Like on the map?"

"Not like on yer map." Dirty Bob let out an exasperated huff. "You don't know what the Code is? The Custom of the Coast?"

Jocelyn shook her head.

"The Jamaica Discipline? The Charter Party? The Code of Brotherhood?"

The girl shrugged. She didn't know a thing about it, which truly was a gross oversight on her part. I'm sure it was mentioned a time or two in her adventure books, but she often skipped over the least bloody parts—not that I much blame her for that.

Dirty Bob threw up his hands. "I knew when ye signed me that you and yer men were a bit green, but by thunder, I never woulda guessed you don't even know what the

Code is!" He caught Roger's eye. "I'll bet the boy knows, though—don't you, boy?"

Roger gave Jocelyn an apologetic look. "I did hear my father say a thing or two about it. Yes."

"All right then, everyone knows except me," Jocelyn snapped. "Perhaps one of you could fill me in?"

"I'll tell you," Bob said. "The Pirate Code is a code of conduct, a list of rules, so to speak. Each ship *should* have her own..." He gave Jocelyn a pointed look. She responded by yawning in his face. He scowled and continued: "But even if'n they don't, there's still a general sort of code that every pirate subscribes to. Things like 'Every man is to obey his cap'n,' 'A pirate's primary concern should be getting more gold, best if procured by theft and/or murder,' and 'No women or children are to be brought aboard the ship.'"

Jocelyn opened her mouth to object, but he plowed right on. "Now, since you're the cap'n and all, an' the daughter of Hook hisself, I looked the other way on that one. Maybe I was right to do it; maybe I wasn't. But the others, those can't be gone back on. Which brings me to my reason for coming to you: It's time to go out, sack a ship or two, and fill our coffers. Your men need more experience fighting, and you need the money."

Jocelyn was no fool. She knew that piracy meant stealing from merchant ships. But in the course of that, people often got hurt. Innocent people. Sailors—sailors like

Roger's father—sometimes didn't come home because of pirates. Jocelyn had no desire for that kind of life. "I'll have plenty of gold when we find the treasure."

"But the Code—"

"I'm not interested in you, or some Code, telling me what I am supposed to be. If I wanted someone ordering me around all the time, I'd go home and spend my days at finishing school."

"Cap'n—"

"That's right, I *am* the captain. And your precious Code says you must obey me. You would do well to remember it." Jocelyn took a step toward Bob, deliberately crowding him. He took a small step back. She might have been a young girl, but at the moment, every inch of her was a captain. "I've nothing more to say to you just now, but watch yourself, Dirty Bob."

He tapped his ash to the deck again. "Aye, Cap'n," he said, but his eyes held a challenge.

She looked at the mess with distaste. "You've just earned yourself extra deck-swabbing duty this week. You are dismissed."

Without a word, Dirty Bob climbed down from the deck.

"That didn't go so well," Roger said.

Jocelyn sighed, removing her air of captainship as another might remove a hat. "I know. I hope things will settle down when we get the treasure hunt under way.

Speaking of which..." She stepped to the front of the poop deck and surveyed the crew just in time to see Dirty Bob go below deck, slamming the hatch with a bang.

In the ship's lights, she spied Jim McCraig seated nearby, his "wooden leg" propped up on one of the new dinghies Blind Bart had purchased in the pirate village. Jim was carrying on an ear-assaulting conversation with his parrot. Bart, presumably because of his sensitive hearing, had wrapped his head in wool blankets and climbed to the crow's nest, where he was ever so gently pounding his forehead into the railing. One-Armed Jack had gotten his plunger stuck to the mizzenmast and was loudly appealing to Nubbins to set him free. Nubbins obliged by whacking the stick end of the plunger with a meat cleaver, freeing Jack from both his predicament and his substitute limb.

The girl had grown quite fond of her crew, but at times she wondered about them. For a bunch of grown men, they certainly acted like children.

Her eye found Mr. Smee, who was taking no notice of the shenanigans happening around him. He was calmly making his rounds, inspecting the ship's sails.

"Mr. Smee, a word?" Jocelyn called.

The man gave her an injured look.

"I mean, Smee, get your scurvy-riddled carcass up here! I need to speak with you."

Smee beamed. He clambered onto the deck as quickly

as his portly body would allow. "Aye, Miss Cap'n. Happy to be of service. What can I do for you?"

"I have a question. When Roger and I visited the mapmaker, we learned something about how to find the treasure."

"Ah, the treasure! Johnny and me, we wish we could be more help to you on that one, but the captain never let us know a thing about it. He didn't want to have to kill us for knowing too much. Wasn't that good of him?" Smee teared up, overjoyed at the memory of not being murdered.

Roger began to laugh, but a look from Jocelyn convinced him to turn it into a cough.

"Not killing you was good of my father," Jocelyn said. "And good *for* him as well. He couldn't have gotten by without you."

Smee nearly burst his buttons, he was so swelled with pride (and a lifetime of extra dinner helpings).

"Still," Jocelyn went on, "Roger and I think you might be able to help. There was a hidden message on the map, a clue to solving the code. We thought you might know what it means." Jocelyn recited the clue for the man. "Do you have any idea what key he is talking about?"

"Behind my face...behind my face..." Mr. Smee scrunched up his own face, thinking.

"The part about a key is not likely to be a way to open locks, but instead, how to solve the code," Roger said.

"Behind my face..." Smee's cheeks grew red with effort. Jocelyn grew concerned.

"I've got it!" he shouted, and the girl's excitement soared. "To my way of thinking," he went on, "the key has got to be on the back of his portrait."

Jocelyn's excitement crashed to the ground. "We thought about that," she said, "but there wasn't anything there." She opened her locket and held it up. "Unless you have another one?"

Mr. Smee barely gave it a passing glance. "If you don't mind me saying so, miss, I didn't mean that one. I was talking about the great one he had hanging over his bed on the *Jolly Roger*. The captain loved that painting with all his dark heart. He wouldn't even let me dust it, 'cept for only once or twice a year. Too important to him to risk anything happening to it, he said."

"That has to be it!" Jocelyn cried, nearly dancing with glee. "All we have to do is find that painting. The key to breaking the code is sure to be on the back. We'll finally be able to read the map, and the treasure will be as good as ours!" But then the rest of Mr. Smee's words caught up with her, and she frowned. "But Smee, where is the *Jolly Roger*? What happened to it after my father died?"

"I'm afraid only one person knows the answer to that, miss. You'll have to ask Peter Pan."

CHAPTER SIX

Cursed by a Lost Boy

One does not always know the worst possible scenario until one is faced with it. Up until recently, if you were to have asked me the most dreadful way to spend an afternoon, I would have said swabbing the splintery deck of the largest galleon in the Portuguese fleet, under a blistering hot sun, using my tongue for a mop—but that was before I'd spent any time with you.

Just as I have come to adjust my idea of terrible ways to while away an afternoon, Jocelyn needed to adjust her worst-case thoughts regarding the *Jolly Roger*. In the few seconds between when the question formed on her lips and the answer came forth from Smee's, she'd feared that he would tell her the ship had sunk, making the search for her father's portrait rather difficult. Still, the idea of recovering the ship from deep inside Davy Jones's locker was far more appealing than having to ask that irritating Peter Pan about it.

And yet Jocelyn was never one to shy away from a job to be done, no matter how awful, so she made up her mind to go find Pan and learn from him what she must. As Roger and most of the crew at one time or another had all been lost boys, and as each had been banished by Peter Pan, Jocelyn decided to go alone. It would be hard enough getting that boy to tell her what she needed to know without bringing banished lost boys into his camp.

By the time the ship was securely hidden in the cove, and after everyone had taken a few hours' rest, it was early afternoon, and Jocelyn could put off the task no longer. As the girl made ready to go, Mr. Smee pulled her aside.

"With all the fluster and fuss over getting away from Krueger," he said, "I nearly forgot to give you this." Smee presented her with a soft parcel wrapped in brown paper.

"What is it?" she asked, but didn't wait for a reply before tearing the package open. Inside was a new white dress—extra long so as to give plenty of yardage for tearing away sections of hem, as the need might arise—and a jacket, similar in styling to the one that had belonged to her father, but sized to the girl, and in her favorite shade of blue. The clothes were so perfectly suited to Jocelyn's needs and taste that she couldn't restrain herself from throwing her arms around Mr. Smee in a hug.

"There's no need for that, miss," he said. "I'd accept a kick to my backside as thanks enough." He patted her back awkwardly, then pulled away. "Anyway, I did it as much for myself as for you. I couldn't have anyone thinking I wasn't doing right by my captain. That wouldn't serve at all now, would it?"

Jocelyn made her face look stern. "No. Not at all, Mr. Smee. Glad to see you have remedied the situation at last."

He beamed with gratitude. "Thank you, Cap'n. Oh, and I made some new things for your young navigator as well. He's down below now, putting them on."

Jocelyn slipped into her cabin to do the same. When she emerged, the whole crew gathered around to see her off. She twirled for them, showing off her new skirts, and they clapped appreciatively, though none louder than Roger.

She stopped to take a look at his new clothing. He was attired in a linen shirt with broad blue and white stripes, which made a striking contrast against his brown skin. Even better, however, were his remarkable new breeches. Smee had nearly gone overboard in his application of pockets: front pockets, side pockets, back pockets, knee pockets, hem pockets. Pockets sized to carry a single coin and pockets large enough to fit a spyglass, fully extended. Expandable pockets. Pockets inside pockets. And one custom-sized to fit his compass. The boy reached into it, withdrew its contents, and pressed the familiar cool brass case into Jocelyn's hands, along with his Neverland map. "Here, take these with you, so you don't get lost."

"Thank you, Roger. I'll take good care of them."

"I know you will. But take good care of yourself, too." He gave her his just-for-Jocelyn smile. "Are you sure you don't want me to come along?"

She did, but she was the captain. There were things she simply had to do on her own. "I'll be fine. I'd best get this over with."

After receiving a few last-minute directions on how to find Peter's camp, she had little to do but leave. Jocelyn stood still while Meriwether gave her a thorough coating of fairy dust.

Roger tugged at her new jacket. "Have fun," he said with a wink. "Don't forget about us."

Jocelyn grinned. "Not a chance."

Jocelyn hoped she never got used to the feeling of flying. Once you were used to something, it threatened to become routine, perhaps even dull. But how could the ability to lift off from the earth, breaking all the laws of gravity—oh, how the girl loved to break things—ever become mundane?

She took her time, playing tag with flocks of birds on their afternoon migration and punching holes in clouds. Even so, like all good things, it was over far too quickly, and she found herself outside Peter's camp. Between Roger's directions, the map, and the compass, it hadn't been difficult at all to uncover.

A nearby wood held a flurry of lost boy activity. So engrossed were they, the boys didn't notice Jocelyn watching. A lost boy wearing jackalope fur—Jocelyn recognized him as Ace—was high in a magnolia tree, attempting to build a tree house. Things did not appear to be going well, as he was trying to construct the main support by sticking branches together with nothing more than spit and hope.

Fredo, still wearing a far-too-small jacket of pieced-together squirrel skins, stood below the tree and hollered, "How about we use this for the floor, Ace?" He held up a leaf nearly as large as himself. Fredo attached it to a dangling rope, and Ace hauled it up, laying the leaf between two tree limbs. It sagged in the middle.

Ace scratched his head and surveyed the new floor. "It looks good, but do you think it will hold her? Mother doesn't look very heavy."

The twins, two boys who couldn't have looked more different, were attempting to saw a log with a large white goose feather. They stopped and joined Fredo at the base of the tree.

"Let's have the baby test it out," the tall, dark twin suggested.

"Yes, let's!" the short, ginger twin agreed. "Baby, get up there."

The "baby" was a new addition to the lost boys since Jocelyn had seen them last. He looked to be a baby in the same way that the twins were twins. The boy must have been at least three, perhaps as old as four, and he was so sweet-looking that even Jocelyn, who was not particularly interested in young children, couldn't help but stare. The child noticed her gaze and peered back with deep blue eyes rimmed in long lashes. He flashed a shy, secret smile, his teeth a row of perfect baby pearls.

Jocelyn wondered if a more angelic-looking child had ever graced the earth. She had only heard of one who could possibly contend—her own mother as a girl. This boy was a living embodiment of the perfection Jocelyn's grandfather, Sir Charles, had always described.

The child toddled over and reached for her. She couldn't resist scooping him up. He flashed those perfect pearls again before placing a chubby thumb into his sweet mouth.

"Oh, hey, it's that girl. Hello, girl," Fredo said. "Are you here to be our mother now?"

Jocelyn rolled her eyes. "You boys need to get over your preoccupation with mothers. It's not healthy." She shifted the little boy to a more comfortable position on her hip. "But to answer your question, no, I am not."

"That's good, since Peter already got us one. Right, Ace?" the ginger twin said.

"Right. And we are building her a little house of her very own, isn't that right, Fredo?"

Jocelyn spoke before he could answer. "I'm glad you have a new mother, but I'm not here about that. I need—"

Fredo spoke right over her. "Right. And Mother is waiting in the home under the ground so as not to spoil the surprise."

"Peter said girls love surprises. Almost as much as they love babies, right—"

"Yes, yes," Jocelyn interrupted. "And now you will say, 'Right, Baby?' But I don't really care. I—"

"Oh, no, girl." The dark-haired twin's eyes were wide. "We'd never ask the baby."

"Tully isn't allowed to talk," the other explained.

Jocelyn scowled at him. "And why not? Because he has to pretend to be a baby? That's ridiculous!" She turned her back on Ace and spoke only to the baby. "Tully, is it? Do you want to talk?"

Tully nodded his head, making his curls bounce.

"Don't, girl!" Ace yelled, hurrying down the ladder.

"Don't tell me what to do!" Jocelyn yelled back. "Go ahead then, Tully."

The little boy plucked his thumb from his mouth.

The lost boys edged away, covering their ears.

Tully opened his bow-shaped lips and released a stream of the loudest, shrillest, *foulest* words Jocelyn had ever heard. She nearly dropped the child in shock. It took him some minutes to exhaust his supply of curses, but once finished, he batted his long lashes and tucked his plump thumb back into his adorable mouth with a contented air.

The boys uncovered their ears. Jocelyn stood still, her jaw hanging open.

"We told you," Ace said, shaking his head.

Jocelyn felt it best to change the subject. "Where is Peter?"

Fredo answered. "He went to get a present for Mother: Tiger Lily's favorite, all-white, wolf pup."

"Tiger Lily must think highly of Peter to give him such a gift," Jocelyn said.

"She's not going to give it to him..." said one twin with a chuckle.

"He's going to *steal* it—right, Ace?" said the other.

"Right! That's how Mother will know it means something."

That was a perfect opening to the subject Jocelyn really wanted to talk about. "Speaking of stealing, I'm looking for my father's ship, the *Jolly Roger*. Peter was the last to have it. Do you know where it is?"

The twins answered in unison. "We don't. Do you know, Fredo?"

"I've never heard of it. Have you, Tully?"

"Don't ask Tully!" the rest of the boys shouted together.

Tully smiled and graced them with a new series of swears, both classic and invented. Jocelyn put him down and took a step back, feeling faintly sick.

Ace uncovered his ears. "One time Peter told me about when he was a pirate and he killed another crew with his bare hands and took command of their ship. Then he sailed it all around the world, twice, *and* stayed up far past his bedtime. But I don't know what he did with it when he was done."

Jocelyn sighed. She had hoped to avoid meeting with Peter Pan altogether. "I suppose I'll simply have to ask him myself."

As if he had been summoned, Peter Pan flew between the tree branches. The small amount of headway Ace had made on the tree house came crashing to the ground in his wake. Pan landed in front of Jocelyn, a wriggling white wolf pup in his arms. "Ask me what?" he asked. Without waiting for an answer, he turned and greeted the lost boys. "Good news, boys! The raid was a success. I have the white wolf!" He held up the pup so they could get a good look at her. She let out a mournful howl.

Peter set her on the ground, placed his hands on his hips, and turned to Jocelyn, acting as if he had just noticed her. "Oh, hello, girl. Are you here to have a war? I'm busy tonight. Can you come back Tuesday?"

I have it on the highest authority that Peter had just learned about Tuesdays and was eager to show off his great knowledge. But Jocelyn, as ever, was unimpressed with him.

"I simply wanted to ask you a question. Mr. Smee said you took command of the *Jolly Roger* after my father died."

He gnashed his teeth and spat, "That's a dirty lie!"

Jocelyn hated to flatter the boy, but finding her father's ship was the first step in finding the treasure. She needed whatever was behind that portrait in order to translate the map. "So you didn't become a great pirate captain and steal the ship of the most feared man to ever live?"

Peter smiled. "I certainly did! Anyone who says I didn't is a liar."

"Right. So where is the *Jolly Roger* now?" she asked.

"I told you, I didn't take it. And it should be right where I left it."

Jocelyn felt a headache coming on. "Which is where, exactly?"

Peter scratched his head. "Let me think. . . . Oh yes! In the middle of Notgonna."

"Notgonna?" she asked, reaching for Roger's map.

"Yeah. Not gonna tell you!" Pan laughed so hard he

nearly choked. "Come on, boys, let's go give our mother her new puppy."

Peter picked up the wolf pup and, without a backward glance, walked away, the lost boys trailing in his wake. Tully brought up the rear. He opened and closed his hand in a babylike wave, bidding Jocelyn a sweet farewell.

She ground her teeth and muttered a few of the new words she'd learned.

CHAPTER SEVEN

In Which a Fierce Battle Ends in Disappointment

The idea came to Jocelyn as she flew back to her ship. She didn't even mind crediting Peter with it. *Much.* His stealing of the wolf pup had inspired it, after all. She gathered her crew around her and laid out the plan.

"Kidnap Peter's mother?" Smee asked, an excited gleam in his eye. "Now we are talking, miss! I hope you don't mind me saying so, but I believe your father would have done the same himself."

Dirty Bob cleared his throat. "I hate to talk out of turn—"

"Then don't, ye dirty rapscallion." Smee fairly growled at the man, but I for one won't hold it against him. "This doesn't concern you! Does it, Johnny Corkscrew?" He unsheathed his sword, appealing to it. It seemed to agree.

Jocelyn placed a hand on Smee's arm, coaxing him to lower his weapon. "Put your blade away and let Bob speak."

Bob took his time, lighting a fresh pair of cigars before making his point. "I don't agree with Mr. Smee here. I knew Jim Hook, we was close as brothers for years, and kidnapping little girls wasn't something he'd have been interested in doing, not unless there was gold involved."

"Gold is involved," Jocelyn said.

Dirty Bob raised an eyebrow. "So we'll ransom the lass? If that's your big plan, I'm afraid it won't work. I doubt that Pan boy has two coins to rub together."

Jocelyn placed her hands behind her back and began to pace on the deck. She was determined not to let Bob's attitude get under her skin. "You are likely right about Pan," she said. "But we'll be ransoming her for *information*, not gold. Information that may help us break the code on the treasure map." Jocelyn still didn't trust her men to be responsible with all the details, but she felt this explanation should be enough.

Bob took a long draw on his cigars and slowly blew out the foul-smelling smoke. "Gold or no, I can't see Jim, or any respectable pirate, mind you, playing nursemaid to a girl—present company excluded, Cap'n. If you want gold, we can go take it. There are merchant ships out there, just ripe for the picking."

Jocelyn stopped pacing and turned to face him. "I said no to that before and I've not changed my mind."

Bob glared at the deck. "Yes, *Cap'n*." He hurled the title like an insult. "Even so, I don't think we should do it."

"Neither do I," Roger spoke up from behind her.

Jocelyn whirled around in surprise. "Roger! You know how important this is."

He shrugged. "I know. But I think there may be a better way. If you were to speak to her, maybe we could get her to come with us on her own. Kidnapping doesn't seem fair."

"Lots of things are unfair, Roger. I can't risk her saying no and telling Peter my plans. I want my father's treasure. I won't let anything stand in my way." She gave him time to agree, but when he didn't, she plunged on. "We will attack Peter's camp before nightfall."

Jocelyn sent Meriwether ahead as scout. He was not gone long, swiftly bringing news that Peter and the lost boys were showing their new mother the tiny ruins of an ancient fairy race. The ruins were scattered along the edge of a long, flat meadow surrounded with short, grassy hills—a prime place for an ambush.

Jocelyn and her crew followed Meriwether to where he had spied the enemy. She commanded they crawl the last hundred yards to the crest of a hill, in order to look down upon their target and get a lay of the land.

"Oh dear," Mr. Smee whispered. "Looks like we'll have to wait our turn."

Jocelyn felt oddly left out to discover that Peter and the lost boys were about to begin a battle, but not with her. The boys, with the exception of Peter, stood in a line, attired in armor made of sap and tree bark. Their purpose seemed chiefly to defend their mother. Jocelyn pulled her spyglass from its pouch at her waist and brought it to her eye for a closer look at the girl. She looked to be a bit older than Jocelyn, with light brown hair and a merry yellow dress.

The boys made a wall of protection in front of her.

On second thought, *wall* might be a bit strong. Knowing Pan's lost boys, I'd wager it was more of a picket fence.

Either way, though, Jocelyn thought the boys looked resolved to hold it. Even little Tully stood firm, his face arranged in grim determination.

Peter neither wore the armor nor stood in the line. His purpose seemed chiefly to be annoying. He flew about, crowing in excitement, his actions more closely mimicking the white wolf pup—as it ran around and around the girl's legs, barking—than any great general.

Peter's fairy was a blur of light, a dancing sunbeam bent on mischief. She darted here and there, tweaking the young mother's ear, tugging at the pup's tail, and making a general nuisance of herself. Meriwether chimed a few choice insults, something that sounded to Jocelyn like *conceited pest*. The girl felt much the same way about Peter Pan.

Jocelyn swung her spyglass to the opposite end of the meadow, getting her first glimpse of the enemy, and gasped at the sight. A small group of warriors had already begun their charge. Their mounts were horselike, but as with so many things on the Neverland, they were more fantastical than any Jocelyn had ever seen, even in her books. Muscles rippled beneath hides that shone as bright as burnished copper. Polished back hooves struck the hard-packed ground, sparking like flint against steel. Steam billowed from their nostrils. Fiery manes and tails streamed out behind—not fiery-colored, mind you, but made of actual flames—though they did not appear to burn the riders upon the animals' backs.

Leading the charge was a fierce-looking girl with long black braids. Though the Neverland boasted many groups of people, Jocelyn was certain the girl could be none other than Tiger Lily. A half dozen mounted braves, armed with bows and arrows, war clubs, spears, and rawhide shields, followed her lead.

Jocelyn returned her gaze to the lost boys. She expected to see them scattering to avoid such a formidable army, but such was not the case. On their side of the meadow, the boys held both their ground and fistfuls of squirming...

Jocelyn rubbed the lens of her spyglass and looked again. That couldn't be right.

She passed it to Roger. "What are the lost boys holding?" she asked.

"It looks like bunches of... snakes?" He shrugged and passed the spyglass back.

When the fiery horses got within range, the lost boys loaded their wriggling ammunition into slingshots and fired. The reptiles flew through the air, landing rather harmlessly—and anticlimactically—in the grass. It seemed fairly pointless, until the horses noticed the snakes. Tiger Lily's was the first to rear, dumping the girl on her, well, *her* rear. The great steed turned tail and headed for the hills, inspiring its blazing brothers and sisters to follow suit.

In a blink, the battle had changed. While the warriors had appeared sure to win moments before, now the outcome was uncertain. The boys' armor protected them some from flying arrows, and now that they were finished with the snakes, each held a knife or sword.

Jocelyn stood. "We attack now. While the boys are

distracted by battle, it will be easy to slip in and kidnap their mother."

"But Captain, are you sure?" Mr. Smee asked. "Unless we've arranged our alliances beforehand, we usually wait our turn. We should come back tomorrow."

"We're taking her now." Jocelyn ordered Jim McCraig and One-Armed Jack to fetch the cannon from where they had left it at the bottom of the hill. They hauled it up, its wheels tangling in the long grass. Upon Jocelyn's order, Jim fired, the cannon blast splitting the air and signaling their intent to join the battle. The girl led her men toward the fray, their own swords drawn. Jim McCraig, slower than the rest due to his "wooden leg," rode the cannon like a wagon down the short slope, his parrot perched atop his head, both screeching in glee. One-Armed Jack followed, waving his new prosthetic—a butterfly net, well suited for capturing things—and whooping with excitement.

With the arrival of the pirates, Peter's side was sorely outnumbered. Jocelyn found she didn't need to slip in and capture his mother after all. As soon as he heard the cannon blast, Peter called for a retreat. And in their excitement, he and the lost boys simply left the older girl behind. Tiger Lily and her braves gave chase, leaving Jocelyn and her pirates alone with Peter's mother. To her vast disappointment, Jocelyn was able to apprehend the girl with absolutely no trouble at all.

I pity young Jocelyn. What fun is a kidnapping with no trouble? It's like tea with no honey! Christmas with no pudding! A tomb with no corpse! A corpse with no jewelry! Hardly worth bothering about, if you ask me.

CHAPTER EIGHT

Peter's Mother

Jocelyn approached the captive, whom Nubbins held rather gently by the arm, and, trying to salvage the moment, declared, "You are our prisoner now! You have been shanghaied into service upon the *Hook's Revenge!*"

"Never!" the girl replied. "I'd rather die first!" She giggled, making a smattering of freckles dance across her slightly upturned nose. "This is exciting!"

The wolf pup clearly agreed. It ran circles around the girl's feet, yapping with unbridled joy.

Jocelyn huffed. "It's not supposed to be exciting! It's supposed to be terrifying!"

"Oh. Right. Terrifying! I can be terrified." She made

her dancing eyes go wide. "How's this? Do I look frightened?"

Roger snorted. Jocelyn shook her head, a feeling of shame growing inside her. Before she could think of a new, more terror-inducing tactic, Tiger Lily returned with her braves. The little wolf stopped barking, her eyes fixed on her mistress.

"Come, Snow," Tiger Lily commanded solemnly. The puppy ran and leaped into her arms. In a blink, the warrior was gone, replaced with a laughing girl. "Stop that, you," she said as the little wolf endeavored to lick every inch of her face. "I know. I know. I missed you, too!" She hugged the wriggling ball of fur tight before placing her on the ground. The pup stood on her hind legs and did a funny little hopping dance. Tiger Lily laughed, then commanded the wolf to follow as she approached Jocelyn and her crew.

"I thank you for your help in reclaiming my little Snow. I am Tiger Lily."

Jocelyn nodded. "I thought as much. I'm Jocelyn Hook."

"You are the daughter of the Captain Hook who once took me captive and attempted to drown me." It was not a question. "Are you also in the habit of doing such things?"

"Me? No! I would never!"

Tiger Lily looked pointedly at Nubbins, still holding

the arm of Peter's mother. "Oh?" she asked, one eyebrow arched.

Jocelyn found she couldn't quite look Tiger Lily in the eye. She pretended to be very interested in a patch of grass near her feet. "Right. Well. This is different. We're not going to drown her—"

"I'm a good swimmer anyway," Peter's mother said, flashing a pair of dimples.

Jocelyn ignored the girl. "We were simply going to invite her back to our ship and...er...keep her there until Peter tells me where he put the *Jolly Roger*."

"And how do you feel about this?" Tiger Lily asked the girl.

"I think it sounds like a grand adventure. Who wouldn't want to be captured by pirates? It's thrilling! Unless they were planning to drown you, I mean."

"As long as you are in agreement, then." Tiger Lily turned to Jocelyn and continued. "Young Hook, your involvement in this battle was a service to me. I will not free your captive." Snow barked, prompting a smile from the princess. "I must say, I take some pleasure in Peter Pan losing something important to him—as important as any of his endless parade of mothers may be, that is. Come. Return with us to our village and share our fire tonight. There will be feasting and dancing as we celebrate our victory!"

On the one hand, Jocelyn was eager to get back to

her ship and quickly ransom her prisoner. On the other, she was fascinated by Tiger Lily and the way she made leading her warriors look so easy. And it was close to dinnertime. . . .

"We would be honored," she said.

Her captive seemed to be in complete agreement. "Today has turned out to be absolutely delightful!"

Jocelyn determined that her first order of business, once they returned to the ship, would be to teach this girl how to be a proper prisoner. This was embarrassing, for both of them.

Jocelyn and Roger flanked Peter's mother, following Tiger Lily and her people over grassy plains. The rest of the crew trailed behind, trading war stories. Jocelyn was certain that before dinner's end, each of her men would be claiming to have been half killed, or more, in the day's nonbattle. At least they had enjoyed themselves.

They weren't the only ones. Their prisoner was still obviously beside herself with glee, chattering on about how exciting it was to be kidnapped by pirates. Jocelyn rolled her eyes, but Roger shrugged and grinned. Turning to the girl, he held out his hand and said, "We haven't been properly introduced, have we? I'm Roger, navigator of the *Hook's Revenge* under Captain Jocelyn Hook."

"Pleased to meet you," the girl replied. She dropped into a brief curtsy, somehow managing to do so while continuing to walk along. "Then you must be Jocelyn. What a lovely name! I'm Evie. You look impressively young to be a pirate captain. How old are you?"

"Thirteen," Jocelyn said, with no small amount of pride. "How old are you?"

"Fifteen," Evie replied. "Or at least I will be in only ten and a half months." She stooped to pick a large yellow daisy from a clump of snow and tucked it behind her ear. "Isn't it lovely here?"

"It's all right," Jocelyn replied, unsure why she felt so irritated with Evie. Was it her unflagging optimism? The way that flower in her hair was a perfect match to the color of her dress? Or the fact that Roger seemed to look at the girl far more than was necessary? Whatever the reason, Jocelyn found herself anxious to be rid of her. Besides, she was eager to find out where the *Jolly Roger* had been abandoned and get the key to decoding the treasure map.

"I'm sure Peter will ransom you soon," she said to the girl, "in case you were wondering."

"Oh," Evie said, "how silly of me. A ransom hadn't occurred to me. I'm having far too much fun to be concerned about going back to Peter and the boys just yet."

Roger was definitely staring. Jocelyn resolved to write a ransom note to Peter and be rid of this girl as soon as she got back to her ship.

CHAPTER NINE

Tiger Lily's Village

Before long, the party arrived at Tiger Lily's village. Jocelyn recalled the time when she and Mr. Smee had come looking for the girl, only to find her camp deserted. As the group made their way into the village this time, Jocelyn was delighted to see it bustling and full of life.

An entire herd of the flaming horses grazed on blackened grass in paddocks at the edge of the village. Their manes and tails crackled, scenting the air with brimstone. Nearby, a group of boys ran alongside a rolling hoop, taking turns trying to throw a spear through it. Tiger Lily paused to call out a few words of encouragement, causing the boys to puff out their chests and double their efforts.

In the village proper, grandmothers, their long, white braids hanging down their backs, sat in front of brightly painted tipis sewing soft leather into dresses and breeches. They smiled and waved hello, eyes nearly disappearing in the cheerful wrinkles round them. Though their materials and style of clothing were different from any Jocelyn had ever worn, the sight of women sitting together to gossip and sew was quite familiar. She was not at all tempted to join them—Jocelyn had always preferred sword points to needlepoint—but there was a certain comfort in watching.

Evie seemed to feel the same. "Look at how fine their stitches are! My headmistress at school would never reprimand my needlework again if I had half their skill."

Jocelyn felt her annoyance with the girl softening. It truly wasn't Evie's fault that the battle had not happened the way Jocelyn had wished. And any girl who knew the wrath of an irritable sewing mistress might be a kindred spirit, at least a little. "My headmistress liked to give me a rap on the head with her thimble for every crooked stitch. She was a monster."

"You can't be serious!" Evie said. "Mine has the same habit! Do you suppose they all go to some sort of How to Be Horrible to Your Students academy?"

"If they do," Roger said, "the one from Jocelyn's school could make extra money teaching evening classes there."

Presently, the group reached the center of the village

and Tiger Lily excused herself to change from her rumpled battle clothes. She invited Jocelyn and Evie to wash, if they liked, but Jocelyn felt quite happy the way she was. And, as Evie was a prisoner, Jocelyn declined on her behalf as well, hoping to set a good example for her.

In order to keep her crew out of trouble, Jocelyn offered to have them assist with preparations for the feast. They were set to work chopping firewood. Village boys, their hoop game now abandoned, arranged the wood in a large fire pit, and within minutes they had a bonfire blazing.

It is a universal fact that where a fire is present, so must be a boy with a stick. Even I, as a young lad, could not resist its siren call.

As if by magic, a stick materialized in each boy's hand and studious coal prodding began. Roger, being a boy himself, was no exception. Not even Meriwether was exempt from the lure of the flames. A log popped, shooting out a small smoking cinder. The little fairy pulled a splinter from a bit of dry wood and sat himself in front of the ember, poking at his fire just as seriously as the human boys did theirs.

Not being thus occupied, the village girls and women took part in one of their favorite pastimes: directing the men in the placement of heavy furniture. First a bench was placed here—"No, that's too close to the fire"—now there—"Oh no, that is too far back"—before they finally settled on a perfect arrangement. The benches were then piled high with layers of deerskin and buffalo robes, creating quite a cozy effect.

"Have you been to a Neverlandian feast before?" Evie asked Jocelyn.

"In a way," the girl replied, thinking of the Karnapinae people. "Only that time I was the guest of honor."

"That must have been such fun!"

Jocelyn remembered how the cannibals had held her captive. Only her wits had saved her from becoming the feast. "You know what?" she said. "It actually was." The girls shared a smile.

Tiger Lily soon emerged from her tent, wearing a white deerskin dress decorated with seashells and tiny blue beads. A gleaming silver knife adorned her waist. She had loosened her hair from its braids, and it fell in dark waves, nearly to her feet.

I'm quite certain the only reason the Neverlandian mermaids kept themselves to the sea was to avoid an unfavorable comparison, for even they would have had to agree (begrudgingly, of course) that Tiger Lily was beautiful.

She joined Jocelyn and Evie, Snow silently padding along next to her. "The feast is nearly ready," she said. "I hope you don't mind waiting a short while longer."

The smell of wood smoke and roasted meat wafted about, making Jocelyn's mouth water. It seemed like ages since she'd had her midday meal. Still, something about

Tiger Lily made her want to try something utterly foreign to her: politeness.

"I don't mind at all," Jocelyn replied. "I'm not terribly hungry just yet."

Jocelyn's mouth may have been attempting good manners, but her stomach had no new scruples. It let out a growl loud enough to be heard over the sound of the crackling fire.

Evie burst out laughing, and Tiger Lily joined in, her voice warm and rich. Jocelyn's cheeks flamed, but she pretended that she had no idea what was so funny.

Roger looked up at the sound of their laughter. Seeing the three girls together, he abandoned the fire, though not his stick, and came to stand nearby. The boy didn't say anything, but stood staring at Tiger Lily, his mouth slightly open.

"What are you doing?" Jocelyn asked him.

"What? Who, me? Nothing." He glanced again at Tiger Lily, then quickly turned his gaze upon his feet. "I just thought I'd come join you in . . . ah . . ." He motioned to Evie. "Guarding our prisoner."

Evie giggled. "Indeed. I am a fierce one."

If anything, Roger looked even more uncomfortable. "Perhaps we should all just . . . er . . . sit down and wait for dinner."

Jocelyn gritted her teeth. "Yes. Perhaps we should."

Tiger Lily laughed again, though Jocelyn couldn't see

what was so funny. She was glad when the girl excused herself to see to final feast preparations.

Jocelyn, Evie, and Roger found a bench near the fire. The fur robes were even more comfortable than Jocelyn had expected. She sat between the other two, though Roger kept leaning around her to peer at their captive.

"Why are you staring at her?" Jocelyn hissed.

"What, don't you see it?"

"See what? That she's pretty?" She balled a wad of buffalo fur in her fist.

"She is, isn't she?" Roger said.

Jocelyn merely said, "Humph," and turned her back on the boy.

"No, I mean, she's pretty because she . . . well, she looks a bit like . . ."

"Never mind. I don't care."

Roger laid a hand on her arm. "It's just that she looks something like you."

Jocelyn's insides warmed. Was Roger saying she was pretty?

She turned back to face him, wearing a hint of a smile. "I suppose that's why you are staring at Tiger Lily, too? Because *she* looks like me?" She raised an eyebrow.

Roger ducked his head and mumbled, "I don't know what you mean. Anyway," he said, straightening up, "about Evie," he went on, "you two could be sisters. You both have freckles and that nose that turns up at the end.

Only she's a bit taller, a bit older, and more, you know . . . girlish."

Jocelyn's smile hardened on her lips. "I'll show you girlish." She grabbed his stick, threw it into the fire, and moved to a new bench. Tiger Lily looked up from a conversation she was having with one of the women preparing the feast. Her face wore an expression of mirth. Jocelyn's cheeks flamed.

There was something about Tiger Lily that Jocelyn admired and disliked all at once. It wasn't only that she was pretty in a way Jocelyn felt she would never be. Tiger Lily also seemed so sure of herself, and her people obviously loved her. She didn't look as if she worried about how to lead them; she simply led. It was irritating. Even so, or perhaps because of this, Jocelyn felt the need to impress her.

Jocelyn shifted in her seat and felt the crinkle of the map in her pocket. Perhaps Tiger Lily did have qualities that Jocelyn did not, indeed perhaps never would. But Jocelyn had something of her own. She had a map to Captain Hook's greatest treasure.

She imagined the look of admiration Tiger Lily would give her if Jocelyn were to show her the map. Maybe she could risk showing it to Tiger Lily, only to ask if she knew where it led. Granted, Jocelyn didn't *really* need to ask for help. Once she cracked the code, she'd know everything about the treasure's location. Then again, asking might save her some time. Surely, that was a good enough reason to show it to her.

She struggled for a few moments, stuck between discretion and winning the other girl's respect. After carefully weighing the consequences of each action, she chose what she felt was best. She stood and pulled the map from her pocket.

"Excuse me, Tiger Lily, do you know where this is?" Jocelyn shoved the paper in the older girl's face. "It's a map to Hook's treasure. He left it for me, in a way. It's my legacy, you know."

Tiger Lily took it from her, but before looking she stopped to scold a group of children for playing too close to the fire. "Go find your nursemaid and tell him to pay closer attention." The children ran off, giggling. They caught up to a man who was already burdened with a small child attached, starfishlike, to each leg, a baby strapped to his back, and two toddlers in his arms. The newcomers tackled the man, nearly making him fall. Tiger Lily smiled and shook her head at their antics, then turned her attention back to the map.

She stepped closer to the fire to get a better look and frowned, concentrating. "I'm afraid I do not. The memory of my people is long, and we are closely tied to the land here. I am surprised to say it, but I do not know this place."

Jocelyn took the map back and returned it to her

pocket, disappointed in both Tiger Lily's lack of jealousy and her lack of knowledge. Having to wait to break the code was so frustrating.

"I'm sorry I could not be of any help to you." Tiger Lily continued, "No one knows this island better than I, though Peter Pan would like to think he does. You could ask him, but I doubt he will tell you anything useful." Her face darkened. "Besides, he's likely off looking for a new mother to steal for." Her hand gripped the knife at her waist for the briefest of instants. She relaxed her hand and straightened her back. "Shall we feast?"

CHAPTER TEN

A Revelation

Many people love surprises, though I am not one, as the friends and family who once attempted to throw me a surprise birthday party could attest. I don't care what the magistrate said; when a group of people burst forth from hiding in a dark room screaming "Surprise!" and throwing confetti, any reasonable person would have perceived it as a threat and taken measures to defend himself. I am nothing if not reasonable.

Speaking of fires (we were, weren't we?), Tiger Lily signaled to the women to pull the meat from the flames and serve her guests. They carved hunks of smoking roast buffalo, piling them, along with sweet wild onion and some root vegetable Jocelyn couldn't identify, into giant abalone-shell bowls. The meal was hot and rich, and Jocelyn felt it was the best she had ever eaten. She attacked it with gusto, relishing every bite and wiping the evidence on her new jacket sleeves. Meriwether perched on the edge of her bowl, finishing off her vegetables when she was too full to eat another bite.

Roger only picked at his food, distracted, but across the fire the rest of Jocelyn's crew seemed to be having a wonderful time. They had a group of young women gathered round and were no doubt regaling them with tales of their exploits and cunning. One-Armed Jack had replaced his prosthetic arm again, trading his butterfly net for a short spear decorated with intricate beadwork. He seemed to be in the midst of some exciting tale, and he gesticulated wildly, nearly taking off the nose of an older woman trying to serve him more meat. Jocelyn hoped he got the hang of it before he injured someone.

As the meal wound down, the village boys added more wood to the flames and took up their poking again. Roger watched them mournfully until Jocelyn brought him a peace offering by way of a new stick. Roger grinned, their skirmish all but forgotten.

Meriwether, on the other hand, developed a sudden foul mood. The fairy gave the boy a jealous pinch on the arm and flew to the top of a nearby tipi. The spot afforded him a perfect angle for flashing his light in Roger's eyes.

Jocelyn laughed off his bad behavior and reclaimed her

seat between Evie and Roger. "Look at him! Jealousy is such a ridiculous emotion!"

Before Roger could reply, Tiger Lily stood and walked to the center of the circle of benches. The fire was at her back, darkening her features until she looked more shadow than girl. A sudden hush came over the camp. The flames danced higher and higher, and a feeling of expectation hung in the air. Somewhere outside the camp borders a wolf howled. Tiger Lily's pup answered with a howl of her own. Jocelyn's blood pumped. She had the wild urge to raise her voice and join in.

"It is time for the evening's entertainment," Tiger Lily announced. "First, we will have Two Bears reenact today's battle in song and dance." A drum beat out a rhythm, and Jocelyn's heart kept time. The warrior's movements were smooth, fluid. Jocelyn felt as if she could read the entire fight in the motion of his body. He flicked his hand and she saw Peter scratch a man with his short dagger. He spun in a circle and Jocelyn saw her own arrival, leading the pirate crew. He swayed and bent, and Jocelyn saw an arrow graze a lost boy's backside as he retreated. His skill was mesmerizing.

No one applauded when he finished, but the silence held more awe and respect for his performance than a standing ovation. The very wind through the trees cried *bravo*, and the stars above cheered.

The girl was startled from her enraptured state when

Tiger Lily motioned toward her. "And now our guests will entertain us."

Jim McCraig jumped to his feet and said something unintelligible. His parrot translated by repeating it more loudly.

"Quiet that infernal chicken," Mr. Smee said. "Beggin' your pardon, Captain, but Jim is volunteering to favor us all with a song."

Jocelyn liked Jim's singing, particularly because it was the only time she could understand a word out of his mouth. Yet, after that magical performance, she couldn't offer something quite so ordinary to Tiger Lily's people.

"Thank you, Jim," she said "but I think I would like to do this one myself." After all, her voice had tamed a mermaid, and that was not something just anyone could say.

She got to her feet and faced Tiger Lily. "This is a song that my grandfather sang to me at night when I was young." She cleared her throat and began to sing in her clear, high soprano:

Over the mountains
And over the waves,
Under the fountains
And under the graves...

Evie stood and joined her, adding a rich alto harmony that blended beautifully with Jocelyn's voice. Even so,

Jocelyn glared at her in irritation. *This was supposed to be a solo!* She fumbled over the next word but, not wanting to disappoint her audience, recovered and sang on.

> *Under floods that are deepest,*
> *Which Neptune must obey,*
> *Over rocks that are steepest,*
> *Love will find out the way.*

Both girls slowed their tempo and repeated the last line, imbuing the song with a sweet tenderness, just as Sir Charles always had. A sudden longing for home, to see her grandfather again, pricked Jocelyn's heart.

The last notes echoed through the air. The music had been so transporting that Jocelyn had forgotten her audience, but she saw them now. They smiled at her, respect for the music showing on their faces. More than one person had been moved to tears. Jocelyn gathered Evie into a quick hug. She felt a sudden kinship with her, born of their harmony.

They rejoined Roger on their bench, and the next performance began. A group of men, with bells strapped to their wrists and ankles, danced in the moonlight. It sounded like an entire crowd of fairies, all clamoring for attention.

Meriwether settled onto Jocelyn's head to watch, softly ringing in appreciation.

Roger leaned over and whispered, "Your song was amazing."

The tinkling bells of the dancers kept Meriwether's attention so well, he didn't attempt to retaliate.

Jocelyn smiled. "Thank—"

"Thank you, Roger." Evie spoke over her. "It was pretty good, wasn't it?"

"It was. . . . I mean . . . Jocelyn sings all the time—"

Jocelyn sent him a murderous look.

"And I like it! I really do, Jocelyn! It's just that the two of you together, well, that was something extra special."

Any feelings of goodwill Jocelyn had felt toward Evie popped like a soap bubble. "Yes, well, Evie appears to be good at stealing the show."

"Oh, Jocelyn, I'm sorry! That was awful of me, wasn't it? But when I heard that song, I couldn't stay silent. My father sang it to me when I was a little girl, telling me his lullaby would keep any bad dreams away."

Sir Charles had said the same thing to Jocelyn.

The dancers picked up the pace, the rhythm of their bells and their pounding feet beating a staccato tempo that Jocelyn felt all the way to her bones.

Evie reached over and pulled Jocelyn's hand into her own. "If I had had a little sister, I think I would have liked her to be someone very much like you."

"I'm not sure a sister could look more like you than Jocelyn already does," Roger said.

Ringing filled Jocelyn's ears.

"And she could even be named Jocelyn! I've always loved that name."

Thoughts started to tumble in the girl's mind. She and Evie did look similar—very similar. And they knew the same song, sung to each of them to keep bad dreams away. Evie . . . She couldn't be. Could she?

"Your name . . . is it . . ." Jocelyn swallowed, her throat dry. "Is Evie short for something?"

Evie flashed the dimples in her cheeks. "It is! My full name is Evelina Helene Hopewell. How did you guess?"

Jocelyn stared at her, caught in a war between fascination and horror. A fitting reaction, I think, to standing face-to-face with a young girl—only a year older than yourself—who also happens to be your mother.

Now *that* was a surprise.

CHAPTER ELEVEN

Wherein Jocelyn Acquires a Nursemaid

"I need to get some air." Jocelyn said, stumbling backward. "The campfire smoke is making me feel ill."

"I'll join you," Roger said, his voice sounding as shocked as Jocelyn felt.

"I think I'd rather be alone." She leaned in close and added in a lower voice, "Don't say anything. Please."

Roger nodded and Jocelyn fled from the fire, barely registering where she was going. She reached the edge of the circle of tipis and stopped, looking out into the night. There she stood, fingering her locket, lost in thought. The distant wolf bayed again, but this time it sounded less wild and free. It simply sounded lonely.

How could her mother possibly be here? And frolicking about with that obnoxious Peter Pan? What could

Evie—Evelina?—possibly see in that boy that was worth *mothering*? Jocelyn ground her teeth. It wasn't fair!

The girl was so wrapped up in the shock, the injustice, the very ridiculousness of what was happening that she didn't hear footsteps approaching. Even so, her reflexes were sharp; when someone grabbed her arm, Jocelyn had her sword out before she even turned around.

The nursemaid she had caught a glimpse of earlier held her loosely by the arm. Up close it was apparent that the man had not been born into Tiger Lily's tribe. Even in the moonlight Jocelyn could see that his skin was too pale, his build too stout. Nautical tattoos peeked out from his sleeves, and his eyes were squeezed into a perpetual squint, the result of a life spent under the sun, wind, and waves.

This was no nursemaid. This was a pirate.

Isn't that just the way life is? It throws something in your path, something momentous, something that must be pondered, mulled over, and truly considered in order for you to make sense of it, but before you have a chance to do so . . . *Snap!* A wild-eyed pirate has caught hold of your arm.

Jocelyn jerked hers away from the man and leveled her sword at him. "If Krueger sent you, his sense of timing is as terrible as his breath. I'm in no mood to be tangled with."

The pirate scowled. "So you've gotten yourself mixed

up with Captain Krueger, have you? I might have guessed it, the way you've been waving that map around."

Jocelyn was no novice when it came to looking innocent. She had played far too many pranks on tutors and governesses for that. "What map?" she asked with wide eyes.

Likewise, the man was no novice in the ways of children. He narrowed his eyes. "Isn't that just like a child? Presented with irrefutable facts and they want to play pretend! The map in your pocket, missy. The map to Hook's gold."

Jocelyn pressed the point of her sword into his stomach. Her voice was low and threatening. "You can't have it."

He spat on the ground, unperturbed. "I don't want it. That map has already caused me more trouble than it's worth. The gold is cursed, you know. Even in death, Hook won't give it up."

"I don't believe in curses."

The man laughed, but there was no joy in it. "You will grow to believe."

She gripped the sword more tightly, her knuckles growing white. "If you don't want the map, why did you mention it in the first place?"

"I know where it leads."

His words hit Jocelyn like a jolt of electricity. If this was true, he might know everything. She wouldn't have to find the *Jolly Roger* in order to break the code. He could simply tell her what she needed! The treasure was practically hers! Still, she tried to keep the man from knowing how much she wanted to believe him. She resheathed her sword and made a show of brushing off the front of her jacket. "I presume," she said, with an air of near disinterest, "you are willing to tell me this?"

He laughed again, a hard, brittle sound. The girl was rather certain he could see through her ruse. "I might be persuaded," he said, "in exchange for something you can provide."

Jocelyn shrugged, unwilling to give up her charade. "I am very close to decoding the map, so you see, I don't really *need* your information, though it may be a small amount of use to me. Name your terms and I shall think it over."

He wiped his hands on his breeches and attempted a casual smile. Jocelyn got the impression that she was not the only one feigning less interest than was felt.

"I want to leave this place," he said, "but my service isn't exactly voluntary. Day and night, without cease I must care for their sticky-fingered children: give them baths, and meals, and grammar lessons until I'm half-mad."

Jocelyn stared at the man, puzzled. "Who are you?"

"Pardon me, forgetting my manners—easy to do when each day is spent in the company of children—such ill-mannered beasts." He held out a hand. "The name is

Starkey, Gentleman Starkey. A long time ago I was an English schoolmaster, but I left that life for one less dangerous: piracy under the black flag of Captain James Hook."

Jocelyn ignored his hand. "You sailed with my father?"

He put his hands in his pockets and nodded. "I did. Right up until the end. Smee and I were the only ones to survive that last battle between our crew and Pan's lost boys. I thought he was dead and gone like all the rest, until I saw him here tonight, sitting by the fire, fat and happy as could be." Starkey curled his lip. "Doesn't look like our downfall hurt him any."

Jocelyn felt oddly protective of her bo'sun. If he was to be insulted, she should be the one to do it, just as he liked. "You leave Mr. Smee alone! He has suffered in ways you'll never know."

Starkey raised his voice. "Yet he's faring quite well, while here I sit, a nursemaid!" A dog barked from inside the camp, prompting Starkey to lower his voice again. "We should have never captured those children and brought them aboard the *Jolly Roger*. The lost boys were bad enough, but the girl, that Wendy . . . Any sailor worth his salt knows that girls are bad luck at sea."

Jocelyn lowered her eyebrows. "I would tend to disagree."

He sighed. "Of course you would. Children are such disagreeable creatures."

"If you hate us so much, why are you even talking to me?"

"I've already told you. I need your help to escape. I'm not a nursemaid. I'm a pirate. It's in my blood, and I need to get back to the sea."

The girl put her hands on her hips. "Why should I help you?"

"I've told you that, too. Do try to pay attention when I'm speaking." He pinched the bridge of his nose and spoke slowly. "I know where that map leads. Help me and I'll tell you."

Jocelyn considered him for a moment. "Why should I trust you?"

"Because I'm a pirate, just like you. We're bound together under the Code of Brotherhood."

Jocelyn wasn't sure how she felt about this Code of Brotherhood. So far, it seemed to be merely a device used to try to talk her into doing things. Even so, she did want to know where the map led. "I suppose I have nothing to lose. I'll do what I can."

Jocelyn returned to the fire, choosing a seat alone, in the back. She hardly noticed a trio of young women somehow singing together in four-part harmony. Roger turned and gave her a questioning look, but she waved him off, unready to talk. Her mind felt a jumbled mess, crowded with thoughts of treasure, escape plots, and the presence of Evie—her *mother*—in the Neverland.

When the music died down, Tiger Lily stood. "My family, my friends, today has shown us a victory. We should have taken it regardless, for Pan is no match for us in our times of war, but our losses might have been heavy. Captain Jocelyn and her crew supported us in our need, and"—she looked shrewdly at Evie—"have taken Pan's mother from him just as he took my Snow from me." The pup gave a sharp bark in acknowledgment of her name, and Tiger Lily reached down and gave her a pat.

"Captain Jocelyn and her prisoner," she went on, "have also given us the gift of song. I would like to offer a gift in return." She turned to address Jocelyn directly. "You may ask a boon of me. Anything you like."

That caught Jocelyn's attention. "I can choose anything? And you will just give it to me?"

Tiger Lily gave a single, regal nod of her head. "I will, with the exception of Snow." She picked up the pup and nuzzled her. "I would hate to lose her again."

Jocelyn pretended to think it over. Starkey stood at the edge of the firelight, a toddler attached to his ankle. The pirate's look was pained and pleading. "I choose . . . that man over there. Your nursemaid."

Tiger Lily raised her eyebrows. "But surely you are too old for a nursemaid?"

Color flooded Jocelyn's cheeks. "Of course I am! But he sailed with my father. I may have need of him."

The princess's face was grave. "I did not expect this. My young mothers will not be pleased to see him go. However, I did say you could choose anything." Her eyes twinkled, and her lips twitched as if holding back a smile. "You may take him."

Starkey shook off the children attached to him—none too gently, I might add, though likely more so than the little blighters deserved. A few mothers, their faces more tired than they had appeared moments before, gathered their crying children.

The crew was curious about the new addition to their ranks, particularly when Mr. Smee greeted him like a long-lost relative: with a slap on the back and an appeal for a loan.

In the meantime, the children, freed from the constraints of their nursemaid, began to run amok: wiping dirty mouths and hands on buffalo robes, pulling dog tails, crossing eyes and making faces at their mothers. Things were swiftly slipping into chaos. The exasperated looks Tiger Lily's people shot in her direction convinced Jocelyn that it was time for her and her crew to be on their way.

After thanking Tiger Lily for her hospitality, they made ready to leave. "Men, gather your things," she commanded. "We must return to the ship at once. And don't forget the prisoner. Roger, you may guard her as you navigate." The girl hadn't yet decided whether or not to tell Evie the true nature of their relationship, and she didn't feel in the mood for casual chitchat.

Jocelyn let the others get ahead while she fell back with Starkey. The puzzle of her mother would have to wait. She wanted to talk about where the treasure lay. "Do you need to see the map again to refresh your memory?" she asked.

"I do not. I know precisely where it is." He spoke in a whisper, drawing farther back, creating distance between them and the rest of the crew.

"Even so," Jocelyn replied, "the land may have changed since the map was drawn. Will you lead us there?"

"No need. I daresay you are likely to know your way there better than anyone."

"I doubt that is true."

"Well then, little miss, you would be wrong—though you are likely used to it. However..." His eyes darted about, as if to ensure they were alone. The others were far ahead of them now. "I won't be telling you after all. I made a blood oath not to reveal it. Solve the map's puzzle and you'll know all you need." With that, he stepped off the path and slipped into the trees.

Jocelyn gave chase. "Wait! What about the Code of Brotherhood?" she yelled after him.

"Never trust a pirate!" he called back just as the girl lost sight of him.

Jocelyn and the crew searched—Meriwether even called for his soldiers to assist—but Starkey had simply disappeared, taking his knowledge of the map with him.

A crafty one, was he. Never trust a pirate, indeed.

CHAPTER TWELVE

The Hows and Whys of Different Whens

If you have ever deeply believed one thing to be true—for example, when your mother said that you were clever and wonderful—only to discover the opposite to be true, you may have an idea of what Jocelyn felt as she tried to reconcile the Evelina she had grown up hearing about—ladylike, docile, polite, perfect—with the Evie she was now getting to know. The Evie who at that very moment had her legs hooked in the ropes of the ship's rigging, from which she dangled, upside down, chatting amiably with Jim McCraig about his parrot. Apparently, his incomprehensible speech was not a problem for her.

Mr. Smee approached his captain armed with parchment, ink, and a feather pen that looked suspiciously like it had been made from a Karnapinae nose feather. "Well then, miss. Do you want to dictate the ransom letter to me, or should I write it and have you sign it?"

"Ransom letter? Oh, right, to Pan. Er . . . I'm not ready to send it yet."

"Ah, I see. You want to make him sweat it out a bit first? Have him worry about what it is you might be asking for? Then, when he finds it's nothing more than telling you where he left the dear captain's ship . . ." Smee took out a handkerchief and dabbed at his eyes. "As I was saying, when the boy learns all he has to do is tell you something, he might hand it over easy."

Jocelyn fiddled with the buttons on her jacket. "Yes, yes, of course that's what I meant."

"Good thinking, Miss Captain. Only, don't let it go too long. That boy is awfully forgetful—right, Johnny?" Smee gave his trusty sword a nod and a loving pat. "Peter Pan is liable to forget where the ship is, or that he brought the girl here in the first place."

Jocelyn rolled her eyes. That boy was such a nuisance. "Thank you, Smee," she said. "I'll let you know when I'm ready to send the letter."

Which will probably be never, she thought. She ground her teeth, frustrated that the adventure she so longed for was stalled yet again. It didn't help matters that Jocelyn truly had no idea what to do with her captive. She really *couldn't* send Evie back to Peter. That boy didn't deserve to be mothered by her, even in pretend.

Perhaps she could invite Evie along on the search for the treasure. It might be nice to spend time together, get to know each other. Except, without ransoming her, how would Jocelyn make Peter tell her where the *Jolly Roger* was?

The girl stomped her foot in annoyance. She was no closer to finding the treasure than when she left the map-maker's shop. *Curses on that nursemaid!* If only he had kept his end of the bargain, she would at least have an idea of where she should go. But no, the treasure hunt was stalled again, the *Hook's Revenge* still anchored in the hidden cove.

Jocelyn was startled out of her melancholy thoughts by something Evie, continuing to converse with Jim McCraig, said—something that seemed to open up a whole new set of problems: "I love being a pirate and I love the Neverland! I'm never, ever going to go back home."

This just goes to show that when you begin to think things couldn't possibly get worse, they generally do. Why dither over an unreadable map when one's very existence could hang in the balance? For if Evie didn't go home, she wouldn't meet and marry Captain Hook. And if she didn't do that, they would never have a daughter.

In that case, what would happen to Jocelyn?

★ ★ ★

Sneaking into the pirate village, under cover of night and alone—without even Meriwether to accompany her—should have felt exciting and clandestine. Jocelyn arranged it all perfectly. She waited until everyone else went to bed, then sprinkled a dash of pepper on Meri's spiderdown pillow, causing him to sneeze and shower her with fairy dust. She excused herself from the little fellow under the guise of washing up, but instead stole into the night sky. Even Mr. Smee, keeping the night's middle watch, didn't notice her slipping away.

As I said, the whole affair should have been thrilling—all right, it *was* thrilling, but only a little. The girl felt sure it would have been more so if it hadn't been for two things: First, she was going to see someone she disliked. Jocelyn would have been happy to never see the harbor-master and his ridiculous ledger book again. However, he seemed more knowledgeable than anyone about different Whens. The girl hoped he could clear up her questions about Evie.

Second, it was hard to be excited about anything, pre-occupied as she was with said questions. This only goes to show: Even if one's mother is little more than a year older than one, she may still have a way of putting a damper on illicit excursions. Mothers are like that.

Jocelyn may not have been excited, but she was alert.

She knew Krueger was out there somewhere, always moving, relentless in his hunt for gold. The girl had no idea how many spies the man had in his employ. This time, she would exercise caution in the pirate village.

Jocelyn landed near the dock and waited in the shadows, hoping the harbormaster would soon make his rounds. It was quite late, but she did not imagine he had gone to bed. Men such as him rarely sleep, not when there is governmental work to attend to. After several long moments, the fluttering of pages drew her attention.

Jocelyn cleared her throat.

The harbormaster looked up from his ledger book and peered into the shadows. "I say, is someone there?" he called. "Are you registered? Come out in the light where I can see you."

Jocelyn stepped forward. "Keep your voice down," she commanded, and then, exercising some manners in the hopes of getting the answers she needed, added, "please."

He tipped his hat. "Ah, it is only you, young Miss Hook. Your paperwork is all in order. There is no need to for me to make any inquiry of you. Good night."

"It's not good yet. I need to ask you something. Something about how the Neverland works."

"Indeed! I like to see young people employed in scholarly pursuits! I will try to explain in such a way that even one as young and uneducated as yourself may understand."

Jocelyn turned her grimace into a smile, trusting the evening shadows to keep the man from seeing the look of annoyance in her eyes. "Please," she said through gritted teeth, "tell me more about travel to and from different times on the mainland."

"Ah, yes. A fascinating subject. As I mentioned when we first met, people can come to the Neverland from any different When. The Neverland exists outside of linear time. Indeed, it could be said that it exists in the Never, but perhaps that is too complicated an idea?"

"I think I just might be able to grasp it. Carry on."

"Very well. People arrive here from many different times, carrying within themselves a sort of internal clock. They stay for whatever length of time they choose before returning home to their own Whens, plus however long they stayed. So if one were to leave home in February of 1300, and stay in the Neverland for four months, he or she would return home in June of 1300—just in time to read the newly published travels of Marco Polo, though I daresay Polo's adventures would pale in comparison. Are you following this all right? It is quite a heavy subject for a young girl."

Jocelyn huffed. "I am keeping up quite well, thank you very much."

"You are entirely welcome. Now, some have attempted to use the Neverland as a sort of way station for travel to different Whens, but it is nearly impossible. If you have a home, it holds a piece of your soul, like an anchor, so to speak. Upon leaving the Neverland, your home will draw you back."

This wasn't quite the information Jocelyn needed, but she felt that rushing the man would get her nowhere. And she was curious about one point. "How does Peter Pan travel to different Whens? And the courier crows?"

"Ah, well the crows are one thing and Peter Pan is quite another. Any creature native to the Neverland—the crows, for example—can travel to any time it likes. As can anyone, like Peter Pan and his lost boys, who has forgotten his home. Such a one becomes untethered."

"So forgetting home sets them free to go anywhere?"

"I suppose you could call it that, but that freedom comes at an exorbitant price. One who is untethered from his or her home will never feel at home anywhere else. He or she will forever be searching for what he or she has lost, feeling no true joy, no true peace. Why do you think Peter Pan is always in search of a mother?"

That reminded Jocelyn of what she had come to learn. "What would happen—hypothetically, of course—if someone came to the Neverland from one When, and, say, for example, their future child came from another, but they were both on the Neverland at the same time? Has that ever happened?"

The harbormaster flipped through the pages of his ledger. "It is rare, but not unprecedented. There would be no trouble, provided neither forgot who he or she was and both returned home in a timely manner."

"Interesting. But what if one, perhaps the mother, chose to stay in the Neverland? What would happen to her daughter?"

"That is an interesting puzzle. Surely, there is no way to know for certain, but simply for the sake of rhetoric, it stands to reason that the daughter would also have to stay on the Neverland, for if the mother never returned home, she could never truly finish growing up. Non-native Neverlandians do age here. That is to say, they do grow older. But growing up—becoming a certified adult—is a thing reserved for the mainland."

Jocelyn nodded, finally understanding why her crew was so childlike. The men had gotten older on the Neverland, but hadn't grown up, not really. Although that explanation only led to more questions. "But what about Peter Pan? He doesn't seem to age at all. And my father, Captain Hook, he was a proper adult. For that matter, you also seem to be fully grown up, and even more so than most. No offense."

"None taken. Your father, myself, and a handful of others in the village reached adulthood before we came to the Neverland, and thus we became, as you say, 'proper adults,' although I would argue that some are not exactly proper.

"As for Peter Pan, he has not only forgotten his home;

he forgets most everything. One cannot age at all here on the Neverland without experience. For Peter, each day is much the same as the last. If he cannot learn, he cannot grow."

"The same thing happened to my friend Roger, for a time. But why have I not forgotten anything?"

"You may have noticed that young girls grow more quickly than boys? They are often in such a hurry to grow up. Maturing at a high speed makes it more difficult to stop. As such, they do not forget as easily—not unless they are determined to do so."

"That all makes sense, I suppose, but..." Here was the question that Jocelyn needed most to understand. "What does all of this mean for my—I mean *the* mother and daughter?"

"Yes, well, of course, should the mother retain her day-to-day memories, she would age, but she would not truly grow up. As such, she would not have adult experiences, such as marriage and children. Thus the daughter could not come into existence. She could perhaps continue to exist here, for the Neverland is filled with impossible things, but were she to try to leave and return to her home—or anywhere on the mainland, for that matter— she would simply cease to exist, like a candle blowing out."

Jocelyn's heart leaped to her throat. She didn't want to go home just yet, but she might want to go one day—after finding the treasure and receiving the freedom it would afford her. Either way, she certainly wanted to choose for herself—not have something foisted upon her.

But if she couldn't find a way to convince Evelina to return to the mainland, she would be stuck on the Neverland forever. They would both grow old, but never grow up.

Even so, how could she send Evie back, knowing that the choice would eventually kill her?

Quite a pickle, isn't it?

CHAPTER THIRTEEN

Rebellion, Riot, and Ruin

Jocelyn timed her return to the *Hook's Revenge* to coincide with Roger's turn at watch. There was no one she'd rather go to when she needed perspective and advice. She filled him in on all the information she had learned from the harbormaster and waited for him to find a solution to her problem, as he had done so often before.

"I think what you have to do is pretty clear, don't you?" he said. "What other choice do you have but to tell Evie everything and let her decide?"

Jocelyn considered how that conversation might go: *Oh, hello, Evie. Remember how you said you would have liked to have a younger sister like me? Well, how about a daughter? Surprise! You're a mother. Or at least . . . you will be.*

Who knew how Evie might take the news—or what she might choose once she learned the truth? No, it was better that Evie not be told. There had to be another way to resolve things, and as Roger didn't seem to have one, Jocelyn would think of it on her own. Somehow.

Jocelyn stumbled from her cabin late the next morning. What little sleep the girl had managed to catch after speaking to Roger had been troubled and filled with nightmares. It was nearly noon when at last she awoke, her mind as tangled as her ratty hair, her emotions as sour as the drool dried on her cheek, her stomach as empty as your own witless head.

Mr. Smee, once more armed with pen and paper, greeted her in the galley, where Nubbins had prepared a porridge he called "cardamom-scented mush" for Jocelyn's breakfast.

"Are you ready for me to pen that ransom letter now, miss?" Smee asked. He held up his hands, revealing bandages on all his fingers. "I filled my ink bottle with something special, to add just the right amount of menace. Better get started before it coagulates."

"Oh dear," Jocelyn replied. "I can see you went to quite a lot of trouble, but I have changed my mind. I won't be sending a ransom letter."

Dirty Bob sat at the table, cutting slices from an apple

with a small silver knife. He waved it in her direction and asked, "No ransom after all, eh? What is your plan then, Cap'n?"

Her plan was to come up with a plan, but she couldn't very well say *that*.

"Well..." She took a bite of her porridge, stalling. "I still intend to get Pan to tell me what I need to know, but as for how..." She took another bite. "Um...it's a secret." *Even to me*, she thought. "After I do so, we will go after the treasure. But let's talk about something else right now. The ship looks absolutely top-notch! Did you all do this while I slept?" Even through her bleary eyes, Jocelyn hadn't missed the gleaming deck and untangled rigging that had greeted her when she left her cabin.

"I'm of a mind that it never hurts to be prepared," Dirty Bob replied. "I tightened up her stays, and now the old girl's ready to dance, should the opportunity arise." He cleared his throat. "Indeed, she's running so fine, I daresay she could overtake nearly any ship not traveling too light. But who would want to overtake those?" He laughed, a great booming *ha-ha*, then fell silent.

Jocelyn flicked a smattering of crumbs off the table. "Yes. Well, I don't think we will be in need of that, as I have mentioned, but it is good to have everything in working order."

Dirty Bob pounded the table, causing Jocelyn's mush to splatter the front of her jacket. "Maybe next you'd like me to set up a tea party? Judging by the number of little girls aboard the ship, that seems fitting." He didn't wait for a reply, but stormed from the galley.

Smee stood, his hand on his sword hilt. "Want me to go after him, Captain? Make the dirty blighter show some respect?"

"No," she sighed. "Give him some time to cool off first." She dabbed at the mush on her jacket. "Later this evening you may inform him that since he seems so willing to waste food, he will be on half rations for a week."

"Anything else? Flogging? Marooning? Keelhauling? Making him change the bandages on Jim McCraig's infected toe?"

"I hope we won't have to resort to those things. I'm sure he will be fine once we begin the treasure hunt."

"Speaking of which, miss, I was meaning to ask you about that. We are running low on supplies again. We'll all be on half rations afore long. Do you think we'll be under way soon?"

Jocelyn worried the edge of her jacket between her fingers. "I certainly hope so."

"What do you hope?" Roger entered, bringing Evie with him.

"I hope Nubbins doesn't mind me asking for seconds," Jocelyn replied. She didn't want to confide the situation to Roger in front of the other girl. "Looks like I've more mush on my jacket than in my stomach."

"Oh dear. Do you want me to get you a table linen?" Evie said. "I don't see any."

Dirty Bob's comment about throwing a tea party still stung. Jocelyn responded rather sharply, "We don't use table linens on a pirate ship!"

Nubbins called from where he stood by the stove. "Oh, Captain, I nearly forgot to tell you, I bought some in the village! Nice floweredy ones. I thought they might brighten up the place. I was saving them for a special occasion, but why wait?" He brought Jocelyn a large linen square and placed it in her lap. "There now, isn't that something? Classy!" He beamed at her. "And if'n you were wanting seconds on the mush, feel free to take what you like." He set the whole pot in the center of the table.

Roger burst out laughing, which only served to irritate Jocelyn further. On impulse, she scooped up a spoonful of mush from her bowl and launched it at him. The cardamom-scented blob struck him full in the face, sliding off and hitting the table with a sickening plop. Everyone froze.

Roger wiped his face with the back of his hand, then ever so slowly reached into the pot. He pulled up a sticky fistful of goo and wiped it in Jocelyn's hair. With that, all bedlam broke loose. Jocelyn screamed with laughter and flung mush at Evie. Evie bounced up and down on the balls of her feet, giggling wildly, and poured a ladleful

over Mr. Smee's head. Mr. Smee seemed unsure what action to take, not retaliating until Jocelyn ordered him to do so, at which point he fired a glop at Roger and hit him dead center in the chest.

"Did you see that, miss? 'Twas a direct hit!" he crowed, and was rewarded with return fire striking him in the open mouth.

Nubbins, scandalized at the improper use of his cooking, tried to put a stop to things, but he slipped in a puddle of mush and fell flat on his back.

"Man overboard!" Roger yelled, causing Jocelyn and Evie to laugh until their breath came in gasps.

When the last bit of porridge had been flung, Jocelyn surveyed the damage. Nubbins cowered under the table, shaking his head and muttering about his wasted effort. Mr. Smee, goo dripping from his beard, attempted to clean his spectacles on his shirtfront, but only succeeded in smearing more mush over the glass. Every inch of Roger, Evie, and the entire galley was covered in a layer of porridge, already beginning to harden as it dried. The girl had seen some messes in her day, but nothing quite as ruinous as this. It was absolutely glorious.

There was only one thing to do. "Anyone have a table linen?" she called out. The three children burst out laughing again, Evie loudest of all, with a very unladylike snorting guffaw. No matter how much of a bind it had

put Jocelyn in, for the moment, at least, she was glad
Evie was there.

Jocelyn excused Mr. Smee and the poor, traumatized
Nubbins while she, Roger, and Evie set to work cleaning the galley. It was not an easy task. The mush hardened into a thick, scabrous layer that covered absolutely
everything. Hot water and hours of vigorous scrubbing
were the only known cure. Once things had been set to
rights again, the three children returned to the upper
deck to rest.

Evie looked down at herself and giggled. "What would
my father say if he could see me? I'm as filthy as a scul-
lery maid!"

The labors of the afternoon had taken Jocelyn's
mind off Evie's true identity, but mention of her father
brought it all back. What *would* Sir Charles say? Jocelyn
was used to him being disappointed in her own lack of
refinement, but he had always spoken of Evelina with
reverence. Would he even recognize the girl who sat on
the deck next to Jocelyn, hands rubbed raw from scrubbing, and dried porridge making a baroque sculpture
of her hair?

"Jocelyn," Roger said, drawing her attention away
from Evie, "I'm afraid we may need to find a new place to
anchor." He stared intently at his Neverland map. "This

part of the island is changing. There won't be a cove here much longer."

Jocelyn peered over his shoulder and confirmed what he was seeing. The inlet would soon be more of an outlet. This was inconvenient, but at least moving the ship might give them all the illusion of progress. It was better than sitting and waiting for inspiration to strike.

"See if you can't find us a better place to moor for the time being," she said. "I'll alert the crew."

Jocelyn ordered the *Hook's Revenge* out to the open sea. It was a windy day, and the waves were rough. She warned Evie that since she was still a landlubber, not having had enough time to get her sea legs under her, she might become seasick, but unfortunately, the girl seemed to have an iron stomach. It seemed nothing could dissuade her from having the time of her life.

If only Meriwether had had the same constitution. At the first sign of rough waves, the poor little fairy changed from blue to green and flung himself atop an apple barrel, moaning like a cowbell.

As soon as they'd weighed anchor, Blind Bart had perched himself in the crow's nest, claiming it to be the safest spot on the ship—as it was farthest from the water. He now climbed down and spoke to Jocelyn. "Captain, I hear a ship out there. It sounds like it is coming directly for us at a fast clip."

"Do you know who it belongs to?" Beads of sweat

formed on her lip, the girl's body seeming to know the answer before her brain did.

"If my ears are not mistaken, and they never are, it's Krueger." Bart adjusted his eye patches, ensuring they were on tight. "He appears to have found us and is not turning away."

Jocelyn's stomach dropped. She didn't want to face Krueger again. That wasn't part of her plan. Or, at least, her plan to think of a plan. Still, she knew that she couldn't pick and choose the things that came along.

You would be well to learn that lesson yourself, and while we are talking about picking and choosing, kindly remove your finger from your nostril.

"Mr. Smee," Jocelyn called. "Gather the men."

"Who is Krueger?" Evie asked, but Jocelyn didn't have time for explanations. She left the task to Roger while she climbed to the poop deck, preparing to address her crew.

"Men, steel yourselves," she said. "Krueger has found us."

They reacted in much the same way the girl would have liked to react herself: with abject fear bordering on blind panic. But Jocelyn pushed aside her own anxiety and reached for the words she hoped would inspire her men. "We will do what we can to outrun him, but if it comes to battle, I believe—nay, I know—we will prevail! You've been here before, and you were victorious."

Roger agreed. "That's right, fellows. Remember? You

may have needed some help from the lost boys then, but things are different now. You're ever so much more experienced."

"Cap'n," Dirty Bob spoke up, "I wouldn't say the men here were top-notch—"

Jocelyn interrupted. "Right. That's because you're better than top-notch. You've new experience *and* you have something even more superior."

One-Armed Jack swung his newest arm—a croquet mallet—through the air. "I have this!"

Jim McCraig with a Wooden Leg said something to his parrot. The bird repeated it, loudly, but it was Smee who translated. "He says, 'And I have Petunia.'"

"Arrrrr! And I have perfected my recipe for key lime pie!" Nubbins called out in his fiercest voice.

"Well, yes, but I'm not talking about those things. I'm talking about heart! Sharpen your blades and polish your courage. We will not be defeated!"

While the men cheered, Smee leaned in and whispered, "That was a right rousing pep talk, miss."

Jocelyn's own spirits lifted a bit. She whispered back, "Do you think they could possibly do it?"

"What, defeat that black-hearted sea devil?" He nodded, an absent smile on his face. "Not even a little."

CHAPTER FOURTEEN

A Valiant Effort Comes to No Good

Though she had been irritated with him that morning, Jocelyn was now grateful that Dirty Bob had put so much effort into improving the speed and agility of the *Hook's Revenge*. They might not have been pursuing a merchant ship as he'd intended, but they were doing a fine job of keeping ahead of *Calypso's Nightmare*. For a time it looked as if they would outrun her, but Blind Bart heard their pursuers jettison their cargo and supplies, lightening their ship. Krueger began to gain on them.

Jocelyn was thunderstruck at the news. "That's insane! They've thrown out everything? Even their barrels of fresh water? If the winds die down, they could be stranded out here for days. How will they survive?"

"I've sailed with Krueger," said Dirty Bob. "I know his methods. Without food or water aboard, the men have no choice but to catch their prey. When they do, they'll have our supplies."

"We can't allow that to happen. We'll have to do the same ourselves. Mr. Smee, order the men to throw everything that is not nailed down overboard."

Nubbins tried to show a brave face as his food supplies were tossed from the ship, but when his favorite crepe pan hit the waves with a splash, he couldn't stop a tear or two from spilling over. Jocelyn wanted to assure him that she would replace it once they got back to land, but with no gold, how could she? Still, they had to escape, if they could. Lives were at stake—and to some people, lives had as much importance as a crepe pan.

Having tasted Nubbins's crepes, however, I'm not certain I'm inclined to agree.

Notwithstanding their efforts, *Calypso's Nightmare* continued to gain at an alarming rate. Jocelyn asked Roger to consult his map, hoping to find some way of escape.

"We are rather close to a ships' graveyard. Looks like the wreckage is from a reef, not far under the sea. When ships try to cross it, it probably tears out their hulls, leaving them stranded."

"I don't see how that would be all that helpful," Jocelyn said. "Wouldn't we have the same problem?"

"It will be dangerous, but the *Hook's Revenge* has a far shallower draft than Krueger's ship. We may just be able to get through. Could be our only chance."

Jocelyn ordered the heading change. Before long, the first ghostly outlines of wrecked ships appeared on the horizon, splintery ribs and rotted beams cast about like the skeletal contents of a plague pit.

Dirty Bob and One-Armed Jack rolled up a portion of the mainsail, causing the ship to slow, to ease navigation through the dangerous passage. The water was quite clear, and Jocelyn could see to the bottom. Bloodred coral formations reached toward them with sharp, bony fingers. As the ship passed over a particularly shallow area, Jocelyn felt them scrape and scratch along the hull, like an animal wanting to be let in. Much shallower and they would be torn apart. Jocelyn felt certain Krueger, in his larger ship, would be unable to pass.

Would you be terribly disappointed to discover the girl was wrong? You would? In that case, I'm happy to report that she was.

Krueger's devil ship rolled right over reef after reef, crushing the razor-sharp coral formations under its reinforced hull.

"All right, men, that's enough!" Jocelyn commanded. "It was a valiant try, but we must now change our tack. Strike the sails! Drop anchor and show our broadsides. Ready the cannon! We stand and fight!"

Jim McCraig and Evie worked together to lower the remaining sails, slowing the ship further. One-Armed Jack and Roger dropped the anchor. The *Hook's Revenge* turned about, bringing the starboard side to the oncoming ship.

Jocelyn wiped her sweaty palms on the front of her jacket. "Wait until they get into range and fire!" she commanded.

One heartbeat. Two.

They were silent, watching with mounting tension as *Calypso's Nightmare* drew steadily nearer. When it was within range, Jocelyn gave the order. "Fire!"

Smee relayed the order through the open hatch. "Fire, Jim!"

Jim's aim had improved by leaps and bounds since their last sea battle—but not enough. The cannonball dropped harmlessly into the sea.

"I think he might've splashed them, though, Captain," One-Armed Jack said, motioning toward the enemy ship with his newest arm, a whaling harpoon. "That should help, right? Fighting with wet clothes could cause them to chafe."

Jocelyn ignored him. "Wait until they start to turn; that will give us a bigger target."

Smee passed the order on. They waited. The *Calypso's Nightmare* drew ever closer.

Evie stood wide-eyed and gripping the railing, though

Jocelyn hardly noticed her. She was watching Krueger. He stood at the bow of his ship, his eyes locked on Jocelyn. His white scar stood out against his sun-browned face. It looked as sharp and dangerous as the knife that had made it.

When he was within spitting distance (Jocelyn tested, hitting a lanky pirate on his gangly arm), Krueger ordered the crew to drop the sails and anchor. His ship began to turn.

"Fire at will!" Jocelyn cried.

"Which one of them is Will?" One-Armed Jack asked. No one responded.

Smee repeated Jocelyn's order to Jim McCraig. This time the man's cannonball found a target, glancing off the side of the hull. The wood splintered, but there was little damage. Still, he hit it! His cries of joy echoed through the hold. The morale of the entire crew flew higher.

"Hit him again, Jim, between the wind and the waves!" Jocelyn commanded.

Jim fired again. His shot was high, crashing into the railing and rolling across the deck. The ball bowled over a half dozen hard-bitten pirates as if playing at ninepins. The rest of Krueger's crew did not bat an eye. A few men started swinging grappling hooks.

The *Calypso's Nightmare* completed her rotation, bringing her cannons into firing position. Krueger gave the order to fire. His ball connected, punching a hole high in the side of the *Hook's Revenge*.

"Mr. Smee, go belowdecks and give me a damage report. Everyone else, ready your arms"—Jack opened his mouth to reply, but Jocelyn cut him off—"or arm, for heaven's sake!"

"Captain Jocelyn, may I have a sword?" Evie asked. "I think I could swing it enough to help."

Jocelyn had nearly forgotten the girl was there. What would happen if she were killed? Jocelyn had to keep her safe. "No!" she replied. "It's too dangerous! Go below deck!"

"Why? You're here. Roger is here." Evie put her hands on her hips. "I'm older than both of you. I'll fight and do my part."

Jocelyn let out an exasperated breath. "I can't let anything happen to you!"

"I didn't know you cared so much." Evie beamed at her.

Jocelyn squirmed. "I don't. I mean I do. But it's complicated."

"Friendship always is. But you're my friend, Jocelyn. I will fight for you."

A lump formed in Jocelyn's throat. What *was* she going to do about Evie? She would have to figure that out later, once they were free of Krueger. "Bob!" she called out. "Arm her!"

He muttered something about tea parties, but gave

the girl a deadly-sharp dagger. She ran to the railing and brandished it. "You dogs will pay for your attack upon young Captain Hook!"

The rival crew hooted and jeered. "Are you ready to dance, little lady?" one called out, waving a wicked-looking cutlass in her direction.

"I am! I'll lead!" she called back.

"Good one, Evie!" Roger called.

Jocelyn gritted her teeth, annoyance flaring. "This is no time for chitchat!"

One of the men swung his grappling hook. It landed on the railing next to Evie. He leaped from his deck, swinging over the water, and hit the side of their ship with a thud.

"Oh dear!" Evie cried. "He's climbing up!"

Jocelyn rushed forward, but the older girl was quicker. She brought her dagger down on the rope, slicing through as if it were made of butter. The pirate fell harmlessly to the sea. "That's right!" she shouted. "Who else needs a bath?"

Nubbins smelled under his arms. "I think I might."

"Not you, Nubbins!" Evie said. "I was talking to them!" She motioned toward the enemy pirates.

"Oh. Them. Right." He raised his voice. "Yeah, who needs a scrubbing? You can borrow my bathing cap!"

The men's reactions were more confused than anything. Each one stopped what he was doing and stared.

Finally one broke the silence: "Keep your stinking bathing cap!" The rest of the pirates growled and shouted curses. Only Krueger remained calm. He held up a hand, quieting his men, then issued his most terrible command yet: "Enough play. Board her."

The crowd parted, allowing passage to several men carrying planks long enough to bridge the gap between the two ships. Large iron brackets were affixed to the planks' ends. Before Jocelyn could formulate a plan, the men used them to hook the two ships together. Krueger's crew began to swarm over the makeshift bridges.

"Stop them!" Jocelyn yelled, but there was nothing left to do. There, in the ships' graveyard, beneath the chill shadow of other fallen vessels, the *Hook's Revenge* was overrun.

All was lost.

CHAPTER FIFTEEN

"Throw Her Overboard!"

I'd like to tell you that the crew of the *Hook's Revenge* was victorious in battle—that they fought back with a ferocity that took Krueger's men by surprise. That they gave those devils their just deserts and sent them to meet Davy Jones. I'd like to tell you that because it is untrue and I very much enjoy lying to children.

However, I fear I must continue rightfully telling this tale until it is finished. Here is the truth: The crew of the *Hook's Revenge* fought hard, with heart and courage, but it did little good. They simply didn't have enough skill or manpower. Krueger's men flocked over them like seagulls on a bread crust. The pathetic fools didn't stand a chance.

At one point, when it was clear that they would lose

the ship, Jocelyn tried to rouse Meriwether and get him to sprinkle everyone with fairy dust. It was of no use, however; the little man was too seasick to fly. The girl tried shaking him, which was rather unkind of her, given the condition of his stomach, but desperate times and all that. It yielded little result anyway. Perhaps enough fairy dust for one person, but that was all.

The battle ended rather quickly after that. One by one, Jocelyn's men were disarmed. Near the end, Jocelyn used the fairy dust on herself and flew to the deck of *Calypso's Nightmare*, attempting to draw Krueger and his men back to her, but they did not pursue.

"You'll pay for this, Krueger!" Jocelyn called.

At the sound of her voice, Meriwether roused himself from his seasick stupor and made one last-ditch effort—an attack on Krueger's face. He hurtled himself toward the pirate, but Krueger simply reached a steady hand into his jacket pocket and pulled out what looked like a fancy perfume bottle. He pumped the atomizer's bulb once. It released a small cloud of violet mist, enveloping the little fairy. Meriwether dropped to the deck at the man's feet.

"Noooo!" The scream clawed its way out of Jocelyn's throat, a wild beast born of terror and rage. She wanted to claw Krueger's eyes out. She wanted to fly to Meri, scoop him up, and make sure he was all right—just as she had on the day they met. She did neither. Fear kept her rooted to the empty deck of *Calypso's Nightmare*. Not fear of Krueger, but fear that Meriwether, her own wonderful fairy and friend, had had his light put out, never to shine again.

Krueger most certainly saw that terror on the girl's face. He stretched his lips across his foul teeth in an approximation of a smile. "Your fairy isn't dead," he called to her across the gap between the two ships. "Not at the moment anyway. He's merely sleeping. I had a special solution made up after our last meeting."

He stooped and plucked up the little man, holding him between his thumb and forefinger as one might hold a pair of dirty undergarments. Meri did not shine at his usual brilliance, but there was a glow about him. Jocelyn felt she could breathe again.

Krueger pulled a silver flask from his pocket and stuffed the fairy down in. "I think I'll keep him close by. Could be useful. Now, pay attention and I'll show you how a real pirate does his business."

He turned to address the wart-faced pirate Jocelyn was most familiar with. "Tie the new girl, Benito. I don't trust her. Women, even half-grown ones, are wily creatures. We'll sell her to the salt mines."

Though Evie fought valiantly, the pirate was large and strong. He trussed her up with relative ease.

"As for the rest of you," Krueger said, surveying his captives, "if any of you wish to join my cause, you are welcome. I am always in need of good men."

Benito cut in, "Captain, we already have a crew surplus. We are in need of no more. I say we send some new souls to Davy Jones!"

"Excellent suggestion," Captain Krueger said. He pulled a gold-plated pistol from his holster and casually pulled the trigger. The blast rang out over the waves, but it was Benito himself who fell overboard. "It seems I have at least one position to fill. The post of first mate has just been vacated. Who will join me?"

Roger was the first to speak. "I'd rather die first!"

"As would I," said Smee. "And Johnny, too!"

Dirty Bob held up his hands. "Let's not be so hasty," he said. "I'll be keeping my life, if you don't mind. Still a no from me, though. I haven't forgotten you marooning me when I was last in yer service."

Krueger fingered the hilt of his pistol. "Nor have I. I should have killed you then, but I'll get around to it sooner or later." He turned his attention back on Jocelyn. "Shall we make it sooner, lassie?"

"No!" she cried. She pulled the map from her pocket and waved it in the air. "Come get the map. You can have it! Just give me back my fairy and leave everyone else alone!"

Krueger ran his tongue over his pointed teeth, greed washing his face. "Bring it to me."

Jocelyn hesitated.

He raised an eyebrow. "Take the other girl and make her walk the plank."

"I've seen this before," Mr. Smee said to no one in particular. "Never turns out like you think it should."

No one responded to Smee, but one of the pirates did grab Evie by the arm and drag her onto the plank. "Take your disgusting hands off me!" She pushed him, her shoulder catching him unaware. The pirate lost his balance and fell to the roiling sea.

Krueger laughed. "See what I mean about wily?" He leveled his pistol at Evie but spoke to Jocelyn. "Bring me the map."

"Don't hurt her!" Jocelyn nearly screeched in her terror. "I'm coming." She flew from Krueger's ship to her own, landing in front of the vile captain. Her hand shook as she held the map out to him.

"Don't give it to him!" Evie cried.

"You." Captain Krueger pointed at a particularly ugly pirate, covered from head to toe in scurvy sores. "Throw her overboard."

"I'll save you the trouble. Fly, Jocelyn!" Evie yelled, before executing a perfect swan dive (which was rather impressive, considering her hands were still tied).

"And there she goes," Smee said, "just like another I once knew. Darling girl, she was."

Evie hit the waves with a splash. Roger launched

himself over the railing after her. In a slight breach of protocol, considering he had no authority to command, One-Armed Jack called, "Abandon ship!" before bounding into the drink, followed by Nubbins and Mr. Smee. Blind Bart screamed in terror but was nudged overboard with a loving tackle from Jim McCraig. The parrot squawked and flew after him, a flash of green and yellow above the blue sea.

Last to go was Dirty Bob. He looked as if he'd rather another option present itself, but when one did not, he shrugged and followed the rest of the crew into the bitter, cold embrace of the ocean, which, I'm certain, was not unlike that of my sweet mother.

Krueger snatched the map from Jocelyn's hand, rousing her from her stunned inaction. She had to get to Evie! Jocelyn took to the air, desperately flying back and forth, watching the waves. At last she caught a glimpse of yellow, a bit of Evie's skirt billowing on the water's surface for just a moment; then it was gone. Jocelyn dove.

The cold water took her breath away, but she tried not to lose focus, intent on finding Evie. Though her eyes burned in the salt water, she refused to give in to the urge to close them. Below her she saw a dark shape, growing smaller as it sank. She kicked with all her might, desperate to catch the older girl. She reached out, her fingertips barely brushing Evie's dress; then it was gone. Jocelyn stayed under, searching until she thought she would faint from lack of air, then forcing herself to search a moment more.

Jocelyn likely would not have come up at all if someone hadn't hauled her to the surface. She gulped air and opened her eyes.

Evie held her tight with one arm and paddled with the other, keeping them both afloat. She swam toward the remains of a schooner, still relatively intact, though abandoned on the reef.

"How—" Jocelyn began.

Evie didn't let her finish. "I hid the dagger down my dress front. It was a bit of a trick to get it out without dropping it—not to mention cutting my ropes underwater—but I managed all right in the end." She grinned at Jocelyn. "I told you I was an excellent swimmer."

CHAPTER SIXTEEN

Wrecked and Wretched

Anger and fear are close kin, even closer than my brother Danforth and me. As children, we were nearly inseparable. At least that's what the surgeon said—though with skill and effort he eventually prevailed.

Jocelyn's fear at the thought of losing Evie, both for the older girl's sake and for her own, hardened to anger once everyone had been accounted for and gathered together safely aboard the same wrecked ship. When she saw Krueger and his men sailing away, taking both *Calypso's Nightmare* and the *Hook's Revenge* with them, that anger exploded.

Jocelyn whirled to face Evie. "What were you thinking,

jumping into the sea like that? You could have been killed!"

The girl appeared to be caught off guard by Jocelyn's verbal attack, but she rallied and reacted in kind. "He was going to push me anyway! I simply took away his opportunity. I'd rather choose poorly, of my own accord, than have someone choose for me."

Guilt tugged at Jocelyn's conscience, but she shoved it away. She placed her hands on her hips, affecting her captain stance. "That's not the way it works on a pirate ship! You don't choose. You wait for orders!"

Evie mimicked Jocelyn's posture, looking down on the girl from a two-inch height advantage. "If I had waited for you to tell me what to do, Krueger would have taken your map!"

"Your brilliant plan failed! He took it anyway! If he hadn't, do you think he would be leaving us alone?"

The two girls were full-on shouting now. Everyone else stood by, watching in uncomfortable silence.

"You let him take your map? Why would you do such a thing?" Anger colored Evie's cheeks scarlet.

"Maybe, for some insane reason, I was more worried about you than it!" Jocelyn put her hand on the hilt of her sword.

Roger stepped forward. "Jocelyn, Evie, please, don't fight."

"Stay out of this!" they both yelled.

Roger put his hands up in a gesture of supplication. "I'm just trying to help," he said.

"It's not working," Jocelyn snapped. "Stop trying to fix everything!"

He stepped back, a pained look on his face. Jocelyn immediately regretted her words, but there was nothing she could do at the moment. She was responsible for the crew. Everyone would be looking to her for what to do next. The only problem was, she had no idea.

"What are you all staring at?" she growled. "Go . . . swab the deck or something!"

Jocelyn stormed to the opposite side of the ship to give herself time to think of a way out of the mess they were in. She sat on the slick and rotting decking (which really *could* have used a good swabbing) and watched until the two ships Krueger now commanded disappeared on the horizon. The *Hook's Revenge* was still seaworthy, but the damage made it move slowly. The ship remained in her sights for several long minutes, giving plenty of time for dampness and despair to settle in, chilling her to the core. Her hopes and dreams felt nearly as dead as the wreckage beneath her.

Above the chattering of her teeth, Jocelyn heard footsteps approach, but to her disappointment they were too heavy to belong to Roger. Mr. Smee groaned as he lowered himself to sit next to her. "Well now, Captain, things aren't so bad, are they?"

"What do you mean, not so bad? They're awful! I'm quarreling with my closest friends. Krueger has Meri, my ship, and the map. What have I got, other than this unsailable wreck?"

Smee looked at her over the top of his spectacles. His eyes were kind. "You're not dead. Not even a little. That's something, isn't it?"

Jocelyn smiled a bit in spite of herself.

"And," he continued, "you *do* have your friends." He absentmindedly patted his sword. "No one can take them away. Though, I suppose, you can give 'em up, if you choose."

He stood, brushed off his backside, and offered her a hand. Jocelyn took it and allowed him to pull her to her feet. She felt shame wash over her. She had spoken far too harshly to both Evie and Roger, and she knew it. Then, to make matters worse, she had gone off on a sulk. With her ship or without, Jocelyn was still the captain. She needed to start acting like it.

The girl returned to find that her prior display of leadership had been a poor influence on the crew. Inspired by their captain's outburst, contention had spread. Blind Bart clung to the stump of the ship's broken mast, mumbling a blistering castigation of anyone and everyone, and most particularly the sea itself. Dirty Bob cursed him right back, not bothering to hold back his contempt regarding a pirate afraid of the sea. Jim McCraig and his parrot were loudly bickering (at least it sounded like bickering), and One-Armed Jack and Nubbins were engaged in a tussle of their own.

Jocelyn arrived just in time to see Jack take a swing at Nubbins with yet another prosthetic: a wooden-handled egg beater attached to the stump of his arm.

Nubbins sidestepped him. "How dare you try to beat me with me own whisk? I said give it back!"

"And I said it isn't yours! It belongs to me!" Jack cried.

"Well, where did you get it?"

"I found it bobbling along in the sea." He made a motion with the whisk, mimicking the way it had floated on the waves.

"Yeah. It were there after you dumped it overboard! Give it back!" Nubbins reached out as if to grab it.

"You can't just go taking a man's arm!" Jack waved it menacingly.

"You can't go taking a man's whisk!"

It was well past time Jocelyn took things in hand (no pun intended).

"Men!" the girl bellowed. "Stop that this instant! All of you!" She glared at each person in turn. When she looked at Roger and Evie, sitting quietly together apart from the others, she felt both a stab of jealousy and a prickle of guilt, but she stuffed them both down and doled out commands.

"Nubbins, you have no need of a whisk at the moment. Jack does need an arm, unsuitable as it may be—"

"Yeah!" Jack said.

"Quiet, you dog," she growled. "I'm not finished. Once we get back to land, Jack will find something else and return your whisk to you."

"How do you propose we get back, Captain?" Blind Bart asked.

That was the question, wasn't it?

There would be no swimming back to the island. They were miles away at sea, with man-eating sharks, giant cephalopods, cruel mermaids, and who knew what else between them and the main island. And not a one of them could fly. All the fairy dust Jocelyn had been wearing had washed away, and there would be no more with Meriwether a captive of Krueger.

Jocelyn's shoulder felt empty without the little fairy there, ringing in her ear. She hoped the toxin he had been sprayed with had no lasting effects and that the bottle that held him had enough air. She gripped her hands into fists. She was determined to rescue Meriwether— somehow. And while she was at it, she'd reclaim her ship and her treasure map. That map had been left to her by

Captain Hook, the greatest pirate of all time. Krueger didn't deserve to have it simply because he had been able to take it.

Krueger might be stronger. He might have a fierce crew and a fast ship. He might even be a better pirate. But he had no claim on her father's treasure. Jocelyn would find him and take back what was hers. She would find a way to make him pay.

But first, they had to get back to land.

"We will have to salvage what we can from this wreck and build a raft. Jim McCraig, take One-Armed Jack and see what tools you can find: rope that hasn't rotted through, mallets, nails, and bolts. Nubbins, you go see if there is any salvageable food in the galley. The rest of you"—she found she couldn't quite look at Evie and Roger, so she made a rather broad gesture taking them in—"start pulling up planking. We'll get as much done as we can before dark and finish up in the morning."

Jocelyn, being young and inexperienced, didn't know what a gift she had given the crew. In the absence of hope, work is a fitting stand-in. Keeps the despondencies away. In the absence of both hope and work, torture will do. At least, it always cheers me right up. But I digress.

While everyone else scurried off to follow her orders, Jocelyn sat to plan. It wasn't enough for them to simply get back to the main island. She had to think about what would happen after that. She hadn't made much headway, however, when Roger returned alone with an armful of planks.

He began to pile them carefully on the deck. "I got these from the driest place I could find below, but they are still rather rotten," he said without looking at her. "I'm not sure a raft made from them would hold us. I thought in the morning I'd swim out to some of the other wrecks to see if I can get any better."

That Roger always was an optimistic one, but the fact of the matter was, he would be unlikely to fare better elsewhere. They were lucky to have found refuge where they did. Though the wreck was fully unable to sail due to a large breach in the hull, it had settled on the reef in such a way that most of it was above water. The craft was a far cry from cozy, but at least it offered some measure of security out in the middle of the lonely sea.

Jocelyn felt it best not to discourage Roger so soon after their fight. Instead she asked, "Where's Evie?"

"She's with Jim McCraig and the parrot, searching the hold."

Jocelyn cleared her throat. "I'm sorry."

Roger turned and faced her, wearing his just-for-Jocelyn grin. "I know. And I'm sorry for trying to tell you what to do. I know none of this is easy, but you'll figure things out. Let's not argue anymore, all right, Captain?"

Jocelyn smiled back. "Deal. It's too awful when we are cross with each other."

She spit on her hand and held it out, ready to make it official, but Roger pushed her hand aside and threw his arms around her in a hug. It felt as warm as coming in out of the rain.

"Deal," he said, squeezing her tight.

Over his shoulder Jocelyn saw Evie climb up from the lower deck, carrying a burlap bag and wearing an enormous straw bonnet. The hat was dripping in ribbons and decorated with an ostrich plume dyed a deep vermilion. Jocelyn quickly pulled back from Roger, sure her face must have been as red as the feather.

"Well, well, well. Don't let me interrupt you two." Evie laughed.

Jocelyn and Roger spoke at the same time.

"We weren't—"

"It's not—"

"Not to worry! I know an innocent, friendly embrace when I see one." She pushed the bonnet back on her forehead. The brim must have stuck out at least a foot on all sides from her head. It was a wonder she fit through the hatch. "Not that I could see all that much wearing this."

Making up with Roger had helped Jocelyn want to make things right with Evie, too, but she didn't quite know how. She still thought that Evie's dive into the sea had been foolish and dangerous. She would not apologize for that.

Jocelyn settled on changing the subject. "I like your hat," she said.

Evie flashed her dimples and dumped her bundle at Jocelyn's feet. "I was hoping you would feel that way about my hat," she said, excitedly pulling something from the bag, "because I found some for you two in a trunk below. They aren't likely to be very helpful to our current predicament, and they smell rather mildewed, but I couldn't pass them up."

She handed a white, curly wig and tricorn cap to Roger. "Now you can look like an aristocrat," she said with a twinkle in her eye.

When he placed them on his head, a cloud of wig powder billowed up, making him sneeze. "Just what I always wanted," the boy said with a slight bow.

"And for you, Jocelyn. I knew this was yours as soon as I saw it." She passed Jocelyn what was surely the most amazing and detailed hat ever created. It was modeled after a frigate, the high brim serving as the sides of the ship and the crown covered with masts and rigging. The ship hat was perfectly detailed right down to the last cannon.

Jocelyn couldn't help wondering who might have worn such a wonderful, ridiculous thing, but when she saw the ship's name, *La Belle Poule*, embroidered neatly at the aft, she shook her head at her own ignorance. Who else could it have been but the French?

The hat was incredibly heavy, but somehow, wearing it, Jocelyn felt a bit lighter. She hooked one arm through Roger's and the other through Evie's. "Let's go show off our finery and see if Nubbins has come up with anything for us to dine upon this evening. Perhaps after dinner, we may even throw a ball."

As they walked off together in search of the crew, one of the other vessels in the ships' graveyard caught Jocelyn's eye. It had been massive, at least a twenty-gunner. If only she had a ship like that—larger and better suited for battle than either the *Hook's Revenge* or *Calypso's Nightmare*—she would have a more than fighting chance of besting Krueger and taking back what was rightfully hers.

Now, more than ever, Jocelyn needed the *Jolly Roger*.

CHAPTER SEVENTEEN

Of Fine Dining and Chats in the Moonlight

Everyone's spirits were much improved that night. Roger built a merry fire in a large brass kettle dragged to the upper deck from the galley. Also in the galley, Nubbins discovered a dry cask of beans, a few spices, and some hardtack, which he managed to turn into a wonderful meal.

Once everyone had eaten, they danced under the moonlight to the sounds of both song and an orchestra provided by the aftereffects of their meal. Jocelyn stuffed her worries down deep inside, for she hoped if she looked unconcerned, her men would feel likewise. It seemed to work. After the dancing ended, the crew found places to curl up on the deck, wrapped in pieces of old sail. One by one, they drifted into untroubled sleep.

Jocelyn laid her hat aside and took first watch. She sat alone at the edge of the wreck, feet hanging between the bars of the railing. The full moon made a shining path on the water, like a road. How she wished they could all just climb on and follow it back to land.

Evie joined her, dangling her bare feet next to her. A nearby splash made the older girl pull them back. "Do you suppose that was a shark? And if so, how high can they jump?" she asked.

"I don't think they can jump this high," Jocelyn replied. "And that splash is more likely to have been a mermaid."

"A mermaid..." Evie practically sighed the word. "How I would love to meet one."

Jocelyn wrinkled her nose. "They are not as impressive as you might think. When I encountered some, they suggested I drown myself. Beastly things."

Evie dangled her feet over the side again. "I hope you won't take this the wrong way, but you are so lucky."

Jocelyn cracked a smile. "I know."

Both girls giggled, and Jocelyn felt the last of their earlier tension ebb away.

"I'm sorry we fought," Evie said.

"So am I," Jocelyn replied.

There didn't seem a need to say more about it. Out of habit, Jocelyn reached up and fingered her necklace. Moonlight glinted off the jeweled sea serpent embedded in the pendant's face, catching Evie's eye.

"Your locket is lovely. Is there a portrait inside?"

Jocelyn closed her fingers around it, protectively, but then loosened them. She and Evie were having such a nice time together, Jocelyn didn't want to spoil it. Besides, what harm could it do? It wasn't as if Evie could possibly know what her future husband would look like. "It's my father," she said, flipping the locket open.

Evie leaned in for a closer look, then gasped and drew back. "It's . . . oh, it's so strange."

Jocelyn frowned. "What is?"

"That painting. It looks familiar."

A shiver ran up Jocelyn's spine. *Had* the other girl somehow divined her future in Hook's face? "You recognize him?" she asked.

"Oh no," Evie said, "It's the portrait itself. It's exactly like I would have painted it. I feel as though I have seen a letter I didn't write, somehow penned in my own hand."

Jocelyn's heart thumped. For one crazy moment she considered telling Evie everything, but she simply couldn't. What if Evie learned Jocelyn would be her daughter and she felt nothing more than disappointment?

Instead Jocelyn blurted the first thing that came into her head. "Why did you ever agree to fly off with that irritating Pan?"

Evie laughed. "He is quite full of himself, isn't he?"

"To say the least!" Jocelyn agreed.

"But truly, he's not so terrible. He can be rather amusing, once you get past all that 'Oh, how clever am I' business. Flying away with him offered me things I'd never get at home: excitement, adventure, the chance to forget my old life and do something entirely new. And look what else it got me—a new best friend."

She smiled at Jocelyn, moonlight shining in her eyes. Jocelyn smiled back, but she felt worried. What if Evie forgot her old life entirely? The harbormaster had said that those who forgot their home—who became untethered—were miserable.

Oh, what was she to do about Evie?

Roger interrupted her thoughts. He tiptoed carefully over the sleeping pirates, trying not to wake anyone, and joined them. "What are you two whispering about over here?"

Evie giggled. "Girlish things—right, Jocelyn? You wouldn't understand."

Jocelyn grinned. "Right."

"Oh, well then. In that case, you can educate me." He stretched out on the deck behind them. "What kinds of things do girls talk about when boys aren't around to hear?"

"The usual," Jocelyn replied. "How to get bloodstains out of party dresses."

Evie nodded solemnly. "Whether a sword or a dagger is better suited for our delicate hands."

"Oh yes," Jocelyn said. "And what number of kills will best impress a future suitor."

"I think no fewer than twenty," Evie said, "but Jocelyn believes that if the girl is also a good dancer, she might get away with as little as eighteen. What do you think, Roger? It would be nice to get a male perspective."

He flashed a moonlit grin. "I think you two are certifiably insane. It's one of my favorite things about you both."

Though she wasn't sure she liked having to share a favorite thing with Evie, Jocelyn had to admit that it was fun to spend time with another girl. Evie was unlike anyone she had ever met.

The three sat in companionable silence under the starry sky.

Evie drummed her feet along the side of the ship. "I don't know what it's like where you are from, but where I live, at the ever-so-prim-and-proper"—she spoke in an overly formal, mocking voice—"*Miss Eliza Crumb-Biddlecomb's Finishing School for Young Ladies,* no one else would appreciate this. The girls would be too worried about not looking ladylike enough, and Miss Eliza, she would be livid at the conditions."

"I didn't know you went to school there!" Jocelyn cried in surprise.

"Do you know my school?" Evie asked.

Jocelyn scrambled to recover from her gaffe. "No. I mean, I assumed someone like you wouldn't need finishing school."

Evie laughed. "You must be joking! My father despairs of ever turning me into a lady. That's where Miss Eliza comes in." Evie motioned to the snoring heap of pirates. "She would say, 'No matter the circumstances, a young lady should never engage in conversation with ruffians. No—'"

"Exceptions!" Jocelyn finished for her, laughing.

Evie gave her a bemused look. "Yes. But how could you know she would say that?"

"Oh. Well. I . . ." She looked to Roger for help.

"That sounds like just the sort of thing any stuffy old headmistress would say, doesn't it, Jocelyn?"

"Quite."

Evie stared at Jocelyn as if the younger girl were a puzzle she couldn't quite work out.

"What about other things from home?" Jocelyn ventured. "I know school was awful, but there has to be something you miss."

"I miss my father. I admit that, freely. When we sang his lullaby together, I missed him so much I could hardly stand it, but that was because even then I think I knew that I would not be going back. His plans for me . . . they're not what I want." Below their feet, a school of glowing fish passed by, lighting up the water. "This. This is what I want. Adventure. Beauty. Surprise. I think I'll stay."

Roger raised an eyebrow at Jocelyn. She knew what he thought she should do, but even though she had been tempted a few moments before, the girl simply couldn't bring herself to tell Evie everything. There had to be another way.

"Besides," Evie continued, "my life at home seems so far away now, as if it were nothing but a dream, and the longer I'm awake, the less sharp it becomes. I have a feeling I won't miss it too badly, for I may forget it altogether."

Jocelyn was about to respond, to urge the girl to hold tight to her memories of home, but something on the sea caught her attention and stole her thoughts away.

Sailing directly up the middle of the shining path the moon cut through the water was a ship, but not just any ship. Jocelyn pulled her spyglass from its pouch to get a better look. The vessel appeared to be made entirely of moonbeams and air—and it was sailing straight at them.

CHAPTER EIGHTEEN

Questions and Answers

Jocelyn roused the crew, unsure if the strange ship might prove to be a threat. They all stood in a line at the railing, weapons out, watching the glowing vessel come ever nearer on the reflected trail of moonlight. Even as it grew closer, it remained somewhat insubstantial—all the correct details were in place, rigging and masts, lines and portholes, but they flickered and shimmered under Jocelyn's gaze.

The girl felt her own flicker—one of apprehension in her stomach. Was this a ghost ship? Perhaps that dreadful *Flying Dutchman* she had heard Dirty Bob talk about? Jocelyn gripped her sword tightly in her hand, attempting to draw comfort from its weight, though she knew it would be of little use against spirits intending them harm.

At last the ship reached them, angling a bit so as to avoid hitting the ruined craft with its bowsprit. Its shining hull tapped the side of their wreck with a surprising little bump. Jocelyn had rather expected it to pass right through them. The ship certainly had more substance than it appeared to.

That can be true of people, as well, though not, I'm sure, in your case.

The relative substance of the ship wasn't the biggest surprise. Standing at the wheel was a man—one made not of moonlight, but of flesh and bone, and one whom Jocelyn hadn't expected to see again.

He let out an exasperated sigh. "So. You survived, then?"

Jocelyn couldn't decide whether to be angry with the man for his past duplicity or grateful for the rescue. She settled on what was likely to most annoy him: smugness. "Pleasure to see you again, Gentleman Starkey."

Starkey's ship was a marvel and a curiosity. The entire craft, from timbers to topmast, shone with a flickering light, not unlike that of a firefly. The deck under Jocelyn's feet hummed and pulsed with some faint energy, and when she breathed in, the girl caught a scent like the air after a lightning strike. The ship did not fly a pirate flag. Indeed, no flag at all hung from its mast. And it appeared to be outfitted more for fishing than for sea battles. Nets, woven together from threads of starlight, hung over the sides, dragging the water in the silvery path.

Evie, Roger, and the rest of the crew spread out along the deck, curious about the ship's operations. The reflected light painted them all in pale, ghostly hues. Jocelyn stayed near Starkey at his place behind the wheel, the vantage point of the poop deck making it easy to see all that was happening. As she watched, a crew of men began hauling in their catch: a net filled with faintly luminous, wriggling creatures.

"What—" Jocelyn began, almost succeeding in keeping the wonder from her voice.

Starkey huffed loudly, interrupting the girl, somehow conveying leagues of impatience in a singular puff of air. "Here we go with the questions. You won't rest until you've had them all out, then, will you?" He huffed again. "I'll answer you, but only to pass the time. Don't for a moment fool yourself into thinking I am enjoying your company."

"Nor I yours," Jocelyn said. "I was merely going to ask what kind of ship this is."

He gestured to the netting. "It's a fishing boat, of sorts. We sail the moonlight river, catching electrical eels. That's how I had the misfortune to come upon you. Your shipwreck was clogging up my path."

Jocelyn raised an eyebrow. "Truly?"

The man glowered at the girl. "Yes, truly," he mimicked

in a high-pitched voice. His imitation of whiny child-speak was spot-on. "I didn't come looking for you, if that's what you are thinking. Certainly, I saw Krueger sail into the harbor with your broken ship, and I did indeed hear his men talking about abandoning you out here at the ships' graveyard, but I didn't care. Why should I? I've had enough of the company of children to last me a lifetime. And I don't feel bad about going back on my word when we met before." He crossed his arms over his chest. "If anything, I came to see if Smee survived. He owes me money."

Jocelyn shook her head, clearly disbelieving the man—though he was most certainly telling the truth. A feeling of satisfaction thick as the morning mist rolled off her. Starkey scowled and changed the subject. "At any rate, we were talking about the eels. They only swim in this particular current here, you see."

The fishermen on the deck below swiftly picked the strange fish from the net, dropping their snakelike bodies into an open hatch.

"Is there a market for eel meat on the Neverland?" Jocelyn asked.

The man snorted, taking his turn at being smug. "We don't eat them," he said. "We milk them—rather, we take them to an eel-lectrical plant on the shore and have them milked. The plant bottles it for us, and we ship the bottles to the mainland and sell it by the pound. People there can't get enough of it. Like bottled lightning, it is. They use it to power horseless carriages and candleless lanterns."

"Horseless carriages! That would be a sight." Jocelyn had seen a lot of fantastical things on the Neverland, but as before, she found his claims hard to believe.

Starkey prodded her on. "I know you aren't finished yet. I can smell the questions on you. What else?"

"I was going to ask if this were your ship."

"If this *was* my ship," he corrected. "Grammar is important, girl. And no, it isn't exactly mine, though I was hired on as captain."

Jocelyn remembered that Starkey had once been a schoolmaster. She renewed her dislike of the man. "I thought you were anxious to get back to pirating," she asked, a slight trace of mockery flavoring her words.

He scowled at her. "I tried to get on with a crew out of the pirate village, but no one is hiring. That devil Krueger has everyone squeezed tight, forcing them to surrender all the gold they take. It's hard for a captain to pay a full crew and earn a decent living on silver and jewels alone. Most ships are running with skeleton crews." He put on what must have been his teacher voice. "Those aren't crews made of skeletons, you simpleton, but—"

Jocelyn pulled herself to her full height. "I know what a skeleton crew is. I'm not a mere child. I'm a pirate captain, which is more than I can say for you."

"Perhaps, but only one of us has command of a ship

now, as you can see. I may not be pirating, which is a shame, but I am captain of this here vessel. That's something I can be proud of."

Jocelyn ignored his comment. There was really only one thing more she wanted to talk with him about. She was sure to learn what she needed once she found the portrait on the *Jolly Roger*, but on the small chance the key wasn't there, Jocelyn wanted all the information she could get. "Tell me what you know of the map."

He refused to even look at her. "I won't."

"Not even if telling me could get you back on a pirate ship?"

"I've no desire to sail under you. Besides, we've already established that you have no ship."

"I'm not offering to take you on, but if I were to defeat Krueger, the pirate village would no longer be under his tyranny. The gold would flow through it again, and—"

"And the local economy would recover."

"If you say so. I was going to say that more pirate jobs would become available."

"What is your plan for defeating Krueger?"

"He has taken my map. I intend to beat him to where it leads and set up a surprise attack, defeating him just as I did the Neverland's crocodile." She gave the man what she surely thought was a winning smile. "As interesting as this ship is, you are no fisherman. You are a pirate. Tell me where the map leads."

"I have made a blood oath."

"Oaths can be broken. Someone once told me to never trust a pirate."

The barest trace of a grin grew on his face. "So you know how to listen, do you?"

"When it suits me. Now tell me. The Neverland has changed so much since the time the map was penned, no one recognizes it."

"That's because it's not on the Neverland. That spot of land it shows is back home in good old England."

Jocelyn started in surprise. "England? Where in England?"

"In a series of caves. They're filled with booby traps and I don't know how to get around them—you'll still need to solve the code to discover that—but I do know where the caves are."

"Go on," Jocelyn prodded.

He cleared his throat. "The caves are under a school. Or at least under the site where the school used to be. There was a fire there years ago, burning the school to the ground. It was rebuilt nearer the road, and all that stands above the caves now is an abandoned carriage house."

Carriage house?

Jocelyn's mouth went dry. She had to swallow twice before she could ask her next question. "What . . . what is the name of this school?"

"You know the name of the school. If I'm not mistaken,

and I never am, you were a student there yourself, just as your mother before you."

Jocelyn thought back to the drawing on the map. The coastline, the creek...it had always seemed vaguely familiar. She had been so sure the treasure was on the Neverland that she hadn't been able to see what should have been so plain.

All that time she had spent in the carriage house, and her father's treasure had been right under her feet. That couldn't be a coincidence. He must have put it there for her! Surely he would have left another key to solving the code—a spare key, if you will—there as well! She could just go home and—

But...

The thought hit her like a bucket of cold water to the face. She couldn't go home, not as long as Evie was determined to stay on the Neverland. Unless Evie changed her mind, Jocelyn could never go home again, and the treasure would be lost to her forever.

After revealing the whereabouts of Hook's treasure, Starkey refused to speak any more about it. He claimed that it was past the children's bedtime and ushered Jocelyn, Roger, and Evie belowdecks to sleep in the crew's quarters. The crew was allowed to stay up and help with the fishing because they were adults, of a sort.

Normally, Jocelyn would have refused to be treated

like a child, but she wanted some time to talk to Evie without the crew around to hear. Still, she gave Starkey her fiercest glare and pretended to be unimpressed as he lit a candleless lantern above their heads. The man scowled and made a hasty retreat to rejoin the grown-ups.

When he was gone, Evie asked Jocelyn, "Which hammock do you prefer? Upper or lower?"

It was just the opening Jocelyn needed. "That reminds me of a game," she said, climbing to the upper hammock. She lay there, looking up at the ceiling. "Shall we play a bit before we go to sleep?"

"I like games," Roger said, choosing a bed across from the girls. "How do you play?"

Jocelyn pushed off from the wall, making her hammock swing. "It's easy. We simply take turns asking each other questions about the things we would prefer." She pushed off from the wall again. "I'll begin." She cleared her throat. "Answer this: Which would you prefer? To never eat sweets again, or eat only sweets for the rest of your life?"

"Oh, that's easy." Evie said. "Only sweets. I rather wish that one were true." Even though Jocelyn wasn't looking at her, she could hear the smile in the girl's voice. "How about you, Roger?"

"Does fruit count as sweets?" he asked.

"No," Jocelyn said. "Only things like pudding and pastries."

"Oh, that makes it tougher. I suppose I'd have to say no

sweets. How could I ever walk through an apple orchard and not be allowed to eat some? That would be torture!"

Evie laughed. "You could always pick them and have them made into pies."

"Good point," Jocelyn said. "Why don't you go next, Roger, since you didn't consider that."

"All right, let me think…" He paused a moment. Jocelyn heard him scratching his head, thinking. "I've got one. Would you prefer to walk backward everywhere you went, or ride a goat?"

"Ride a goat? What kind of question is that?" Jocelyn giggled and Evie joined in.

Roger stuck out his foot and gave Jocelyn's hammock a push, setting it swinging again. "I don't know. I panicked!" he said, laughing at himself.

Evie pushed his hammock, in defense of her friend. Jocelyn was about to reach down and push Evie's, but she thought better of it. A hammock war would be fun, but she needed to keep at the game for a bit longer. "Why don't you take a turn, Evie, and show Roger how it's done?" she asked.

Evie knew her question right away. "Would you prefer to belch all your words or never speak again?"

"How's this for a reply?" Jocelyn asked. She and Roger answered in unison: "Buuuuuurrrrrrp!"

It was several minutes before they settled down enough to continue the game.

"Ask another, Jocelyn," Evie said.

It was the moment the girl had been waiting for, but she pretended to think it over. "Would you prefer to live a long life, but not very happily, or die before you get very old? I mean, you'd still be old, but not very. Perhaps in your twenties." She stole a glance at Roger. He was watching Evie.

"My twenties may as well be a hundred years away," Evie said, "they seem so far off. Would I be happy up until that time?"

"I think so, for the most part. You would fall in love and have a family, but you would have some heartbreak, too," Jocelyn answered honestly. "On the other hand, if you lived to be old, you wouldn't have your heart broken, but you would feel like you'd left your true self behind somewhere else. You would spend your life looking for it."

"What do you think, Roger?" Evie asked.

"I think I'd rather hear what you think."

"I think that is an oddly specific question for the game, but I'll answer: I'd rather die early after truly living."

That was what Jocelyn had both hoped and feared Evie would say.

Starting the next day, Jocelyn would begin her plan to convince Evie to go home.

CHAPTER NINETEEN

"Victory for Our Mother!"

Mr. Smee roused Jocelyn, Roger, and Evie before dawn the next morning, after reaching the end of the moonlight river. Starkey had brought his boat to a section of unoccupied beach, far from the pirate village, surely more for his own convenience than out of any concern for Jocelyn's safety. He barely looked at her as she prepared to leave, giving only an annoyed wave of his hand by way of farewell. Jocelyn returned the sentiment with a loud yawn in his direction.

I like to think it was a bonding moment for the two of them.

After disembarking, Jocelyn gathered her friends and crew around her. "Well, men—and Evie," she said, "yesterday was difficult. I won't deny that. But we prevailed!" She chose not to mention that this was mostly due to coincidence and luck. It was likely no one wanted to hear that anyway. She continued her speech. "Now that we are back on the island, we can set our sights on reclaiming what has been taken from us!"

"How can we do that, Cap'n?" Dirty Bob asked. "We don't even have a ship."

"What if I told you we could use my father's ship, the famed *Jolly Roger*?"

Most of the crew broke out into applause at the very idea. Bob did not clap, but there was a light in his eyes, an excitement Jocelyn hadn't seen before. She decided to give everyone something more to look forward to. "And finding the *Roger* won't just give us a ship," she said. "It also contains the key to Hook's map."

"But Cap'n?" One-Armed Jack raised his hand, or rather, his whisk. "We don't have the map. What good will the key do?"

"Everyone knows that aboard the *Jolly Roger* is the largest and deadliest cannon ever forged. We'll use Captain Hook's legendary Long Tom to blast that devil Krueger out of the water; then we'll rescue Meriwether and take back my map." Jocelyn raised her sword dramatically. "Victory and the treasure are both within our grasp! Believe it, men. We won't let anything stand in our way."

The crew cheered wildly. Mr. Smee was overcome with weeping.

"There is just one small detail," Jocelyn went on, quieter than before. "We don't exactly know where the *Jolly Roger* is." Before the men's joy could turn to dismay, she hurried to explain. "But we know who does! It's..." Jocelyn mumbled the name.

"What's that, Captain?" One-Armed Jack placed his whisk to his ear. "I didn't quite catch that. Pebble Ann?"

Blind Bart leaned in close to the girl. "Even with my superior hearing, I couldn't decipher your words. Dieter Graham?"

"No. I'm sure she said 'partridge hen.' We'll need to ask a bird, right, Captain?" Nubbins asked. "Somebody grab the parrot."

"Wrong." Jocelyn sighed. "I said we'll need to ask... *Peter Pan.*"

"That's what we planned all along, ain't it, Captain?" Mr. Smee asked. "Do you want me to write up a ransom letter now?"

"Ransom letter? Of course. I almost forgot I was your prisoner." Evie spoke bravely, though disappointment was evident on her face. "I had begun to feel like a regular part of the crew."

"Evie, you don't have to go back to Peter," Jocelyn said.

"I don't? That's wonderful news!" The older girl's eyes sparkled.

Out of the corner of her eye she saw Roger intently watching the conversation unfold. She forged on. "No. You can go home."

"What? Why?" A frown creased the girl's brow. "I already told you, I'm not going back. Have I done something to upset you?"

"Not exac—"

Evie never heard what Jocelyn was going to say, for she didn't get a chance to finish. At that moment, Peter Pan and his lost boys attacked, running pell-mell out of the trees and onto the beach, their faces smeared with crudely drawn war designs in mud and berry juice, screaming, "Victory for our mother!"

Or rather, the lost boys attacked. Peter, and his irksome fairy, flew above, shouting instructions. Lost boys and pirates quickly paired up for battle. Even little Tully did his part, nearly incapacitating Blind Bart with a string of screeched curses. The poor man covered his ears and moaned.

Only Dirty Bob stood apart, arms folded across his chest and a sneer upon his face, refusing to join in. When one of the twins rushed at him, short sword drawn, Bob deflected him with a scowl. "Hook may have felt it worth his time to fight children," he said, "but I'm more of a traditionalist." The boy turned sadly away, clearly stung by the rejection.

With the exception of those two, the pirates and lost

boys were having a marvelous time. Evie took in the scene, grinning wildly. "It's frightfully exciting, isn't it?" she asked Jocelyn. "So long as no one really gets hurt."

Jocelyn raised an eyebrow. "Oh, but someone might," she said. "You never know how things may go on the Neverland. It's not civilized here at all. Not like at home."

"That is for certain." The older girl's eyes shone with what Jocelyn hoped was dread but feared was delight. "Which side should I fight on? Am I with you, or with Peter?"

Jocelyn pictured Evie being injured or even killed. Still, she knew that Evie would never consent to sit and watch. The only way to ensure her safety was for Jocelyn to protect her. "You're with me, but stay close. We fight together!"

Evie drew her dagger. "That sounds delightful!" she said.

The girls descended upon the battle like a pair of Valkyries, ready to determine who would live and who would die. The sheer fierceness of their combined attack might have been enough to bring the fighting to an end right then and there, if Peter hadn't noticed Evie and dipped down to claim her (and the glory of the fight). "Hello, Mother," he said. "Don't be afraid. We have come to rescue you."

"Oh, hello, Peter," Evie replied. She smoothed down her hair and smiled brightly at him. Jocelyn nearly gagged with disgust at how quickly Evie seemed to fold up her battle lust and tuck it into a drawer.

Evie slid her dagger into her belt and went on. "That is very kind of you—"

"I know," Peter interrupted. "Stand aside while I kill the girl pirate who stole you. When I am done, you may make a sketch of me standing over the body."

Evie gave a small smile and shook her head. "Thank you, but that's really not necess—"

"The only body will be yours, Pan!" Jocelyn cried. "Unless you tell me what you did with my father's ship!"

"Never! Prepare to die for the honor of my mother!"

Evie brushed down the front of her dress. "Peter, really—"

"She's not *your* mother!" Jocelyn roared. "And *you* can prepare to die for stealing my father's ship! You haven't sunk it, have you?"

"I didn't sink that ship! I sailed it wonderfully. Besides, I didn't take it. I've never even heard of it. So, *you* prepare to die!"

"Both of you, stop preparing to die!" Evie's fierceness returned and grabbed their attention. Jocelyn snapped her mouth closed. Peter left his hanging open. "Peter, thank you for coming to rescue me, but I don't need it. I'd rather stay and be a pirate with my dearest friend, Jocelyn. I'll never leave her side."

Now Jocelyn was the one with her mouth hanging

open. Peter snapped his shut, then rearranged his face into a nonchalant look. "I wasn't coming to rescue you anyway. How like a girl to think everything is about her. I'm here because that one"—he shrugged a shoulder in Jocelyn's direction—"promised me a war. I've only come to collect, that's all."

"I did no such thing!"

"Beggin' yer pardon," Mr. Smee called out from where he and Fredo were taking a small rest before resuming an attempt to murder each other, "but, Miss Captain, I've been thinking. It seems to me, and Johnny agrees, that yer men and me are getting in some good exercise. Right, men?"

A chorus of ayes resounded.

"And as such," Mr. Smee went on, "maybe we can come up with a compromising situation—something to make everyone happy."

"I'm listening," Jocelyn said.

"I'm not," said Peter, placing his fingers in his ears and humming a jaunty tune.

"Well, miss, Peter Pan is always going on about wanting to have a war with us pirates, right? Only we've been mighty busy as of late. Perhaps'n we stay and give these miscreants the war they've been wanting—might even let 'em win a time or two—and in exchange, Peter Pan will tell you where to find the *Roger*."

"I'm in agreement," Jocelyn said. "Pan, if you will tell where it is, and if my crew has no objection, I'll leave you to your war. What say you, men?"

Another robust chorus of "Aye," except from Bob, who let out a surly "Nay!"

"Not quite unanimous, but it will do. Do we have a deal?"

"I guess so," Peter said, removing his fingers from his ears, "but wouldn't you rather have something else? Like maybe..." He took a step closer and lowered his voice. "A thimble?" The boy pursed his lips, closed his eyes, and leaned in.

Jocelyn took a step back. "What are you doing with your face? Stop that."

Peter frowned and straightened up. "I was going to give you a thimble! Girls love thimbles!"

"I think you have been misinformed. I must have had a hundred thimbles before I came here. They aren't that special."

His eyes popped open wide. "A hundred thimbles?" Peter seemed to be having trouble fathoming such a large amount.

"I didn't know you were interested in needlework," Jocelyn said. "But I don't care for it. All I want is the location of my father's ship. Tell me, or I'm afraid there shall be no war."

"I knew you were afraid," Peter crowed. "But if those are your only terms, I guess I accept. We have a deal." They spit on their hands and shook, though Jocelyn might not have been quite so agreeable had she known exactly where Peter had left the *Jolly Roger*.

CHAPTER TWENTY

*In Which Our Heroine Leads
Her Friends Into Necessary Hardships*

There are many various surprises a person can feel in life. There's the surprise of finding a diamond ring in your stew. There is the astonishment of noticing that it is still on the finger of its late owner. And there is the amazement of discovering that the cook has begun experimenting with new spices. Paprika adds such a nice, unexpected smokiness to a dish.

Jocelyn anticipated hearing that the *Jolly Roger* was moored somewhere, abandoned and half-forgotten. Those expectations were met. Where it was moored? Now, that was the surprising part.

"At the top of Craggy Peak? How on earth did you get the ship up there?"

"I don't remember. I either flew it there or beached it

nearby and the Neverland grew a mountain underneath. All I know is, I was tired of that game, so I left it. Can I join my war now? Which of your men are staying?"

"All of them, I suppose, except Roger. You will come with me, won't you, Roger?"

"Of course I will."

"So will I," Evie said.

"I won't," Bob said. "I never signed on for these childish games. There's bound to be someone in the pirate village in need of an experienced hand. I'll have no trouble finding work."

Jocelyn considered telling him that finding work in the village might not be all that easy—not unless he wanted to work for Krueger—but she was, quite frankly, relieved to see him go. "According to your Pirate Code, I could have you clapped in irons for mutiny, but I won't bother. I have more pressing issues to attend to. Good luck to you."

"Save your luck. I've a feeling you'll need it." He nodded once, then turned and walked off in the direction of the pirate village.

Peter and the lost boys allowed a brief reprieve in the battle in order for Jocelyn's crew to wish her good luck.

"Bring us back presents!"

"I'd like a new crepe pan!"

"Bring me a new arm!"

Evie kissed each man on the cheek, Roger saluted,

and Jocelyn gave last-minute instructions. "Have fun. Don't die!"

Mr. Smee wrapped her in a tearful hug. "I'd say the same for you, miss."

Good-byes having been said, Jocelyn, Roger, and Evie set off.

"Is that the mountain we need to go to?" Evie asked. They could see it from where they stood. Even at a distance, it appeared to loom over them.

"It looks to be quite a long journey," Jocelyn said. "Wouldn't you say so, Roger?"

The boy pulled his map from one pocket and his compass from another. "Judging distance by sight can be tricky, but we have these. I'd say the best course is north, skirting a bog, a desert, and a dense-looking forest, before turning east. It's a longer route, but much easier."

"Don't worry about making it easy," Jocelyn said, motioning her head toward Evie. "We are pirate adventurers. I'm certain we can take whatever the Neverland might dish out—though of course there is no shame if it becomes too difficult for you, Evie. I think we should be able to find a courier crow to take you home nearly any time you like."

Roger shook his head, not bothering to hide his disappointment at her choice. Evie gave Jocelyn a long, searching look. Jocelyn ignored them both, feigning a deep interest in the stitching of her jacket cuff.

"I'll be fine," Evie said at last. "You have nothing to worry about."

If only that were true. "Well then, that settles it," Jocelyn replied. "We'll take the shortcut. I'm sure the Neverland will be no match for us."

Had I been there, I would have given Jocelyn some advice: never taunt an island.

What happened next was tedious, arduous, and not all that interesting to tell. The Neverland must not have taken kindly to Jocelyn's boast, for the miles stretched before them, never seeming to grow shorter. There were too many blisters, too much rain, and too little food. There was mud—oh, such mud! Stinking, sucking, cold black goo that went on for days, and a desert filled with burning hot sand, without any seashore to make it worth the trouble. Shall I describe it all in minute detail?

No? I see. You want me to skip ahead to the "good parts."

Children are so impatient. You may have noticed Jocelyn herself being guilty of that vice. You all want life to be like a pearl necklace, one shining moment after another. No one ever wants to see the string that holds it all together.

I'll warn you: This next little gem won't be beautiful or pleasant. It will, however, certainly be exciting.

CHAPTER TWENTY-ONE

Abandoned Bits and Pieces

The three adventurers were awakened on the morning of the third day by a cloudburst, passing through on its way to spoil a picnic. Though she wasn't its intended target, Jocelyn definitely felt more cross than usual in the rain's aftermath. Even the ever-jovial Roger seemed in danger of losing his good cheer. He dumped water, along with more than a few rocks and wet sand, from his boots before pulling them gingerly over his sore feet, grumbling a bit under his breath about "rain clouds" and "blisters" and "shortcuts."

Only Evie seemed unperturbed. She wrung the water from her skirts and hair, chattering about where their journey might next take them. Presently they arrived at the forest Roger had seen on his map. The trees grew close together, forming a living wall. They were so tight, there didn't seem to be room for even the smallest horned squirrel or bipedal mouse to squeeze between their trunks, let alone Jocelyn, Roger, and Evie.

Except, in the middle of the wall of trees, there *was* a path. It was strewn with yellow and blue petals, dropped from dozens of trees in blossom. A warm breeze blew around their branches and out the opening, beckoning the children in with a sweet scent that made their mouths water.

As Jocelyn stood looking into that warm and inviting forest, she was filled with a sudden sense of foreboding. The girl had almost decided it would be best to go another way, when Roger spoke. "Jocelyn, I'm not too sure about this. Why don't we go around?"

"Oh yes, let's," Evie agreed. "I don't like the look of these trees. I feel like they are . . . watching me somehow."

Jocelyn reached to pluck a blossom from a low branch. The flower was unlike any she had seen before. Its petals were arranged in alternating layers of blue and yellow, with a deep, dark center. As she watched, two stamens unfolded, thick and black. They reminded Jocelyn of insect antennae or, even more aptly, the eyestalks of a slug.

The hair on the back of her neck stood up. It did feel

as if the trees were watching them. But if Evie didn't like this forest, they most certainly *would* be going in. Jocelyn had to show Evie that the Neverland was not altogether wonderful, and that home might not be so bad in comparison. She was sure she could show Evie the darker side of the Neverland while still keeping her safe. After all, Jocelyn had faced plenty of Neverland dangers before and come out all right.

She dropped the flower, crushing it under her heel, and squared her shoulders. "Don't be a coward, either one of you. This is the shortest way to the ship. I don't want to leave poor Meriwether trapped with Captain Krueger any longer than necessary. Do you?"

"Oh, of course not. I didn't think of that." Evie took a cautious step forward.

Roger frowned, but Jocelyn stepped through the trees and onto the path. "Let's go!" she called. "Captain's orders."

Evie shrugged and fell in line behind her, with Roger bringing up the rear. Jocelyn was glad they hadn't required more convincing. She called back to them, "See? This isn't so terrible."

Here is a little life lesson for you: When someone says something like "This isn't so terrible," you can be certain things are about to get much, much worse.

They trudged on in silence for some time, the only

sound a slight rustling of the trees, though the air was still. No birds called to one another. No small animals scuttled about.

Just as Jocelyn began to grow bored with the unending monotony of trees, a new sound, like the clinking of glasses, pricked her ears. Was there a silent dinner party going on somewhere ahead? The journey thus far had been rather light on sustenance; her stomach growled in anticipation.

"What do you suppose that noise is?" Evie whispered.

"I'm hoping it's our midday meal," Jocelyn replied. "But be prepared. I've learned that the people in the Neverland are not always friendly."

Jocelyn put her hand on her sword and led the way. They rounded a slight curve, and the path ended, opening into a small clearing. The edges were still walled with tightly grown trees, but within those borders, a pretty little garden thrived. In its center, surrounded by a sky-blue carpet of blooming forget-me-nots, a single tree grew—the same variety as the others in the forest, only much larger.

Oddly, it was not yet in full bloom. Someone had tied dozens, maybe even hundreds, of brightly colored bottles into its branches. Though Jocelyn still felt no breeze, the tree swayed gently, making the bottles clink together.

So there would be no lunch. Jocelyn humphed, but

Evie whispered. "Oh, this is lovely. I wonder who put all the bottles there?"

Roger whispered back. "And what kind of tree this is. I've never seen anything like it."

There was a reverence in their voices that made Jocelyn want to shout.

So she did.

"Yes! Very pretty! But we have a ship to find!" It felt good to shatter the stillness in the air—to bring a disordered messiness to the quiet, pristine garden.

The others must have felt the same way, for they laughed, allowing their voices to return to a normal tone. Even the clinking of the bottles grew louder. A few of the buds popped into blossom, right before their eyes.

"I think we can take a minute to look around, can't we?" Roger asked. "That is, with your permission, Captain." He winked at Jocelyn.

She gave a slight smile and a small nod. "All right. But let's not take long."

Roger and Evie waded through the forget-me-nots and approached the tree. Sunlight shone through the colored glass, splashing their skin with strange, dancing lights. The sense of foreboding Jocelyn had felt since they reached the forest deepened, but she brushed it aside and hurried to join her friends.

"What are the bottles for?" Jocelyn's voice was much

quieter here, next to the tree. She had the crazy notion that she didn't want to awaken it.

Evie reached out and touched a bottle. "Look, they're labeled," she said quietly. "The letters are faded by the sun, but I think I can make it out." She leaned close to read. "This says, 'First love, Amelia Nichols, age thirteen.'"

Roger and Jocelyn moved closer, and the three children took turns reading aloud.

Belief in Magic, Edward Winter, Age 9
Fear of Toads, Julie Breckinridge, Age 6
Dislike of Green Vegetables, Annie
    Henderson, Age 12
Reluctance to Leave Mother's Side, Lloyd
    Jackson, Age 2

"What are these things?" Roger wondered aloud.

The answer came in the form of a breathy voice, not far behind them. "They are filled with childhood castoffs and leave-behinds."

A woman approached. She was tall and willowy, looking a bit like a tree herself, with long, thin limbs and wild hair that hung in soft, moss-green clumps. A crown of the yellow and blue blossoms was perched upon her head and she carried a basket full of the colorful bottles.

"Children start out with so many options," she said. "Truly every possibility is open, but over time, they start to lose things." The woman dug through her basket and held up a shining green bottle. "This child forgot his propensity for baby talk, carelessly forgetting it in the backseat of a taxicab." She traded the green bottle for a yellow one. "And, oh dear, this child did not hold tightly to her loyalty to a friend. It was plucked from her hands by a passing wind."

Though she spoke in a soft voice, there was something Jocelyn found repellent, even mildly threatening, about the woman. The girl placed her hand on the hilt of her sword. "Who are you?" she asked, more challenge than question.

The woman gave a dreamy smile, her eyes soft and unfocused. "I am the guardian of this forest. I feed and care for it—as a mother would."

Evie took a step closer to her. "What else is in your basket?"

"See for yourself," she responded, passing it to the girl.

Roger took a peek inside, running his fingers over the bottles. Even Jocelyn, who still felt anxious to move on, leaned close and lifted a bright purple glass. The liquid inside was viscous, like a thick bone broth, and shimmered a bit. "How do you get these?" she asked.

"Once the bits and pieces have been abandoned, I gather and bring them here, to give life to my beautiful forest. It drinks up these discarded scraps of children's lives, and no one misses a thing."

"It drinks their lives?" Jocelyn asked, suppressing a shudder. She couldn't help but think of the vampire stories she had read.

The woman tilted her head and regarded Jocelyn with wide eyes. They were blue, with the irises ringed in yellow. "Only the parts they abandoned," she said.

"But what about the child who lost it?" Evie asked, frowning into the basket. "What about thirteen-year-old Andy Clibber here, who lost his respect for authority, or ten-year-old Mary Farrington, who lost her good cheer?"

The woman's face sharpened, losing a bit of its dreamlike quality. "Perhaps Andy and Mary shouldn't have been so careless," she snapped. "Besides, if those things are truly important to them, and they work very hard, they can grow more. Children do have so many possibilities." She took the basket back and slung it over her arm. "Regardless, these morsels have been abandoned. Why should I allow them to go to waste?"

She removed a bottle, uncorked it, and stepped closer to the tree. Roger followed, curiosity written all over his face. The woman held up her offering, her faraway smile back in place. A tender new shoot wrapped itself around the bottle's lip, tucking its end into the opening. The tree shuddered and made a slurping noise.

"It *is* drinking it!" Roger exclaimed. "Like some sort of plant food!"

More blossoms blinked open, closed, then opened

again. A soft rustling filled the air. Jocelyn took an involuntary step back. Something seemed off. She noticed Evie doing the same, but Roger was fascinated.

He placed a hand on the tree's trunk. "It's warm. It feels more, I don't know, *alive* than any plant I have ever come across." The tree responded to his touch by dropping a tendril to his shoulder. Roger laughed. "I think it likes me."

The woman smiled and carried on affixing bottles to the tree. "I'm sure it does."

Roger continued his examination of the plant. "But why feed only this one?" he asked. "What about the others?"

She paused in her work to answer. "The trees here are connected by their roots. They all receive the nourishment."

Evie reached for Jocelyn, clutching at her jacket. "I . . . I felt something brush against my ankle. I think there may be snakes in the leaves."

Jocelyn pulled her sword, using the tip to push the forget-me-nots aside. "The roots are moving!" They writhed, slowly, like a serpent rousing itself from its cool den, waiting for the sun to warm its blood and enable it to strike.

Roger brushed the curling vine off his shoulder and joined the girls, stooping to look at the roots. "It's amazing!" he said. "I'd like to take a few notes." He fumbled in his pockets for a notebook and lead pencil, but Jocelyn placed a hand on his arm.

"It's time to go," she said. "Now."

"I'm afraid you won't be going anywhere," the guardian said dreamily. "You are so full of life, of possibilities, and my forest is hungry."

The rustling grew to a quiet roar. Insistent. Ravenous.

CHAPTER TWENTY-TWO

An Explosive Temper

A new silver dagger, an emerald-green snake, the barmaid at the Black Spot—I've found that the most beautiful things on earth are quite often the most sinister. Such it was with that lovely yet deadly forest. Like a honey-baited flytrap, it had drawn Jocelyn and her friends in, and there it held them.

Evie was the first to scream, as was her right. She was oldest, after all, and should have been first to do things. "Something is wrapped around my ankle!" she cried.

Roger made a move to help, but stumbled and nearly fell as a vine tightly gripped him by the legs.

"Both of you, fight back!" Jocelyn cried. She drew her sword and hacked at the vines now climbing up her calves. Roger and Evie set to work with their own

blades, but the creepers were as terrible as the heads of a Hydra—sever one and two more seemed to take its place.

Jocelyn screamed, half in fear, half in frustration. "What I wouldn't give to turn this whole forest into firewood!"

The vines withdrew, ever so slightly, then pressed in again more urgently, quite literally rooting the girl to the spot.

"Did you feel that?" Roger cried. "It loosened when you said fire!"

"Can you—" Evie began, but a root wound up her body, squeezing the air from her lungs and cutting off her speech. Jocelyn leaned over and slashed with her sword, freeing the older girl.

"It will be over soon," the guardian of the forest crooned in a voice one might use to comfort a crying baby. "No need to fuss."

Jocelyn felt a great need to fuss, but as the vines wrapped ever tighter round her legs, she decided not to waste the effort. Instead, she frantically looked about for something that she might use to start a fire.

The woman paid little attention to them, humming to herself as she continued to affix the colored glass to the tree.

That was when Jocelyn realized she still held the bottle she had taken from the basket. She turned it over and read TENDENCY TOWARD PUBLIC TEMPER TANTRUMS, JAMES HILL, AGE 7. It was merely the glimmer of a possibility, but if anything was more incendiary than a child's temper, Jocelyn didn't know what it was.

The vines crept ever higher, and Jocelyn furiously attacked them with her blade, hoping to buy a bit of time. When she had fought them back to her ankles, she replaced the sword in her scabbard and tore a bit of hem from her dress.

She tucked the bottle in the crook of her arm, uncorked it, and stuffed the fabric inside, creating a wick. Jocelyn withdrew her flint and steel from its pouch, held her breath, and struck. The spark caught her wick and grew into a flame. The girl lobbed it toward the tree and covered her ears.

"No!" screamed the woman as the flaming bottle sped toward its target. "You can't! You'll ruin everything!" But it was too late.

The glass hit the trunk and exploded in a blaze of flame and heat. Little James Hill must have had quite a temper before he gave it up. The intensity of the blast brought tears to Jocelyn's eyes. Roger, a few steps nearer to the source, had his eyebrows singed nearly off.

Roots and vines withdrew from the children immediately, and a wailing filled the air. Jocelyn couldn't tell if it came from the woman or from the forest itself. She suspected it to be both.

Roger, Evie, and Jocelyn ran then, finding the path on the other side of the clearing. More explosions shook the ground, sending blasts of heat that blistered the backs of their necks. The trees around them twitched and thrashed. Branches tore at their faces and hair. They coughed and gagged as the air filled with thick, oily smoke. Still they ran.

At last, sunlight poked its fingers through the thinning leaves overhead, and they were out. The path gaped wide behind them, a mouth deprived of a meal, but the trio continued to flee, not stopping until they were well out of the forest's shadow. Roger and Evie looked at Jocelyn, their breath as ragged and eyes as wide as hers surely were.

A flood of feelings coursed through the girl: relief that they had survived, guilt that she had led Roger and Evie into such a dangerous place, anger that things were not turning out the way she intended, and more than a little devious joy at the explosions she had created. She didn't know whether to shout or cry or laugh. Roger's face showed a similar mix of emotions.

Jocelyn turned to Evie, expecting she would now be ready to say good-bye to the Neverland and its unpredictable dangers. The older girl trembled from head to foot. Her eyes shone, perhaps with unshed tears? For a moment Evie was too overcome to speak. She opened her mouth, and nothing came out but a squeak.

Clearing her throat, she tried again. "That—" She swallowed. "That was . . . astounding! What do you think will happen next?"

Jocelyn's hopes fell. She scowled and began marching onward, Craggy Peak in her sight. "Next? We simply keep walking."

Have you ever ridden on a seesaw? I spent many a happy childhood hour on one, playing with my baby cousin, Hilda. As I was much older, and therefore much heavier, I had to take great care to get on my end in just the right way—in order to maximize the baby's flight time after launching her into the ether.

Jocelyn and Evie were on a sort of emotional seesaw. The higher Evie's spirits flew, the lower Jocelyn's sank— and Evie's sprits were dangerously high, so ready was she for more adventure. She didn't even mind when a group of fairy schoolgirls flew by, each taking it in turn to pelt the three adventurers with volleys of pond-slime balls. (It appeared that news of Meriwether's capture had spread.) Indeed, Evie seemed charmed by their pigtailed hair, dainty bluebell uniforms, and jangled curses.

Roger wiped the sludge from his face with the back of his hand and reached in one of his pockets for a handker-chief. Instead he pulled out a small blue bottle. "I guess I'm turning into quite the pirate, after all," he said. "It appears that this has worked its way into my pocket."

Evie took it from him and read the label: "'Courage, George Watson, age nine.' Oh dear. Poor George," she said with a smile.

"Not so bad for us, though," Roger said, taking it back and tucking it into his pocket once more. "Never know when we might need some extra courage."

"No indeed. Though I do hope it's soon!" Evie replied, laughing. "I can't wait to see what else this island has in store for us."

Jocelyn glowered at them both.

Whatever the island did have in store for the young adventurers, it wasn't dinner. Jocelyn was certain she had never been hungrier. Thus far, they had managed to subsist on nuts and wild fruit, but none had been found since before the forest. All they had eaten that day were a few dried-up wild turnips discovered along the way. Jocelyn supposed the turnips were better than death by starvation, but not by much.

As soon as they found a place to camp—a mostly dry clearing in a thicket of sugar maples dressed out in their most colorful autumn finery—Roger offered to forage for dinner while Jocelyn and Evie got a fire going.

He wasn't gone long. "We're in luck," he said, joining the girls around their campfire. "I found us something to eat." He gave each of them a handful of green leaves, with a few stems mixed in. "Wood sorrel, chickweed, and dandelion leaves. Let's call it a salad."

Jocelyn had been hoping for something more substantial. "Let's call it a bunch of weeds," she mumbled under her breath.

The evening was cool and damp, the ground was hard, their stomachs were empty, and yet Evie seemed happier than ever. Jocelyn's plan to make the older girl miserable had backfired.

In fact, no one seemed to be more unhappy than Jocelyn herself.

"Eat something," Roger told her. "You are always out of sorts when you are hungry."

"I have plenty of other reasons to be 'out of sorts,'" she grumped at him, but she did put a few of the leaves in her mouth. They tasted as bitter as she felt.

"I think I saw some berry bushes while I was gathering firewood. I'll see if any are ripe, and we can have them for dessert," Evie said.

"Don't go far," Jocelyn told her. Knowing Evie, she'd likely find a den of tigers and decide it would be fun to wrestle them. Still, Jocelyn let her go. She wanted a moment alone with Roger.

As soon as Evie was out of sight, she took a deep breath and dove right in. "That was a close call back there, in the forest. It never should have happened."

He looked up from where he sat, poking his fire with a stick, and gave her his just-for-Jocelyn grin. "I'm glad to hear you say that. It's not easy to admit when you have been wrong. I accept your apology."

She frowned. "My apology? I wasn't wrong. I was talking about *you*. If you had left when I said to, instead of being so wrapped up in learning about that ridiculous tree, we wouldn't have gotten so, well, wrapped up in that ridiculous tree."

"You think that was *my* fault? If you'd listened to me and gone the easier route in the beginning, we might be at the *Jolly Roger* finding the key behind your father's portrait and cracking the map's code even now." He softened his voice. "Look, Jocelyn, I understand why you want Evie to go home, but why the sudden urgency? Instead of trying to make her hate the Neverland, why not let her come along with us and hunt for the treasure? Maybe once she's had enough adventuring, she'll be ready to go home on her own."

"She can't come on the treasure hunt! The treasure isn't on the Neverland."

Roger frowned at her, confused. "What? Where is it? And how do you know?"

"Starkey told me it's in England—right under Miss Eliza's school, of all places. Evie can't go with us because it's not in her When. Who knows what would happen to her if she tried. And if she stays here, while I go, I'll snuff out like a candle! Is that what you want?"

Roger's voice was quiet. "Of course not, Jocelyn! Why didn't you tell me where it was before?"

She fiddled with her locket, popping it open and snapping it closed. "I didn't want you to worry. I'm the captain—that's my job." She scuffed her boots in the dirt. "I also didn't want you to think I was trying to be rid of Evie merely so I could go after the gold."

He squinted his eyes at her. "Aren't you? A little, at least? Are you more concerned for her, or about not getting the treasure?"

"For her, of course! I don't want it to be like this. I don't want her to have to go home and die young, but Roger, that is what happened. My mother died. Or, at least, she will. I wish I could change that, but I can't." Sudden tears stung her eyes, but Jocelyn dashed them away. "All I know is, if she stays here, she'll grow to be miserable—and I'll be trapped. I'm trying to set things right . . . to put them back the way they are supposed to be. But don't fool yourself into thinking I like it."

Roger blew out a breath. "I'm sorry. Maybe that was unfair of me. But Jocelyn, can't you see? You have to tell Evie the truth. Isn't that the whole point of you wanting the treasure? So you can decide your own future? Why not give her the same option?"

Jocelyn shook her head. "No. We've been over that. I can't do that!"

"Why not? Aren't you tired of lying to her? I know I am."

"Not telling is not the same as lying! Besides, if I do tell her who she is, I know she'll go back."

Roger rubbed his eyes with the palm of his hand. "Isn't that what you want?"

"Yes, but not like that. If I tell her who she is and what her staying here means for me, she'll go home. *For me.* And when she dies, it will be *my* fault. She has to choose it on her own."

"All right," he said, suddenly looking very tired. "What would you like me to do?"

"Part of what makes having adventures so fun is having them with friends. I hate to do this . . ." Jocelyn hesitated. "We need to stop being so friendly to her."

Roger shook his head. "That's not fair. I won't be unkind to her."

Sometimes it's better to just let things lie. For example, sleeping dogs, long-dead bodies, and disagreements with your best friend. However, Jocelyn felt that too much was at stake. She employed a surefire friendship tactic, used by children the world over: coercion.

She stood and took a breath. "I didn't want it to come to this, but need I remind you that I am your captain? You signed on to my crew the very day we met."

Roger stood as well, using the extra inch of height to

his advantage. "That's funny. I remember it a little differently. I remember becoming your *friend* on that day. Sure, I said I'd be on your crew, but that was only pretend."

"Well, maybe you were pretending to be my friend, too!"

Roger visibly recoiled at her words. "I can't believe you would say that. After everything we have been through together—" He crossed his arms over his chest. "You don't mean that."

"I do, Roger. And I am ordering you, as your captain, to stop being nice to Evie. If you don't, perhaps you are not part of my crew or my friend!"

He stared at her for just a moment, hurt and anger written all over his face, then stormed off on his own. Jocelyn wished she could take back her words, but why didn't he understand that she *needed* him to do this? She would love for the three of them to go on having fun and adventures together, but they just couldn't—as much for Evie's sake as for her own.

CHAPTER TWENTY-THREE

Wherein Our Heroine Is Given
Something to Chew On

For centuries, philosophers the world over have debated whether doing something wrong for the right reasons justifies that act. Morals can be such burdensome things. That is precisely why I am happy to remain unafflicted by them.

Jocelyn had no such luck. The girl sat alone at her fire, waiting for Evie to return with her berries and for Roger to simply return. She alternated between anger at him for not going along with her plan and shame that she had tried to force him to.

After what seemed like hours of waiting, but in reality was likely no more than ten or fifteen minutes, Jocelyn decided to storm off herself, though she regretted no one was around to witness it. Had someone been, the girl was certain hers would have gone down as the most dramatic leaving in history. Being alone robbed her of that honor and she added it to the list of reasons she should be irritated with Roger.

Jocelyn wandered the woods, most certainly not searching for *him*—even though it was growing dark and he had been gone a very long time. She decided it likely that Roger had caught up with Evie and made her his new best friend. They were probably laughing together over some rich, warm, meaty stew.

Jocelyn imagined the scene so clearly, she could smell the stew meat. Her stomach growled and her mouth watered in response. As she walked on, peering around trees and up game paths—not looking for Roger—the smell grew stronger. Perhaps it wasn't her imagination after all!

She scrambled to the top of a boulder to get a better look around. Through the trees, not far in the distance, she spied a flicker of firelight. It couldn't have been Roger and Evie, for several figures were silhouetted around the crackling flames. And judging from the delicious smell on the air, whoever they were, they had something far better than twigs and leaves for supper.

Normally, approaching an unknown group in the dead of night is a bad idea, unless, of course you are planning on ambushing them—which, if it came down to it, Jocelyn most certainly would have done. She was determined to share that meal by invitation or by force. The girl was a pirate, after all; it was time she began acting like it.

Jocelyn crept ever closer, near enough to spy a leg of venison rotating slowly on a spit, its juices dripping into the flames with sweet little pops and hisses. Her stomach rumbled and she prepared to strike, but before she could formulate an attack, an attack came to her.

A small, fierce creature dashed out of the circle of firelight and leaped on the girl, knocking her over. It focused its attack on Jocelyn's face—not with bites, but with a vigorous and violent licking.

"Snow!" a young woman called. "Get off her. That is no way to treat a friend!"

The wolf pup relinquished its seat on Jocelyn's chest and moved to stand beside its master.

"What are you doing wandering the woods alone? It's nearly dark out," Tiger Lily said. "What would your pirate nursemaid think of this?"

A wise man once said: A full belly diminishes all other problems. That wise man was me.

Though it was true in the case of Jocelyn, diminishing is not the same as removing. Upon hearing that Roger and Evie were out in the woods alone—and without supper—Tiger Lily sent one of her warriors to find them. When they arrived, everyone sat around the fire, eating the wonderfully rich stew. Throughout the meal, Roger refused to look at Jocelyn, which was vexing, mainly because she wanted him to notice that she was not looking at him.

After each bowl was empty—and, in Jocelyn's case, licked clean—Tiger Lily spread out extra buffalo robes and invited the children to share her camp for the night. Evie and Roger climbed into theirs right away, but Jocelyn stayed near the fire. She found a stick on the ground and used it to poke at the coals, discovering that boys were onto something. It was rather soothing.

She was full and she was warm, but she was not content.

"You look like you could use some company." Tiger Lily joined the girl, sitting on the ground next to her. "I am surprised to see you out here. Are you searching for the place on your map?"

"No. I found out where the map leads. It's not even on the Neverland, but we are on the treasure hunt, in a way. What are you doing out here?"

"I have brought my best braves with me on a quest to find a silver grizzly bear. They say those who catch a glimpse of him will have good luck in all the next year's hunting."

"You'll find him. My mo—" Jocelyn looked over at Evie, stretched out on her buffalo bed. "*Someone* once told me that anything was possible if you first decide what you want, believe you can have it, and don't let anything stand in your way."

"That is very good advice."

"Yes. And it worked when I was hunting the Neverland crocodile, but it's much harder now. I want to find my father's treasure. I believe I can. It's just . . ." She looked over at Roger. He was lying propped up on his elbows, using a piece of string from his pocket to teach Evie how to make a cat's cradle design. "What if the thing that is standing in my way are the people that I care about?"

Tiger Lily nodded. "That is difficult. But consider this: If that is the case, perhaps you want the wrong thing. Or you are going about the wrong way of achieving it." She took up her own stick and stirred the coals. "Sometimes believing in yourself isn't enough. You have to believe in others as well." She tossed her stick in the fire and brushed off her hands. "I wish you luck on your journey, wherever it takes you. Good night, young captain."

Jocelyn said her good nights and joined Roger and Evie, her thoughts all abuzz. Roger rolled over, away from her, though Jocelyn could tell by his breathing that he had not yet fallen asleep.

Evie filled the cracks his silence might have otherwise occupied with her cheerful chatter. The girl lay in her blanket, marveling over the night sky. She praised the stars for their sparkling talent, pointing out her favorites. The stars could not resist such flattery and began to twinkle extra brightly, each hoping to gain her attention.

Even Jocelyn's spirits were lifted somewhat by the show playing out above her. Orion, the hunter, held his bow steady, flexing his starry muscles. Taurus, the bull, pawed the sky with one cloven hoof, steam twinkling from his nostrils and dissipating into the Milky Way.

"I love the Neverland! There is nothing at all like this in England," Evie said, turning Jocelyn's mood sour again.

Younger stars, not attached to any constellations, began to show off, as young things are wont to do. Soon the sky was filled with streaks of light.

"Quick, everyone, make a wish!" Evie said. "What did you wish for, Jocelyn?"

"Wishing on stars is stupid," she said. "They never come true the way you want them to."

"I don't know about that. I think things have a way of working out just the right way, even if we can't see it when we are in the thick of it."

Jocelyn hoped that was true, though she couldn't imagine how. Just then, Orion loosed his arrow. The brightest star the girl had ever seen hurled itself from one end of the sky to the other, and she couldn't resist: *I wish that things* would *work out in just the right way. And I wish it wouldn't cost me my friends to make that happen.*

CHAPTER TWENTY-FOUR

Impossibilities

Morning sunlight squeezed between Jocelyn's lids and poked her in the eye. She sat up, blinking in the dazzling light of day. Tiger Lily and her warriors were gone, off to find their silver bear. A ceiling of clear blue sky hung above, and Craggy Peak loomed directly over her. The Neverland had done some rearranging when they weren't looking.

The three quietly munched on a breakfast of nuts and dried berries, left for them by Tiger Lily, then neatly piled their buffalo robes in a place where she would be able to find them when she came back through. Once that act of housekeeping was finished, they started up the path. Roger walked ahead and Jocelyn let him, unsure of how to approach the boy. Evie strode along next to her.

Every few moments she patted her dress pockets as if she were searching for something.

"What is the matter?" Jocelyn asked.

Evie drew her eyebrows together, concentrating. "I have that unsettling feeling that I have lost or forgotten something. I don't know what." She shook her head. "Never mind, it will come to me, I'm sure."

Jocelyn felt a stab of concern over Evie's forgetfulness. "If you were at home right now, what would you be doing?" she asked.

"What do you mean?" Evie asked with a frown. "I am home."

"I don't mean this home," Jocelyn said. "I mean where you live with your father, Sir Charles. You do remember him, don't you?"

Evie lowered her eyebrows, concentrating. After a moment she shook her head. "Perhaps I have had too much sun. I nearly forgot my own father! But my life there seems so far away, like a dream."

"Maybe it would help if we talked about it," Jocelyn said. They spent the next half hour chatting about Hopewell Manor—Evie's favorite places to hide from her governess, her ongoing war with the manor cat, and her fears that she would never live up to her father's expectations. Jocelyn had not known how many things she and her mother had in common. Now that she did, it felt even more important that Evie not forget them.

"You need to be careful here," Jocelyn said. "The Neverland can take all your memories of home if you let it. And home helps you remember who you are."

"I suppose." Evie sighed. "But I don't think I want to be who I was when I lived there."

Jocelyn frowned. Maybe Roger had been right to suggest she should tell Evie what she knew, or at least in part. She decided to share what the harbormaster had said about those who forget their homes, leaving out only that which concerned the true nature of their relationship. ". . . so you see," she finished, "if you become untethered—if you forget—you will be miserable."

Evie bit her lip, thinking. "I don't know. Tiger Lily and her people aren't from here, but they seem fine to me."

Jocelyn was surprised. "They aren't? Where are they from?"

"A woman sang their history at the feast that first night we met them. It must have been while you were getting some air. Tiger Lily's great-grandfather led his people here from the Americas, through a passage they found while fleeing from a warring tribe. They haven't become 'untethered' in all their time here, and"—Evie turned to look at Jocelyn—"neither have you. You've been on the Neverland ages longer than I have."

"Tiger Lily's people remember who they are. They keep that memory alive in the songs they sing and stories they tell. As for me, maybe I remember because no matter what happens, I still want to be myself." She shrugged. "I guess my home is a big part of that." Jocelyn was silent for a moment, then added, "I hope to go back one day."

Evie threaded her arm though Jocelyn's. "Well, *I* hope that's not for a long time. I'd miss you. As for this untethering business, is that the reason you've been trying to get me to leave the Neverland?"

Jocelyn nodded.

"I'm glad to know it. I thought you were angry that Roger and I had become friends. I was worried you didn't know how special you are to him."

"I don't know about that..." Jocelyn said, looking ahead to where Roger walked alone.

"Oh, pishposh. You two will be over this ridiculous quarrel of yours in no time. I'm sure that whatever it's about is of less importance than your friendship." She nudged Jocelyn with her elbow, eliciting a small smile. "And while we are talking of ridiculous things, what about this harbormaster of yours? What makes him such an expert on the ways of the Neverland? Adults are wrong all the time. I'm sure I'll find a way around this untethering business."

For the first time, Jocelyn felt a flicker of doubt. What if the harbormaster *was* wrong and Evie could be perfectly happy in the Neverland?

★ ★ ★

Jocelyn grew colder as they climbed, both inside and out. Roger's mutiny left her feeling hollow. She filled the space with grim determination, marching through knee-high snowdrifts and wading through icy streams. He wasn't speaking to her, but he wasn't speaking to Evie, either. He plodded along ahead, looking every bit as miserable as Jocelyn felt.

At length they came to an ice bridge spanning a deep crevasse. How Jocelyn wished they could simply fly over it. She missed Meriwether, and not just for his supply of fairy dust. If he had been there, he would have been certain to do something to make them all laugh and break the tension.

Jocelyn didn't know how things had gone so terribly wrong, but she knew that finding the *Jolly Roger* would be a start to setting them right. The key to the treasure map's code would be on her father's portrait, just as Smee suspected. It had to be! And they'd have the ship, giving them the means to finally defeat Krueger. She would rescue Meriwether and get her map back. She didn't know what might happen after that, but she believed that everything would work out, just as it was supposed to. She only had to stay the course.

At long last, they scaled a steep incline and it came into view: the *Jolly Roger*. Seeing it took her breath away. She hadn't really thought about what it would be like to stand in its presence at last. Her father's ship! And soon it would be hers. A lump formed in her throat. Jocelyn wondered how he would feel about her taking the helm. She hoped she was pirate enough to deserve it.

"Oh, Jocelyn, it's magnificent!" Evie said.

The ship sat low in the snow, looking for all the world as if it were cruising on an ocean of white. The mountain rose for some ways behind it, like a great ice-covered wave, frozen in time. Jocelyn shivered at the thought of that wave crashing on the deck.

"But," Evie continued, "how will we get her down to the sea?"

Jocelyn stopped short. Her thoughts had been so consumed by finding the *Jolly Roger*, and by her other problems, she hadn't even considered that.

Roger consulted his map and finally broke his silence. "The mountain butts right up to the ocean," he told Evie. "If we weigh the anchor, I think we could ride her down the slope like a great sled."

Evie giggled. "And why not? Snow is nothing more than frozen water. We'll sail her right down to the sea!"

Finding the ship had lifted both Jocelyn's hopes and her spirits. She had been waiting so long to find the key to breaking the treasure map's code, and finally it was within her grasp. She brushed aside the problems of not actually having the map in her possession and the situation with Evie. It would work out. There in the shadow of the *Jolly Roger*, anything seemed possible—even making up with Roger.

She caught his eye and gave him a small smile. He didn't quite return it, but he didn't scowl, either. That was something, at least.

They hurried as best as they could through the deep drifts. Here, the top layer of the Neverland's peculiar snow was as warm as fresh baked bread, not yet having had time to cool. Jocelyn grabbed fistfuls as she walked, warming her cold hands.

She reached the *Jolly Roger* first. There was no gangplank, but a rope ladder hung over the side where Peter Pan must have left it when he abandoned the ship. *He probably sailed a new mother here in it,* Jocelyn thought with a snort. *Or a load of new lost boys. He does seem to have trouble hanging on to his friends.*

Jocelyn didn't want to be like that. She waited for Roger and Evie to catch up, and tried to thaw the ice between them. "Roger, meet your namesake," she said with a grin. "You have always been the jolliest person I know, and I'm happy we are friends. I'm sorry I gave you cause to feel otherwise. As a way of apology, I'd like to give you the honor of going first."

Roger said nothing, but he gave her a half smile and a tiny salute before climbing the rope.

Evie flashed her dimples. "Oh, Jocelyn, I'm so glad we found it. Let's get up there and find the key to your map. Then we'll sail it down to the sea, find and gut that awful Krueger, and get your pirate gold!" She giggled. "I never would have had a chance to say something like that at home. I wonder what Miss Eliza would think."

Jocelyn grinned, both at the thought of Miss Eliza's reaction and that Evie was thinking of home. "I'm sure she would find that to be quite exceptional."

Evie's eyebrows contracted and she stared at Jocelyn. She took a breath as if she were about to say something, but Jocelyn cut her off.

"After you, Evie." She motioned to the rope ladder.

Evie blinked, shook her head, and began to climb.

Jocelyn did not follow right away. She touched her forehead to the rough wood planking on the hull and closed her eyes. Finding the *Jolly Roger* had felt impossible, as impossible as all the other problems Jocelyn was struggling with. But she had done it. Standing here at the ship—her father's ship—gave her hope. She remembered what the harbormaster had said: *The Neverland is full of impossible things*. This ship was proof. In a place filled with impossible things, anything was possible, wasn't it?

Jocelyn opened her eyes, grabbed the rope, and began to climb. Hand over hand, higher and higher she rose. Her arms burned and the ladder swayed a bit beneath her, but she cared little. Everything she wanted was within her grasp. She could feel it.

The girl reached the railing and climbed over, her feet

solid on her father's ship. She stood there a moment, looking out over the snowy sea. Jocelyn felt nearly as much triumph in that moment as when she slew the crocodile. She turned slowly, with a smile on her face. "Let's go find that key."

"Yes. Let's."

But it wasn't Roger or Evie who replied. That would have proven difficult for either, as they were bound and gagged, captive at the feet of Captain Krueger.

CHAPTER TWENTY-FIVE

Here There Be Monsters

This world is filled with terrible things—insects that bite and sting, debt collectors, diminutive monsters that whine and beg for stories—but perhaps the worst of all is the face of someone you trusted right after you discover they have stabbed you in the back. I mean that in the figurative sense, though the face of someone who has literally stabbed you is not much nicer to behold.

At first, Jocelyn wasn't sure what had happened. How had Krueger found them? Then she noticed Dirty Bob standing nearby, a surly smirk on his face. "How dare you!" she shouted at him, but Krueger silenced her by pulling his blade and pointing it at Roger. He paced up and down the deck, always moving, and Jocelyn was once again struck by the waves of malevolence that seemed to emanate from him.

"I'll be doing the talking here, girlie, if you don't mind." His black, pupil-less eyes bored into her. "I believe you still have something I want. You may have given me the map, but it's unreadable without the key. Where is it?"

"I don't know what you are talking about," Jocelyn growled.

"I think you do. See, Dirty Bob here told me all about it, didn't you, Bob?"

Bob spat over the railing. "Aye. The key is here some-where. They planned to find it, then use this ship and its extra-powerful cannon to attack you and take back the map and that fairy."

Krueger pulled the silver flask from his pocket and shook it. It made a dull, metallic clunk. "This fairy? I think I'll hang on to him for a while." He pasted a smile across his face, but having failed kindergarten, his past-ing skills were limited. This left him with a crooked grin that peeled up at the edges. "However," he went on, "once you tell me where the key is, I'll set him free. In fact, I'll let you all go." The smile fell from his face. "But if you don't, I'll kill each and every one of you. Now, what will it be? Life or death?"

Jocelyn stuck out her chin, trying to look brave. "How do I know you won't kill us anyway?"

Captain Krueger laughed then, hard and full of spite.

"You don't. But if you fail to give me what I want, you can be certain that I will. Slowly. And with great pleasure." He pulled his sword from his scabbard and caressed it. Krueger may not have had pasting skills, but he was excellent at cutting. Anyone could tell that, simply by looking at him.

Jocelyn felt herself go pale. "You are a monster."

"And you are a spoiled child. But I won't force an answer tonight. Why don't you spend a night in the bilge and think it over? In the morning, if you make the correct choice, I'll be kind to you. If not, you will stay locked up until there's not enough meat on your bones to even entice the rats. That is, after you watch me pluck the wings from your fairy and"—he pointed his blade at Roger, tapping him lightly on the arm—"do a little carving on your friend here." Krueger pulled the boy roughly to his feet. "Tie him to the mast and throw the girls below. Let's hope those rats aren't too hungry."

A ship's bilge is not a pleasant place. It's dark and dank and foul, filled with stagnant water, sewage and whatever else might wash down from the upper decks, mold, and rats. It is a place unfit for human habitation, as filled with despair as it is with filth. Oh, how I would enjoy giving you a tour of one.

Bilge rats are notoriously large and aggressive. The

ones in the *Jolly Roger* when Peter abandoned ship were, as Miss Eliza would say, no exception. And having been aboard for a very long time without any other food source, they had turned to each other. When the hatch opened, shining light down into its foul interior, it illuminated a single remaining rodent.

It takes a certain skill set to be the last surviving cannibal: above all others, one must be strong, cunning, clever, and ruthless. This rat had all those qualities in abundance. She was also abnormally large and fiendishly hungry.

The rat glared up at Jocelyn and Evie from the small square of light created by the open hatch. Jocelyn felt sick to her stomach. She did not want to be locked up with that creature. What she wanted and what she got, however, were two different things.

Bob removed Evie's bonds, stripped the girls of their weapons, and threw them down into the bilge, one after the other. He slammed the hatch, casting them into near-total darkness. The two girls fumbled for each other's hand in the blackness, then waded through the slimy, stinking water, searching blindly for something on which to climb up and out of the horror they were stewing in. Paddling legs in the water brushed up against Jocelyn. She felt sharp claws try to gain purchase on her stockings. The girl stifled a scream and kicked out, banging her shin on a large wooden crate. She scrambled atop it, pulling Evie up with her, and sat still, allowing her eyes time to adjust to the dark.

"Are you all right, Jocelyn? Did you hurt yourself?" Evie asked.

"A little, but I don't think it's serious. Not that it would matter now if it was." She felt that certainty creep inside her, chilling her to her bones. She didn't want things to end this way.

"Don't give up," Evie said. "We'll think of something. I believe in us. I believe in you."

In the dark, Evie sounded like the adult version of herself, the one that Jocelyn had met after her fairy wish: Jocelyn's mother.

Decide what you want. Believe you can have it. Don't let anything stop you.

Jocelyn knew what she wanted. She wanted the treasure, and the life it would give her. She had believed. But Krueger had stopped her anyway.

She pulled her knees to her chest and wrapped her arms around them. "I don't see any way we can succeed. If I tell Krueger where to find the key, he will probably kill us anyway. If I don't, even if we are somehow able to free Roger, and Meri—I won't leave him behind—and escape, however unlikely that may be, he'll still have the map. There is the barest sliver of a chance we will all survive, and I'm trying to hold on to that, but even so, the treasure is as good as lost."

Evie scooted close to her, placing an arm around her shoulder. "Why is your father's gold so important to you? I attend school with quite a few girls who are obsessed with wealth and status. You don't seem at all the sort."

Jocelyn thought of some of the spoiled girls she had gone to school with, particularly Prissy Edgewater and Nanette Arbuckle. She knew exactly what kind of girls her mother was talking about. "I don't care about the gold for the gold's sake. It's just that . . . I think my father intended for me to find it. Krueger doesn't deserve it."

"No. He doesn't."

"And I want the treasure for myself, too. My grandfather has plans for my future that I simply cannot abide. He plans to see me well mannered and well married to a gentleman of fortune."

Evie signed. "Your grandfather sounds just like my father."

"You have no idea." *Truly.* "But you see, if I had my own fortune, he couldn't object to me doing what I like."

Evie snorted. "Of course he could. If he is anything like my father, it's not merely about wealth. It's about what he sees as proper. It's about the security gained by a high place in society. And on my worst days, I suspect it's about being able to lord something over his gentlemen friends, over cigars. That's why I'm not going back. Being the prim and stately wife of some rich but dull man would be worse than prison. I want freedom. I want adventure."

"But you don't have to do what he wants." If only Jocelyn could tell the girl that she had married—or at least, she would marry—a pirate over a gentleman. Sir Charles hadn't liked it, but he had survived. "You can make your own path. Your father will forgive you. I know it." By now, Jocelyn's eyes had adjusted somewhat to the dark. She read the hunger on Evie's face and wondered how often hers looked the same.

Evie sighed. "You can't know that." She nudged Jocelyn and a smile crept into her voice. "However, if it's true for me, then it's likely true for you as well. No treasure needed."

"You may be right." Jocelyn let the barest hint of hope settle on her heart. "But even so, I'd like to have the gold."

Their conversation was interrupted by the sound of scrabbling claws on the wooden box. This time it was Evie who kicked out. Jocelyn heard a solid thud and a squeal as Evie's foot connected with the giant rat.

Jocelyn shuddered and gripped her hands into fists. "Even more than gold at the moment, I wish I still had my sword."

Evie felt along the side of the crate and pried loose a couple of half-rotted boards, handing one to Jocelyn. "For the time being, perhaps this will do."

The rat was undeterred by the difficulties she had encountered. How those girls must have appealed to her, the scent of their blood as delicious in her nostrils as a Christmas goose in yours. She had conquered all the other rodents, feasting on their flesh and sharpening her teeth on their bones. It was time to feed again. The rat drew nearer.

"I am sorry about all this," Jocelyn said. "You being here is all my fault."

"You must be joking! I have loved every moment of this adventure." She wrinkled her nose. "Except perhaps the carnivorous forest. And the weeds for dinner."

"If I hadn't taken you prisoner, you would be safe, mothering Peter and the lost boys. But now . . ."

The rat attacked, launching herself over the top of the crate and directly for the pulse in Jocelyn's throat. Evie leaped to her feet and swung her board, connecting solidly with the hideous rodent, sending her hurtling into the wall of the ship. The rat hit with a bone-crunching thud and slid into the slimy water.

"But now I'm having a different sort of adventure." Evie set down the board and brushed off her hands.

Jocelyn stared at her, slack-jawed. "How did you know how to do that?"

"Dancing lessons." She smiled and winked. "Now, back to our problem with Krueger. What are we going to do?"

"What can I do? I can't beat him in combat—I don't even have a proper weapon. No offense to your board."

The smile in Evie's voice was evident even in the dark. "Then outwit him. Your mind is sharper than your blade anyway."

"How? He has Roger and Meriwether. He has my weapons. He's bigger and stronger, and I have no idea how to defeat him."

"We can come up with something together," Evie said. "Let's just think on it." Jocelyn wasn't sure how to feel about that. She was the captain. Wasn't it her job to make the plans? Still, it wouldn't hurt to at least listen. "All right, Evie. What are your ideas?"

"Maybe..." Evie paced back and forth on their crate, making a very narrow circuit. "No. That won't work. But what if we..." She tapped her front teeth with a fingernail, thinking. "Ugh! I don't know. If only finishing school taught lessons on how to steal from pirates and escape their clutches. That would be ever so much more useful than embroidery!"

Jocelyn smiled in spite of herself, remembering how her manners training had once saved her life. Still, she couldn't see how becoming conversant in French, being light on one's dancing feet, or having nimble sewing fingers would help in this situation. *Unless...*

An idea struck like a bolt from the blue. She wouldn't be able to do it on her own, and even with Evie's help they would be unlikely to succeed, but it was something. She laid out the germ of an idea to the other girl, listening as Evie made some suggestions of her own.

Their plan was utterly outrageous. It was absolutely impossible. And it was their only chance.

CHAPTER TWENTY-SIX

*In Which Evie Finally Declares
She Would Like to Go Home*

When their plan was as solid as they could
make it, they sat in silence together. Jocelyn
leaned into Evie, taking comfort from her
warmth. She believed they had a chance. That was all
she could do.

The girl had just begun to doze off when Evie asked
her, "Jocelyn, who are you?"

She shook her head, groggily, trying to understand the
question. "I'm ... I'm Jocelyn. Jocelyn Hook."

"I know that. I mean, who are you to me? We have
some sort of connection. My father's song. The painting
in your locket. We even look a little alike. Tell me the
truth. Are you ..."

Jocelyn's heart thudded.

"...my sister?"

Jocelyn couldn't help but laugh. "I—I'm sorry. I wasn't expecting you to say that."

Evie sat up and faced her. "It's not so funny, really. I mean, we could be from different times. Maybe back on the mainland, I'm a lot older than you. Perhaps my father will remarry and you will become my sister. Or ...maybe you are a secret sister he hasn't told me about. From a woman in the village or something. Such things do happen, you know."

Jocelyn turned to look at Evie. *No. You're my mother. If you go home, you'll grow up and marry Captain Hook. But then you'll die shortly after I am born.* The words were there in her mind, but how could she say them? "I'm not your sister."

"Oh. Right. Because Captain Hook was your father. But then who are you? You know something, I can tell. Please don't keep it from me."

"But if I tell you, maybe you won't want to be my friend anymore," Jocelyn said, knowing how much that would hurt.

"Don't be silly. It's not like you're a murderer or some such thing."

"But...what if..." She was going to tell her. It was time to face this. "What if I—"

The hatch above them banged open, bathing the hold with light. Dirty Bob poked his head into the rectangle of sunshine. "All right, girlies, come on up. The captain wants to see ye."

Jocelyn squinted in the glare above deck. The bright morning sun glinted off Krueger's sharp teeth. "Did you enjoy your evening, ladies?"

"Quite. Thank you," Jocelyn replied with a smirk.

He stepped to her, raising his hand as if to strike, then wrinkled his nose, coughed, and gagged. Here in the fresh air of the deck, Jocelyn could tell how terrible they smelled. He took a step back and placed a handkerchief to his nose.

"You stink of bilge and failure. Tell me what I need to know so I can be rid of you. Unless"—he pulled his sword and pointed it at Roger—"you are in the mood for a show. I think I'll start with cutting out his tongue so he won't even have the satisfaction of a proper scream when I move on to his eyes—"

The thought of Roger being tortured stole the smirk from Jocelyn's face. "Stop!" she cried. "I'll tell you what you want to know, but please let Roger and Evie go. You can kill me after if you like, but they are no threat to you. I beg you."

"You beg me?" he replied. "I like the sound of that. I think I'll add it to our deal. You tell me where to find the key, and throw in some begging, and you'll all be free."

Jocelyn didn't believe him. It would be far easier to do

away with them than to worry about them knowing too much about the treasure. But what could she do? "I'll tell you."

Roger sagged against the mast where he was tied—out of relief that Krueger had lowered his sword or disappointment that Jocelyn had given in, she could not tell. Evie began to cry.

Krueger ignored them, intent only on Jocelyn and the information she would provide. "I'm listening."

"It's...it's..." A small tear leaked from Jocelyn's own eye. Sadness at losing the treasure was written all over her face. "It's etched inside the barrel of Long Tom."

Krueger regarded her tear with unveiled suspicion. "Bob. Go inspect that cannon."

Jocelyn wiped her face and arranged it into the picture of innocence. "Yes, Bob. Go do that. But do be careful."

Dirty Bob spluttered and pointed at the girl. "It's booby-trapped, Cap'n! Look at 'er face. She knows it is."

Krueger snarled, baring his razor-sharp teeth. "Enough of this foolishness, girl!" he commanded. "You can both go. Bring back that code, and be quick about it, before I get bored." He placed his hand on the hilt of his sword and motioned with his head toward Roger.

Evie flung herself on Krueger, falling to her knees and clutching at his jacket. "Please," she cried, "don't hurt him. Don't hurt any of us. Jocelyn will give you what you need, won't you, Jocelyn?" The pirate tried to pry the girl off, but she clung harder. "I wish I had never come here! I want to go home," she sobbed.

He shoved the distraught girl roughly from him. Evie fell backward, landing at Roger's feet. She scrambled up and wrapped her arms around the boy, mast and all, her cries turning to wails.

Krueger smoothed the front of his waistcoat. "I'm losing my patience!" he yelled over Evie's hysterics, looking at Jocelyn. "Go. Now!"

Jocelyn obeyed.

CHAPTER TWENTY-SEVEN

Dirty Bob Comes Clean

I'm quite an expert when it comes to betrayal. My life has been filled with treacherous so-called friends, disloyal family members, men I once loved as brothers and women I gave my heart to. In one way or another I've double-crossed them all.

Being young, Jocelyn was not as finely acquainted with those who deal in perfidy, the low and untrue. Like most children, she divided the world into those who were good and those who were bad. She believed in those assigned roles, in fairness and justice. Dirty Bob was giving her quite an education.

Evie's sobs followed the two of them as they climbed down the steep ladder to the gun deck. There were twenty cannons lined up, ten on each side of the ship, but it was easy to see at a glance which was Long Tom. It was third from the end on the starboard side, pointed toward the mountain's summit. The gun was at least ten feet long, and crafted to look as if the cannonballs would shoot from a gargoyle's mouth. At any other time, Jocelyn would have marveled at it, but at the moment Dirty Bob's treachery overshadowed everything else.

Her voice shook, not with nerves but with rage, as she asked, "How could you do this? *Why* did you do this?"

The man turned his head one way and then the other, taking in the ship around them. He caressed one of its support beams with an attitude that bordered on reverence. "All these years, she should have been mine," he said. "Your father stole her from me."

Jocelyn frowned. "Who?"

"The ship herself! Look at her beauty. She should have belonged to me."

Jocelyn shook her head. "I thought my father stole this ship from Blackbeard."

"Aye. That he did. But he stole *the idea* to steal her from me. We were bunkmates, you know. Your father was bo'sun and I was quartermaster—both positions of trust. Positions of power. I got a taste of that, but like with a good grog, one taste wasn't enough. Blackbeard, he was a hard man to serve. He demanded respect and bought it with our fear. Ever so often, for no reason at all, he'd just up and kill someone. It kept the rest of us in line. He was a fine pirate captain—almost like a father to me. Jimmy and me both aspired to be like him."

"So you planned to betray him?"

"How else could you show a man like that the depths of yer feelings but by becoming like him? I decided that the *Queen Anne's Revenge*—that's what the old girl was called then—should be mine, but I couldn't do it alone. I made the mistake of trusting your dad. I laid out the whole plan for him: how we'd get the men on our side, how we'd get a message to the governor, and how I'd demand the *Queen* in exchange for Blackbeard's head. It was perfect."

Jocelyn peered into the mouth of Long Tom. "I think there is something in there," she lied. "I just have to reach it." She put her arm inside and Bob stepped back, tensed for an explosion. "Well, go on," Jocelyn said as she felt around. "What went wrong with your perfect plan?"

"We went ashore, sent the message to the governor, and took ourselves to a local rum swillery to celebrate. Old Jimmy musta put somethin' in me grog. When I awoke, I was doing a turn in the stocks, punishment for drunken and disorderly conduct. By the time I served out the rest of my sentence and paid my fine, Blackbeard was dead, the *Queen* was gone, and Jimmy was no longer Mr. Hook, the bo'sun. He was *Captain* Hook, the terrible. I loved him like a brother—and hated him like one too."

Jocelyn reached farther into the cannon, her arm buried nearly to the shoulder. "So you betrayed me for revenge?" she asked. "Or out of respect, like for Blackbeard?"

"Neither." Dirty Bob spat on the deck, then mopped it up with his handkerchief. "When you saved me from being marooned, I thought I could start fresh and remember, through you, what it was like when Jim and me were young."

"So what happened?"

Bob reached in his pocket, pulled out a fistful of tiny objects, and scattered them on the floor. "This did."

The girl removed her arm from Long Tom and stooped to look. Springs and cogs and bits of twisted metal... they were all that was left of Dirty Bob's pocket watch— the first thing he ever stole. Jocelyn had smashed it in order to silence its ticking after a nightmare about the crocodile. Seeing the pieces on the floor brought back her feelings of white-hot shame. "I apologized. I gave you my father's silver double cigar holder!"

"This?" He pulled the holder from the same pocket. "Aye. And I thought it was so special, until Smee told me it wasn't even his only one. In fact, this one was his everyday holder: tin, covered in silver leaf."

"But it's the only one he left me."

"More's the pity for you, then," Bob said. "And I might have forgiven you yet, seeing as how you were so determined to be your own self and not a copy of him. But since you killed the crocodile, I see more of him in you every day."

"How so? I'm still doing things my own way! I won't even sack ships!"

"Aye! And that's the problem! It's the doing of everything your own way that's so like him. You won't take counsel from anyone. Not from me, not from that fool of a bo'sun you have, not even from your friends! You completely disregard the Pirate Code! I mighta simply walked away, but when I heard you were going after the *Jolly Roger*—my *Queen Anne*—I couldn't let you have her. You don't deserve her any more than your father did. It was no hard choice to sell you to Krueger in exchange for my *Queen*."

Jocelyn placed her hands on her hips. "And you trust him to give her to you?"

"That's my affair!"

She shook her head. "You would have our deaths on your hands?"

"I would have the *Queen Anne's Revenge*! What Krueger does with you after is none of my concern!" He narrowed his eyes at her. "What's taking you so long? Get back to it. I don't want to keep him waiting."

Jocelyn looked inside the cannon again. "There's something blocking it. Maybe if I use this..." She grabbed the cannon rammer—a long metal rod with a fat piece of wood at the end—from its hook on the wall. Her movements thus far had been careful and slow, but now she whirled, quickly bringing up the rod and smashing it into the side of Bob's head. He crumpled to the floor, knocked out cold.

From up above her, the girl could still hear Evie's sobs, artfully loud enough to disguise any sound of struggle from the gun deck. So far, their plan was working. She only hoped the next part didn't kill them all.

Jocelyn opened a small cask of gunpowder and poured it in the cannon's powder hole. Long Tom was much larger than her gun on the *Hook's Revenge*. The girl could only guess at the amount—too little and the ball wouldn't fire, too much and it would explode in her face.

Jocelyn loaded the cannonball, listening for Bob to awaken or Krueger to come below and check on them. She looked out the gun port and positioned Long Tom, hoping her aim was true.

With trembling hands, she struck her flint and steel. A volley of sparks flew toward the fuse, but none hit their target. Bob groaned. Jocelyn didn't have much time. She steadied her hands and tried again. This time a spark landed on the fuse. It flared briefly and went out. Over Evie's wails, she heard Krueger's sharp boots clicking on the deck above.

"Bob, what's taking so long down there?" he called down the hatch.

Dirty Bob groaned a second time, louder.

Jocelyn struck the steel again.

This time the spark caught. The girl wrapped her arms around a timber support and held tight. A hand grabbed her arm from behind. She did not loosen her grip on the timber but turned her head. Bob's angry face was only inches from hers.

"What do you think you're—"

The cannon blast ripped through the rest of his question, making her ears ring. Bob let go of her arm and moved to the gun window. He looked out, then turned back to her, a confused frown on his face. "Why the devil did you shoot a ball? What good did you think it would do?" he screamed, though his voice sounded small and tinny through the ringing of her ears.

Krueger started down the stairs, yelling about booby traps. The girl paid no attention. She was watching the cannonball. It arced gracefully through the air, a smudge of black against the blue sky, before it fell, landing harmlessly in the snow on the slope high above them. A little puff of white erupted into the air at the point of impact—then all was still.

Bob continued to shout, but Jocelyn hardly heard him. The ringing in her ears grew to a roar. Still she watched.

Captain Krueger and Dirty Bob could not have said the same. Their eyes were on the girl. Neither was prepared for the great wall of white about to smash into the ship, but Jocelyn saw it coming.

Her shot had been sure and true. Jocelyn's cannonball had hit the mountain right where its burden of snow lay heaviest. As the avalanche barreled toward the ship, Jocelyn did the only thing left to do. She gripped the post more tightly, squeezed her eyes shut, and braced herself. Rough waves were ahead.

CHAPTER TWENTY-EIGHT

Shipwrecked

The avalanche hit the *Jolly Roger* with the force of a hundred waves, tossing it down the steep slope and over a short cliff. Time slowed as the great ship fell from the sky. When the impact didn't come, Jocelyn wondered if the *Jolly Roger* had somehow gained the gift of flight.

In case you were wondering, it hadn't. This was nothing more than a very long fall. Eventually, the ship smacked into the snow at the foot of the bluff, but it did not rest there. It tumbled over and over, like a pair of wrestling badgers, before finally coming to a rest.

Even after the *Jolly Roger* stopped moving, Jocelyn couldn't bring herself to let go of the timber post, though now she held it with her arms and legs, hanging on like a sloth in a ginkgo tree. She opened her eyes and looked around. The gun deck, or at least what was left of it, was turned on its side—the floor was now a wall—and mostly filled with snow. If she wanted to find the stairs and hatch to the upper deck, she'd have to dig.

Whether it was the avalanche itself or the impact from the fall, Jocelyn couldn't tell, but something had punched a great, ragged hole in the ship's hull, which was now situated more above the girl than in front of her. Dirty Bob and Captain Krueger were nowhere to be seen. It appeared as though they had both been swept through the breach as the ship tumbled about. She did not expect to see either man again.

Jocelyn forced her arms and legs to let go of the post and dropped into the snow. With great difficulty, she climbed the steep slope and out of the wreckage.

Debris marred the pristine whiteness of the ground. Casks, boxes, and barrels, bits of rope and chain, and splintered pieces of the ship itself lay scattered about. The *Jolly Roger*'s entire rudder had been torn aside and was now stuck upright in a drift, like a grave marker.

"Roger! Evie!" Jocelyn called out. But there was no answer.

She quickly made her way toward the upper deck. A bit of bright yellow fabric lay atop the powder—Evie's dress. Jocelyn began to scoop away the ice and snow. She uncovered an arm, then a shoulder, and finally Evie's face. The older girl took a deep shuddering breath and opened her eyes.

"Roger—" she said. "I couldn't hold on."

Jocelyn quickly finished digging her out. "Are you hurt?" she asked as she hauled Evie to her feet.

"I don't think so." Before she had even finished speaking, Jocelyn was pulling her along.

Together they hurried to the other side of the ship. The center mast had snapped when the ship rolled. Its splintered nub stuck out like a thumb from the decking. To this bit, Roger was still tied, suspended only a few feet above a snowbank. He hung limply in the ropes. Jocelyn couldn't tell if he . . . She ran to him, refusing to think of it.

His gag had worked itself loose, but his mouth was slack, unsmiling. Forgetting, she reached for her sword, but her sheath was empty. All she had was the spyglass, mercifully unbroken, in the pouch at her waist. But in this situation it would be useless. "Evie, find me something to cut the ropes with," she commanded.

"Look in his pockets," the other girl suggested. "Doesn't he have a knife?"

Jocelyn frantically began the arduous search, with Evie joining in to help. Given that the boy had a hundred pockets, it was like trying to find a particular grain of sand upon the beach. They unearthed two purple stones, a bit of string, a tin soldier, one of the parrot's green feathers, a live frog and a dead mouse, a handful of dried leaves, and the *I'm sorry* note Jocelyn had written to him the night she left school.

Tears stung the girl's eyes, and she wished she could tell him she was sorry for the quarrel they had just had. After searching three more pockets, and cursing Smee for creating so many, Jocelyn finally found the knife. She sawed through the ropes that held Roger captive, and she and Evie carefully lowered him to the snow.

Evie hovered anxiously nearby while Jocelyn laid her head on Roger's chest. It rose and fell beneath her. She heard the *thump-thump* of his heart. He was alive, but other than figuring that out, Jocelyn had no idea what to do for him. So the girl did the first thing that came to her mind. She punched him on the arm.

Roger's eyes fluttered, then opened. He gaze focused on Jocelyn's face. "So, we're shipwrecked, then," he said. "Like Magellan."

Jocelyn started to giggle. Her giggles turned to laughs and her laughs turned to guffaws. Roger and Evie both joined her, their relief at surviving pouring out in hysterical laughter. Evie stopped to catch her breath and asked, "What's so funny about Magellan?" which struck Jocelyn and Roger as so hilarious it took them quite some time to recover.

Eventually, Jocelyn grabbed her aching side, wiped the

laugh tears from her eyes, and surveyed the wreckage. "It looks like we may have seen the last of Krueger, though I'm sorry to see the map go with him." Jocelyn paled. "And Meriwether! Were you able to get him?"

Evie smiled. "You were right. Finishing-school embroidery does make for nimble fingers—perfect for fine stitches *and* pickpocketing." She pulled a silver flask from her dress pocket, uncorked it, and tipped it into Jocelyn's outstretched palm. The bottle must not have been completely empty when Meriwether was placed in it, for he tumbled into the girl's hand, stood and gave a wobbly bow, then fell over and into a drunken sleep. Jocelyn felt her heart might burst with relief. She kissed the little fairy over and over, grateful to have him with her once more.

Pity for him Meriwether was not conscious and able to enjoy it. Those kisses would have been his fondest dreams come true, but such is life.

After tucking him snugly into her pocket, Jocelyn turned her affection on Evie, gathering her into a tight hug.

"You did even better than I had hoped," she said. "Thank you."

"Don't thank me just yet." Evie giggled and squirmed away. "Wait until you see what else I took." She held up a small leather purse and jingled it. "Gold. Here you go, Captain." She tossed it to Jocelyn. "And speaking of gold...I also got this." She placed the treasure map in Jocelyn's hands. "Now let's go break that code."

Jocelyn made a choice, then and there. She would send her crew, under Roger's command, after the gold, but she would stay behind—with Evie. If her mother, her friend, still wished to never leave the Neverland, Jocelyn would remain always with her, reminding her of where she came from so Evie would not become untethered. Perhaps they would grow old instead of growing up, but they would do it together.

Jocelyn smiled, offering Evie one hand and Roger the other. "Yes indeed. We have a painting to find."

CHAPTER TWENTY-NINE

Wherein the Portrait Gives Up Its Secret

Those who knew him, even casually, before his crocodilian demise were well aware that Captain James Hook was a fastidious man. His boots were always polished, his jacket pressed and brushed, and his hook gleaming, never so much as a spot of blood or gore clinging to it, no matter how busy his day might have been.

That attention to detail extended to his ship, most particularly his private quarters. Therefore, it should come as no surprise to any thinking person—though you may want to brace yourself for this—that while the rest of the *Jolly Roger* lay in ruin, Hook's cabin was in fairly good condition. As my mother was fond of saying, a strong habit of tidiness may even prevail over death and destruction.

The ship was broken nearly in two, twisted at the breach like a wrung-out rag, but Hook's quarters were fairly level. The floor, walls, and ceilings were all in their usual and customary places, even if some of his personal belongings were not. A few cupboards and drawers hung open, their contents scattered about, yet somehow still looking smart.

By unspoken agreement, Roger and Evie hung back, allowing Jocelyn to enter on her own. The portrait of Captain Hook was miraculously undamaged, and still clinging to the wall above his bed, though it was mostly obscured by his slightly disarrayed bed curtains. One visible eye glared at Jocelyn as she picked her way through the detritus littering the floor.

The girl looked away, suddenly nervous. What if the key to breaking the code wasn't there? Her eye fell upon a small leather-bound book, embossed with a *J. H.* on the front. Wishing to put off possible disappointment, she picked it up for a closer look. It appeared to be a captain's log, but when she thumbed its pages, she regretfully found it to be blank. Still, she slipped the book into her pocket. It could come in handy, and keep her from having to tear pages from her own books, should the need for paper arise.

In the doorway, Evie cleared her throat. Jocelyn knew she was stalling. She steeled herself and quickly strode the rest of the way across the cabin. No pomp or ceremony was displayed as she flung the curtain back and pulled the heavy portrait from the wall, not even pausing to examine her father's likeness. It was with trembling fingers that the girl, none too gingerly, plucked the still-sleeping Meriwether from her jacket pocket and shook him over the back of the painting. A sparkling shower of fairy dust rained down upon the canvas. Jocelyn held her breath, watching.

Nothing happened.

Still holding her breath, she gave the painting another, more vigorous, dusting. Meriwether did not wake, though he jingled a sleepy complaint, to which Jocelyn paid no heed.

The back of the painting remained stubbornly empty.

Black spots began to dance before her eyes, but she moved to the wall where the portrait had hung, flinging the fairy about with wild abandon. He opened one bleary eye at this rough handling, and rang out a few dull curses. Jocelyn hardly noticed. The wall, the bed, and much of the room were coated in fairy dust, but it exposed nothing. Roger stepped to the girl and gently removed Meriwether from her hand.

"I think this poor little fellow has been through enough," he said.

Jocelyn exhaled and sank to the edge of the bed, heartsick and rather light-headed. "It's not here!" she cried. "I thought for certain that it would be!"

Roger spoke in a soothing voice, the kind one would use to comfort a child—that is, if one was of that sort of disposition. "I know," he said. "We'll simply have to look elsewhere. We'll find it, Jocelyn."

Without the treasure, what would the girl do? She would have to give up her principles and start sacking ships, or give up piracy and live wild like the lost boys, depending on the Neverland to provide for her. Since she could not return home, those were her only options.

Jocelyn had just allowed Roger to begin leading her out of the cabin when she noticed Evie kneeling on the floor. The older girl lifted Hook's portrait and propped it against a dresser. She reached out and touched it, her fingers sliding over the artist's signature. Jocelyn's curiosity was piqued. She moved closer to the painting. As clear as the horizon on a sunny day, Jocelyn read the initials signed in the lower corner of the painting: *EH*.

"Evie—" Jocelyn felt sick with sudden anxiety.

"I painted this." Evie's voice was oddly devoid of emotion. "EH stands for Evelina Hopewell."

"Yes. Well, sort of." The proof was before their eyes. What else could she say?

"How?" Evie's voice rose. "What haven't you told me?"

Jocelyn knelt next to her friend, feeling a bit dizzy. She twisted her hands in her skirt. "I know some things about your future. And I'm sorry I have kept them from you, but I thought it was for a good reason."

Evie's voice was quite shrill now. "What reason could that be? Is my future terribly unhappy? Do I become someone appalling? Do I die a horrible death?"

Roger quietly slipped from the room, giving the two girls privacy.

Jocelyn paled but said nothing.

"I . . . Maybe I don't want to know."

"But you see, it doesn't matter," Jocelyn said, grasping Evie's arm. "Because if you stay here, on the Neverland, you will be safe. You'll never have to face your future. We can have adventures here forever!"

Evie pulled away. "You sound just like Peter Pan."

The words hit Jocelyn like a physical force, jolting the girl. "I'm nothing like Peter Pan! I want to grow up. I simply want to do it my own way." She took a deep breath, trying to calm herself, to calm them both. "But I will give that up to stay here with you."

Roger called to the girls from the deck outside, but neither acknowledged it. Indeed, they hardly heard the boy, so intent were they on their conversation.

"Why would you do that?" Evie frowned and shook her head. "Go home and have the life you want."

"I can't!" Jocelyn felt like the ground was shifting beneath her feet, like the bottom was falling out of her world. She trembled from head to foot.

"Jocelyn," Roger cut in, poking his head through the doorway.

They ignored him.

"Why can't you?" asked Evie.

"Evie!" Roger insisted.

"Roger, please!" Evie said. "Jocelyn and I need to talk this out. There are things I need to know."

"You'll have to learn them later. The ship is moving!"

The girls scrambled to their feet and out onto the deck. Jocelyn looked over the splintered railing. She wasn't trembling—the *Jolly Roger* was! It had begun moving again, sliding down the icy slope. The ship was picking up speed, and in the condition it was currently in, it would surely break apart any moment.

"We have to fly!" Jocelyn shouted. The ground beneath them began to blur with the speed of their descent.

Roger pulled Meriwether from his pocket. Once more the poor little man was flung about until fairy dust coated all three children. The *Jolly Roger* began to shake violently. Roger and Jocelyn lifted into the air, but Evie stayed rooted firmly on the splintered deck.

"Evie, come on!" Jocelyn commanded.

She shook her head. "I don't know how!"

Jocelyn dipped, taking the older girl by the hand. "Think of something that makes you happy. Anything at all. And then just push off."

"I can't." Evie seemed weighted down. It was clear that seeing the painting had rattled her as much, if not more, than the danger they were currently in.

"You can!" Jocelyn argued back. "You can do anything you want, if you just believe hard enough. Now fly!"

The ship moved faster down the slope. A split formed in the decking near Evie's feet. She screamed, her eyes wide with fright.

Roger reached down from where he hovered above her and grabbed the girl's other hand. He tried to help Jocelyn lift her, but Evie was firmly rooted with fear.

"Evie, you are the bravest girl I have ever met—besides myself," Jocelyn cried. "You can't lose courage now!"

Evie squeezed her eyes shut, as if not seeing the ship breaking apart around her might afford her some protection. The split grew.

"Courage!" Roger yelled. He let go of Evie's hand and patted his pockets until he found what he was searching for: a small blue bottle. He bit the cork, pulling it out with his teeth. With a flick of his wrist, the shimmery liquid started falling. It coated Evie, mixing with the fairy dust, baptizing her with borrowed resolution.

The *Jolly Roger* lost its last remaining strength. A yawning hole opened beneath the girl. Evie's hand was wrenched from Jocelyn's, and into the breach she went. The girl fell into the churning guts of the doomed ship, but she did not stay there. In a heartbeat she returned, eyes open, fearless.

Evie soared.

CHAPTER THIRTY

Jocelyn Gets Her Revenge

Flight has a way of making you see things in a different way, or so I've heard. The ground grows small beneath you, as does everything that creeps upon it. Great lakes take on the appearance of puddles, elephants seem no bigger than mice, giraffes look like really small giraffes, and even that uncle who seems so large and brash in person shrinks until he is as insignificant as your aunt always claimed him to be.

While one part of Jocelyn enjoyed the weightless exhilaration of soaring among the clouds, another part felt encumbered by troubles. She looked over at Evie, gliding along in the air next to her. The older girl giggled at the antics of a sparrow, wings beating furiously in an effort to remain ahead of the children. The little bird muttered to himself about the affront of being overtaken by such gangly, featherless birds. He was having none of it.

Evie's smile was genuine, but like Jocelyn, she had not left her problems behind. She carried them in a new crease between her eyebrows, a tension in her shoulders.

Jocelyn was prepared to tell her the whole truth, and promised as much, but asked Evie to be patient a bit longer. The older girl reluctantly agreed to wait until they reached their destination, when they could talk in quiet and relative comfort.

Though Jocelyn had resolved to stay by Evie's side, she felt uncertain Evie would agree once she knew what had been kept from her. No matter how good Jocelyn's intentions had been, her choice to conceal Evie's identity from her no longer felt like mere withholding. Roger had been right. It felt like a lie.

Jocelyn's other problems were no better. She was uncertain of the treasure—it seemed farther away than ever—and as such, she felt as if she had lost her direction. Without that quest to drive her, what would she do? Worse still, difficulties with Roger pulled and tugged at the girl. He had not mentioned their earlier fight—indeed he was as affable as ever—but still it lay coiled between them, unresolved.

At least she had been able to recover her sword, a fact that brought her no small sense of comfort. Roger had spotted it as they flew over the wreckage of her father's ship. The blade had stood straight in the snow as if waiting for her. Roger drew it out as easily as Arthur did the sword in the stone, returning it to her with a midflight bow, just as poor Meriwether had awakened from his inebriated stupor. He pinched the boy's nose in a jealous fit, then flew a wobbly course some distance away, tinkling curses and holding his head.

Though Jocelyn drew some consolation from the return of her sword, and even more from having her fairy back safe and sound, it wasn't enough to bring her solace. For the first time since coming to the Neverland, the girl longed for home. But since that door was not open to her, she set her hopes on the next best thing.

Jocelyn led Roger and Evie toward the pirate village. They would reclaim the *Hook's Revenge*.

The trio waited until dark fell before conducting a reconnaissance flight over the village. The Neverland, seemingly conciliatory now, provided them with a cover of clouds. They landed on an especially dense one, sinking to their ankles in the vapor. Jocelyn knelt, the cold mist dampening her dress at the knees, and made a hole big enough for the three to peer through.

The pirate village was indulging in an extra bit of merrymaking that evening. News of Krueger's demise had traveled quickly, spread by flocks of gossiping herring gulls. Someone had pushed the Black Spot's piano into the street, and a cacophony of music filled the night. Men and women danced under the light of the full moon, the streets running with rum. Lights twinkled in every window and on every ship—including, there in the harbor, the *Hook's Revenge*.

Jocelyn pulled her spyglass from its pouch and brought it to her eye. Her ship had never looked better. The damage from the cannon blasts had been repaired, and the hull had been touched with a new coat of paint. Even more wonderful, as far as she could tell, the *Hook's Revenge* was deserted.

Like great birds of prey, Jocelyn, Roger, and Evie swooped from the sky and retook command. The three of them weren't crew enough to properly sail the ship, but they were able to get out to sea, far enough that any accomplices of Krueger's could not easily reach them. Roger flew to the crow's nest to keep watch.

Jocelyn gave Evie the blank logbook she had found and asked her to tear out a page and write a note to Smee, telling him to bring his war to a close and prepare the crew to join her. She instructed Meriwether to shake off his headache and get ready to deliver the message.

If felt good to captain again.

Jocelyn was just about to go below deck to see if Krueger had outfitted the ship with any food supplies, when the hatch banged open and a pirate emerged. His hat was pulled low, cloaking his face in shadow, but Jocelyn could see that he was not a member of her crew, and therefore, he did not belong on her ship.

Roger flew down from the crow's nest and brandished his pocketknife. Evie had no weapon, but arranged her face into a particularly fierce scowl. Jocelyn leveled her sword at the man's chest.

"You are trespassing here," she said. "Tell me why I should let you live."

The man lifted his chin, his face catching the light from a hanging lantern. I can't tell you whether shock was greater on his face or Jocelyn's.

"Starkey?" she asked. "What are you doing here?"

He replaced his look of shock with one of derision. "I don't answer to children. I've had enough of that in my life."

"You were going to try and steal my ship, weren't you?" Jocelyn accused.

He felt no need to respond. Only a fool attempts to defend his actions to a child, and Gentleman Starkey was, above all, no fool.

"What am I to do with you?" Jocelyn said. She tilted her head to the side, looking him over. "I freed you from your nursemaid service, but you double-crossed me. However, you rescued me and my crew when we were marooned in the ships' graveyard, and you told me where the map leads. I suppose that makes us even."

He lowered his eyebrows. "I'd say that puts you in my debt."

"We can chalk that up to a simple difference of opinion. At any rate, you did just try to steal my ship—"

"From Krueger, not from you," he interrupted.

Jocelyn ignored him. "—so I could argue that you owe me again. I'll not be returning to the pirate village until I've word that my crew is there waiting for me. It looks like you'll have to stay on until then, or swim."

"I'll do neither. The least you can do is return me to shore. I'd say me telling you the treasure is under that Miss Eliza's school is worth that much."

Evie's eyes grew wide. "Miss Eliza's school? You don't mean Miss Eliza Crumb-Biddlecomb's Finishing School for Young Ladies?"

"Aye," he said, while Jocelyn shot him a murderous look. She had wanted to speak to Evie, to tell her everything, but in her own time and on her own terms.

Evie didn't seem to notice Jocelyn's frustration. She chattered on, thrilled at the prospect of further adventures. "But that puts the treasure at my very own school! Jocelyn, we have to go get it!"

Jocelyn turned away. "We can't. The treasure won't be there in your time, and neither of us can go to mine."

Evie's face fell. "Oh. All right, I won't be able to go. But why can't you?"

Jocelyn kept her back to Evie and shrugged.

Evie grabbed her by the arm and whirled her around, forcing Jocelyn to face her. "What aren't you telling me? It's time I heard everything."

It may very well have been time, but time is funny on the Neverland. Jocelyn opened her mouth to tell Evie all the things she had kept from her. She had quite a speech planned, but she didn't get to give it. Before she could say a single word, a dark shadow passed over the moon. The hairs on Jocelyn's arms stood up.

Something was coming.

CHAPTER THIRTY-ONE

Evie's Greatest Adventure

Jocelyn looked up. The outline of something huge and dark blocked the stars. It wheeled, sinking low enough for the ship's lanterns to give it form: a great black bird with a wingspan as long as the height of a man.

Jocelyn smiled in spite of herself, happy to see Edgar Allan the courier crow once more. It had been a long time since he brought her to the Neverland. He landed on the deck in front of her with a little hop.

"Hello again, young Jocelyn Hook." He nodded politely to Roger, still in the crow's nest, to Starkey, and to Evie, who merely stared in return (quite rudely, I might add; her finishing-school training must have abandoned her at that moment, though her frustration at the interruption is understandable). Roger nodded back.

"Edgar," Jocelyn said, "this is a surprise. What are you doing here?"

"I am doing my job. Delivering letters." He removed a packet of letters tied to his leg. "Please sign here."

Jocelyn signed a delivery receipt, her heart pounding. The last letter he had brought her had been from her father. Could he have arranged for another delivery before he died? Perhaps she would find the key after all, though what good it would do her at this point, she didn't know. The great bird shuffled through his papers and then placed a parchment in her hand. She unfolded it with trembling fingers.

The message was short, scrawled across the page in a reddish-brown ink—or was it blood?

Jocelyn Hook,

The ice and snow only served to freeze my resolve. Hook's gold will be mine. I have taken that pompous fool Sir Charles Hopewell. Such a shame that I will have to torture him into madness before I kill him. Bring me Hook's map, with all its secrets revealed, and I will deliver him into your care. I'm at execution dock—I believe you know the place—in your very own When, waiting, but not patiently. Come alone. Do not cross me again.

—Captain M. Krueger

The blood drained from her face. How had Krueger survived? And how could he have traveled to her When?

Roger climbed down the rigging from his perch in the crow's nest. He took the letter from Jocelyn's hand.

"What does it say?" Evie asked. "What's wrong?"

Roger looked to Jocelyn for permission. When she nodded, he read it aloud.

Starkey grew interested, despite himself. "Who is this Sir Charles person?" he asked.

Evie started to answer. "My fath—"

"My grandfather," Jocelyn said, without thinking.

The two girls looked at each other, and Jocelyn could see understanding dawn on Evie's face.

"It's not possible," the older girl said, then sat hard on the deck. "I'm . . . I'm your . . ."

"You're my mother."

Family reunions can be uncomfortable even under the best circumstances. There's that cousin who's younger and more beloved, the brother who is more skilled at thievery, and the cheek-pinching maiden aunt (no doubt testing to see if one is plump enough for roasting). Still, I doubt there has ever been a reunion as awkward as this one.

"Why didn't you tell me?" Evie asked.

"I . . ." Too much was happening to Jocelyn all at once.

"And how is this even possible?"

Roger stepped in to explain. "People come to the Neverland from many different Whens. You came from your time—or at least the time when you are this age. Jocelyn came from hers, about twenty years later."

"Twenty years from now I'll have a thirteen-year-old daughter? But I'll be so old." She touched her face as if testing to see if wrinkles had already begun to scrawl across her skin.

Tears came to Jocelyn's eyes, though she said nothing.

"But that means I must marry that dashing Captain Hook! Won't my father be scandalized?" She beamed at the very idea. "What kind of mother am I? Are we friends then, like we are now? I hardly remember my own mother, so I only have a vague idea of how it works."

Jocelyn allowed a tear or two to fall. "You are one of the best friends I've ever had."

"I suppose that won't be terrible then, even if I am ever so old." She was obviously warming to the idea, becoming excited, even.

"Perhaps you two would like some privacy?" Roger suggested.

Jocelyn nodded and led Evie into her cabin. It was time to tell her the whole truth. "I can't leave without you, because outside the Neverland I don't exist. That is, if you never go home, I am never born."

"Oh." Evie deflated. "Well, I'll go home, then. I'd rather go on a treasure hunt—can you believe it was below my school all along? But at any rate, that's your adventure, not mine." She blushed ever so slightly. "Besides, it sounds like I have some adventures of my own coming up. I'd better get ready for them."

Jocelyn sat on her bed, her fingers picking at the coverlet. "But that's the thing. You can't go now. I don't want to lose you."

Evie sat next to her. "You won't lose me. You'll just have me in a different way. I'll be your mother." She giggled. "I'm going to dress you in the frilliest pink dresses, just to get back at you for some of your peevishness."

"But you won't—you can't." Jocelyn didn't know how to tell her.

"Of course I can. Who will stop me from doing whatever I like? You'll be a baby and subject to my whims." She nudged Jocelyn with an elbow. "Right now my whims are telling me that you will want to wear giant hair bows."

Tears filled Jocelyn's eyes and she dashed them away.

Evie looked about for a handkerchief to give her, but finding none readily available, she tore off the edge of her own hem. "Look at the example you have set for me." She laughed. "But I'll have my turn in the end."

More tears threatened, but Jocelyn refused to let them fall.

"All right, all right," Evie said. "You don't like hair bows. I'm only teasing. It's nothing to get so upset over."

Jocelyn wadded the fabric scrap in her hands. "I'm not. I mean, I'm not upset about hair bows. I wish you would have a chance to put them in my hair, and dress me in the frilliest, ugliest, pinkest dresses you like, but you didn't. You don't."

"Jocelyn, what are you talking about?"

"If you go home, yes, you marry Captain Hook, my father, and you have me, but..." Jocelyn hesitated.

"But what?"

"But that's it. There is no more. You...you die. When I am still a baby."

Evie went very still. "Oh. I see."

"So you cannot go back. If you stay here, you can grow old. We can grow old together. Maybe not like mother and daughter, but like sisters." Jocelyn's vision swam with unshed tears.

Evie clasped her hands together quietly in her lap. She stared down at them. "We will grow older, but not really grow up. We'll be like your pirate crew, like grown-up children, is that right?"

"Yes."

"I'm not sure now if that's what I want. You wanted me to go home before—what changed your mind?"

Jocelyn felt sick with shame. "I thought having you

go back was simply setting things right. Putting them back the way they were supposed to be. I didn't really like it, but I thought it was the only way. I wanted to be able to go home someday. But having you in my life is more important."

"If I stay, you will never be able to leave the Neverland."

"That is true."

Evie caught Jocelyn's gaze and held it. She spoke quietly, but her words were heavy. Each fell upon Jocelyn with the weight of the world. "If you cannot leave, who will save my father?"

Jocelyn's tears fell freely now. Things had not always been easy between her and her grandfather, but she loved him. She had no answer.

Evie continued to look her in the eye. Jocelyn watched a series of emotions play across her face. The older girl took a deep breath and seemed to steel herself. "Jocelyn, you must go. My father—your grandfather—he needs you. You can't leave this to anyone else, not even Roger."

"Are you sure you don't still have some of that borrowed courage clinging to you, making you say this?"

"I'm quite certain this is all mine."

Jocelyn looked away. "But if you go back, you'll die."

"If I don't, he will. And you will never get to properly grow up." Evie straightened, some of her usual excitement returning to her voice. "The thing is, I won't die right away. I'll get to really live first. I'll get to do a lot of things with my life between here and there. Growing up will be a great adventure. Besides..." She nudged Jocelyn again, prompting the girl to lift her eyes to her face. Evie raised an eyebrow, a mischievous grin on her face. "Captain Hook is in my future, and he is wickedly handsome."

Jocelyn threw her arms around her. "I don't want you to go!" she cried.

Evie hugged her back. "I know. But this is right and good. We do hard things for our family, sometimes even tell them good-bye, if we know we should." She let go and stood quickly then, her mind made up. "That bird that brought the letter, can he take me home?"

"What? Now?"

"It's time," Evie said. She kissed the younger girl on the cheek. "Until we meet again."

"Good-bye," Jocelyn said, choking back her tears. She walked Evie to the deck and made the necessary arrangements with Edgar, paying him with some of the gold Evie had pilfered from Krueger.

Evie took that moment to say her good-byes. "I'm going home now, Roger. Take care of Jocelyn for me." She gave him a hug. "And yourself, too."

He nodded. "I will. I promise."

"And you," she said to Starkey, "if you sail with Hook in the future—my future, at least—I'll likely see you then... though I suppose that has already happened for you." She shook her head. "My, how the Neverland is confusing!"

She settled herself into the hammocklike sling Edgar would use to carry her back to her own time—the very sling that had first brought Jocelyn to the Neverland. "Are you ready?" the great crow asked.

"Just a moment," she replied.

She dug the logbook and lead pencil Jocelyn had given her earlier from her pocket, and quickly scribbled a note inside. She closed the book and handed it to Jocelyn. "I hope this works," she muttered. "Good-bye, Jocelyn."

Edgar rose swiftly, his shadow blocking the moon and the stars. Evie was gone. Jocelyn missed her already.

She looked down at the book in her hands and opened to the note. It read:

Look closely at your locket. Best of luck!
Love, Evie

Jocelyn untied the ribbon holding the locket round her neck. She stepped closer to the light of one of the ship's lanterns. Her heart pounded, and her hands felt so slick with sweat she thought she might drop the pendant. She ran her fingers over the serpent on the front, feeling for the jewel that stuck out a bit farther than the rest. She pressed it, and the locket sprang open. She examined it, inside and out. It appeared no different from before.

She looked closer. Was that a hairline crack between the tiny portrait of Captain Hook and the back of the pendant? She pressed her fingernail into it and it came apart, ever so slightly. She pressed harder, but it didn't budge. Jocelyn looked back at the sea serpent. She would force the necklace open if necessary, though she didn't want to break it. "Come on, open up," she commanded, poking the jeweled monster right in its ruby-red eye. The back of the locket swung open, revealing a second compartment. A tightly folded piece of paper fell to the deck. Jocelyn snatched it up and carefully smoothed its folds.

It was a page torn from a book of fairy tales—the story of Cinderella, to be precise. On one side, in Jocelyn's own hand, was written:

> Dear Mother,
> Whatever happens, I will be fine.
> Love from your daughter, Jocelyn

She had written that very note to Evelina just after she defeated the crocodile. Jocelyn turned the page over.

> Dear Jocelyn,
> Better than fine. You will be great. Now go rescue Sir Charles and get the treasure!
> Love, Evie (Your Someday Mother)

Jocelyn slipped the note into her pocket and wiped her eyes with the back of her hand. She brought the locket close and looked in the new compartment. In tiny writing, painted on the back of the portrait, Jocelyn found at last the key to breaking her father's code.

CHAPTER THIRTY-TWO

Starkey's Tale

The key wasn't the only thing Jocelyn gained that night. She also gained a new member of her crew, likely the best she would ever have.

After Evie left, Roger felt it best to give Jocelyn some space. He squeezed her arm, then made a show of taking time to look over the ship's repairs.

Jocelyn stayed with Gentleman Starkey, staving off heartbreak by contemplating what to do with him. The man was a pirate through and through—and a rather superlative one, I might add—but Jocelyn suspected that he was not entirely heartless, that he had been touched by the bravery he'd witnessed in Evie. She was likely wrong about that, but we can forgive her this once. She was going through an emotional time.

"I knew your mother somewhat, years ago," Starkey told the girl, "back when she was just a bit older than now—and again after she was newly married to the captain. Evelina was one of the most remarkable people I've ever met. I always admired the way she was determined to live each day as if it could be her last. If you are going to save her father, I'll help you, but I won't set foot on those school grounds again, and don't be asking me about it. I have my reasons."

Jocelyn shook her head. "I'm tired of secrets, both my own and others'."

"I don't much care what you are tired of. I've a right to keep it to myself."

"And I've a right to return you to Tiger Lily's village. I'm certain the children would be glad to get you back. How did you know both my mother and I went to school there?"

To Jocelyn's surprise, the man laughed. "You're a dirty extortionist, you are," he said. "I can respect that." He shook his head. "All right. I'll tell you. It makes little difference now. I knew about your mother because I was on Captain Hook's crew while he was building his treasure caves. I never set foot in them, which I believe is part of the reason he let me live. My job was to scout the school grounds, to make sure no one stumbled upon the old carriage house and found their way in before the booby traps were set. To do so, I took a job as an assistant teacher."

Jocelyn found that hard to believe. "If that's true, how was it that Evie didn't recognize you all the times she saw you here on the Neverland?"

"I must have begun teaching after she returned home, so the Evie you knew hadn't yet met me. And when she finally did at school, she was smart enough not to let on. At any rate, if you've finished interrupting, I'll continue."

Jocelyn nodded.

"On occasion, the captain would come ashore with a new building crew. He never liked to leave any of them alive for too long, lest they start getting ideas about mutiny and selling out the treasure location. At those times, he'd join me in walking the school grounds to hear my report. I'm sure he thought often of killing me, but he restrained himself, knowing it would be difficult to place another in my position. Not many pirates have been trained as an English schoolteacher, now, have they?"

"I suppose not."

Since Jocelyn had not added anything interesting to the conversation, he carried on as if the girl hadn't spoken. "On one such evening, as we were walking along, we overheard a young lady, Miss Evelina Hopewell, boasting to her friends that her father had bought a fine new ship and was planning on sending her out on a pleasure cruise for her eighteenth birthday. She named the upcoming date and time, just a fortnight from thence, and expressed her hope that the party would attract the right sort of gentlemanly attention. Captain Hook quietly parted the foliage separating us from the girl and, upon looking at her, declared to me that he was the right sort himself. He made a dramatic entrance to the party, sacking the ship and beginning a formal courtship of Evelina in one fell swoop. The two were married before a month was out."

Jocelyn wondered at this. It didn't sound like Evie, though the details did fit in with what she knew about her parents' meeting. "But why did he let you live, once the treasure was hidden away and he no longer needed you? And how did you know I went to school there?"

"He let me live because, once he married Evelina, she took a liking to me. She insisted that I stay on as crew and made him promise to never harm or dismiss me. It didn't hurt that he knew I'd never go back to the school, not as long as Cook was still alive and working there. Hell hath no fury like a woman scorned. Cook may have hated me, but she was happy to work for him, keeping an eye out for anything suspicious and, later, keeping an eye on you."

Cook had known her father? And even more shocking, had had a love affair with Starkey?

"But how did *you* know that I went to school there?" she asked. "If Cook was so angry with you, she wouldn't have told you, would she?"

"Once, when he was well into a bottle of muscat, Captain Hook showed me one of her letters, telling how you were getting on. I daresay he was pleased."

Her father was pleased with her? Of all the revelations Jocelyn had received, this one seemed the most incredible. She was quite speechless over the idea.

Starkey did not seem to notice her consternation. "So," he concluded, "there you have it. What you'll do with it, I can't say. But as I mentioned, if you require my services in saving Evelina's father, I will do what I can. I think I owe her that much, for my life. But don't be getting any ideas that I'll enjoy serving under a mewling infant, such as yourself."

"Nor would I enjoy your service. But I could use you. I am short a man, thanks to that traitor Dirty Bob. I'll take you on," she said, "but don't cross me again."

"I won't. But you had better not put any sticky hands on me. I don't like it."

And that is how Starkey joined the crew. Jocelyn was reluctant to have him. He was reluctant to sign on. It couldn't have been a better match.

Meriwether delivered Jocelyn's note to the crew, and she was able to round them up without any difficulty. She gathered them together and informed them of her intentions. "The most important thing is that we free my grandfather—even if I have to give up the treasure to do it."

Jim McCraig volunteered to use the information in Jocelyn's locket to crack the code. "Says he's good with languages, miss," Smee translated.

After copying the code key into the logbook, Jocelyn instructed him to write his translations in it. *Blank pages do come in handy for writing,* she thought. She also copied the key directly onto the map. She was hoping to free her grandfather by stratagem, but if it came down to it, she was prepared to meet Krueger's demands in order to save Sir Charles's life.

Both Gentleman Starkey and Mr. Smee had made the trip from the Neverland to the mainland many times and knew the way. Starkey guided them through a rock arch in the middle of the sea. On the Neverland side it was bright and sunny; a soft, warm snow drifted down and hit the decks with a sizzle. But as soon as they came through the archway, the *Hook's Revenge* was plunged into a deep gray fog.

"So, we're back in English waters, then," Smee said.

Jocelyn would soon have to face Captain Krueger again. It was not the chilly air that caused her to shiver.

CHAPTER THIRTY-THREE

Return to Execution Dock

FOR the average young person, thinking of one's mother while in proximity to execution dock might be considered strange. That is, unless one's mother is a wicked and dastardly woman, bent on destruction and world dominion, much like my own.

However, Jocelyn, as you may have gathered, was not an average young person. Evie was very much on her mind as she flew toward execution dock. How the girl wished that both Evie and Roger had been flying along next to her at that very moment, but Evie was gone.

She'd left the Neverland the night before.

She'd died years ago.

As for Roger, he had wanted to come. All the crew had. But Jocelyn could not, would not, risk their lives—or her grandfather's. Krueger had said to come alone. She did so.

Jocelyn mulled over what she knew of Krueger—aside from his lust for gold. She thought it more than likely he would have extra men hidden somewhere, just as he had on the dock outside the pirate village. She knew there was a large chance that even if she met his demands, he would refuse to turn Sir Charles back over to her, happy and whole. If there was one thing she knew about Krueger, it was that he was predictable. Jocelyn hoped she could use that knowledge against him.

Execution dock made its presence known before the girl was able to actually see it. The creaking of the iron gibbets and the scent of rot carried to her through the fog, informing Jocelyn that she was close. She was taken back to the day her grandfather had brought her there to show her the grisly remains of executed pirates, displayed as a warning to others considering the occupation. It wasn't an outing planned for amusement (though I would have enjoyed it); rather, Sir Charles had brought her to the docks trying to impress on her mind that piracy would come to no good end, that happiness lay in the future he had planned for her.

That was the last time she had spent alone with her grandfather. The next day had begun a flurry of arrangements and the packing of trunks. By the end of the week, she had been sent away to finishing school.

That walk they had shared seemed so long ago. Jocelyn disagreed with her grandfather now as much as ever, but she felt a new pity for him. Sir Charles had lost his wife, and then a daughter. He wanted Jocelyn to have a quiet life, secure and safe—if somewhat dull. She understood a bit better now, though she still would not choose the life he envisioned for her.

At last, execution dock came into sight, the fog dampening, but not obliterating, its horrors. The girl landed, watchful for the as yet unseen Captain Krueger.

The gibbets hung from gallows, some high overhead, others dangling just above the waterline. The latter held lesser criminals, their bodies on display just long enough for the seasonal high tide of the river to cover them three times, after which they could be buried. Jocelyn couldn't help feeling a little embarrassed for them, and I, for one, agree with the girl. If only those blighters had applied themselves, they might not have had such a short run of notoriety. Contrast those to the remains of the great Captain Kidd. He had lorded over execution dock for years.

Jocelyn looked about, hoping to catch a glimpse of someone famous, but the ravages of time had left the figures difficult to identify. Still, one hanging over the water a bit farther on looked to be fresh enough. She approached, leaning over the dock's railing, trying to see through the fog. The man's back was to her, but the gibbet slowly turned him about as it twisted in the breeze.

His face came into view, and Jocelyn stumbled back. "Grandfather?"

He reached for her through the bars, an innocent man in the iron shroud of a criminal. Relief flooded through her. In the mist, she had thought . . . At any rate, he was alive. He peered at her with confusion for a moment before recognition dawned on his face. "Jocelyn, my dear girl," he called to her. "You are alive! You have been gone so long. I had feared . . ."

"Grandfather, I'm . . . I'm sorry," Jocelyn cried, but the reasons why were uttered only in her mind.

I'm sorry I left without a word.

I'm sorry that you are here because of me.

I'm sorry I could not—cannot—be all you want me to be.

He seemed to know what she meant, even as the words remained unspoken. "As am I, my dear girl. But . . ." His eyes sharpened. "What are you doing here? This is no place for a child. You must leave. It isn't safe!"

She reached for him, lifting off the dock so that her fingertips could touch his hands. "I came to get you," she said.

"Such a sweet family reunion." Krueger's voice pierced the fog, bringing Jocelyn back down to the dock with a thump. She whirled, searching for him. A dark shape appeared in the mist, gradually developing into the form of a man. He limped slowly toward her. When he drew close enough for Jocelyn to truly see, she let out a gasp.

A startling change had come over Krueger's already terrifying face since the last time she had seen him. He still had those hideous, pointed teeth, the terrible white scar, and the lifeless, dark eyes, but now, his appearance had taken on a new level of horror. His left ear and the tip of his nose were gone, leaving only angry-looking red and scarred skin in their place, and across his cheeks dead, black patches spread like mold.

Jocelyn shuddered with revulsion and retreated a step, feeling the railing press against her back. The fog swirled around the vile man, turning him misty again for just a moment. It brought to Jocelyn's mind the image of her father in the Black Swamp, how insubstantial he had truly been and how her confidence had caused him to simply disappear. She squared her shoulders and put on a brave face.

"You look well," she taunted.

"Your little trick on the mountain cost me three toes, an ear, and a good part of my nose to frostbite, but don't worry, you'll pay for it. I'll buy new ones once I have my hands on your father's gold." He licked his lips, and his black eyes took on a fevered gleam. "You will not thwart me again."

Jocelyn understood now why he had been able to travel to her When. It was apparent that he had forgotten his home—he was untethered, able to slip in and out of any time. She wondered if he had substituted a gold lust for what he had forgotten. The pursuit of it seemed to be the only thing that mattered to him.

Krueger drew his sword and rested it on a rope tied to the dock. She followed the line with her eye; it ran up through a post to a high beam and back down to the gibbet. If he were to cut through the rope, Sir Charles and his iron prison would plummet into the river, where he would sink to the bottom and never be heard from again. Krueger's threat need not be spoken. *Cross me and your grandfather will die.*

"Give me the map." His voice was quiet and slow, but coiled. He would strike without provocation.

Jocelyn had hoped that she would find a way, a trick of some sort, that would enable her to free her grandfather and still keep the treasure from Krueger, but standing here now, nothing seemed worth the risk. She could fly to the gibbet, but a great iron lock held it closed around her grandfather—there was no way she could force it open. She could attack Krueger, but he would surely cut the rope the instant she moved toward her sword. Besides, he had the advantage of physical strength on his side.

There was nothing she could do. She held out the map. He snatched it from her hand.

Krueger peered closely at it, attempting to verify its authenticity. He translated a few words, working them out aloud to test the key Jocelyn had written. "I see you found the way to make it readable. Very good. Your grandfather will live—"

Relief landed like a delicate butterfly on Jocelyn's heart—then flew off, startled away by his next words.

"—but I'll keep him as payment for my missing flesh. I've always wanted a nobleman to scrub my chamber pot. Adds a touch of class. And when I claim the treasure, I'll force him to carry it out. Let him feel the burden of another man's riches across his back." He laughed—a wet, nasty sound emanating from his ruined nose— caught up in his cruel fantasy.

The gibbet creaked. When Krueger looked down again at the map in his hand, Jocelyn stole a glance. There, perched on the cage, was Roger! He had disobeyed her orders and had come to help. Jocelyn felt a mixture of annoyance and gratitude.

The boy lit on the other side of Sir Charles's prison and was stealthily trying to liberate him. He ignored the lock, instead working to loosen the hinges that held the cage together.

Jocelyn edged away from the railing. "I feel sorry for you, you know," she said loudly, pushing Krueger to keep his focus on her.

Krueger's laugh died out, his eyes flashing in anger. He turned his back to the gibbet so he could face the girl directly. "I have your grandfather," he spat. "I have your map. I'll soon have what should in all fairness be your gold. I have won. What reason could you possibly have to pity me?"

Jocelyn took another step back, drawing him after her. He moved, almost unconsciously, keeping her close enough to strike. "Hook's treasure is rumored to be the largest hoard in history. You will have more gold than anyone."

Krueger licked his lips greedily. "You are making a poor case for yourself."

His sword no longer rested upon the rope. Jocelyn wondered, should she strike? Or wait for Roger to open the cage? She feared what would happen to her grand-father should she make the wrong choice.

"You will be the richest pirate on earth, and it will still not be enough." She took another small step back, trying to create a bit more distance between him and the gibbet.

Krueger followed, his eyes narrowed.

Jocelyn stole another glance at her grandfather's prison, hoping Krueger wouldn't notice in the fog. Roger appeared to be having difficulty removing the hinges. She spoke louder, in order to mask any noise. "You know it to be true. You can never have enough. Your hunger for gold has already eaten holes in your soul. It will consume you as completely as the crocodile did my father!"

"I will hear no more!" he barked.

"The gold will never love you back!" Jocelyn yelled.

In the ringing silence that followed, Roger finally succeeded in removing a pin. He attempted to put it in one of his pockets, but his fingers slipped and it fell to the river. Its splash hung in the air.

Krueger whirled around and locked eyes with the boy. "Kill him!" he yelled. "Him and the girl!"

Krueger's men materialized out of the fog and advanced on Jocelyn. Even as Jocelyn drew her sword she knew she would never be able to fight them off. Instead she cast her eyes about for some way to help Roger free Sir Charles, perhaps a tool of some sort, but there was nothing. The girl shot into the air, flew over the railing, and pressed her hand through the bars, grabbing her grandfather's arm. "Roger, hurry!"

He pulled at the pin on the second hinge. "I'm trying, but it's rusted! I can't get it."

"Don't let them get away!" Krueger commanded.

One of the men reached for the gibbet. His fingertips brushed it, but he was unable to grab on.

Another pirate began to untie the rope holding it in place. "Maybe we will just give them all a good dunking, then," he said.

The gibbet slipped a few inches.

Her grandfather squeezed her hand. "Jocelyn, you have to go."

The gibbet slipped again.

"Jocelyn, I can't open it!" Roger called.

She ignored him, focusing on her grandfather. "I won't abandon you."

"I know. But you must leave now."

Krueger drew his pistol.

"Go, child!" Sir Charles cried. "Take her, boy!" He pulled from her grasp and shoved her away, making the gibbet sway.

Jocelyn had spent her life carefully cultivating a habit of disobedience where her grandfather was concerned, but Roger had no such principles. He immediately stopped working with the pin and grabbed Jocelyn's arm, tugging her away.

She fought him, desperate to stay with her grandfather. "No! I won't leave him! I promised Evie I would save him!" She wrapped her fingers around the bar.

Roger tugged, and the gibbet spun, swinging Jocelyn close to the deck. A hand closed over her leg, but she kicked out, hitting the pirate in the teeth. His grip slacked, and she jerked away.

The gibbet slipped a few more inches.

An explosion ripped through the air. Krueger was firing upon them. Roger flinched at the sound. "We have to go! We'll come back for him." He wrenched Jocelyn's hand from the bar. Krueger fired again, but they were already gone. Jocelyn looked back, watching, as the fog swallowed the only family she had left.

CHAPTER THIRTY-FOUR

Back to School

When I was a child, my schoolmaster would occasionally suggest a game of Who Can Be Quiet the Longest? The winner would receive a small piece of taffy the master kept in a tin on his desk. The loser would have his tongue removed—by the winner. How we laughed the day the schoolmaster sat on a tack, screamed, and lost the game himself. Not only did we all feast on taffy that day, but we also learned that arithmetic is a lot more interesting when taught by pantomime.

Jocelyn and Roger kept their tongues (pardon the pun) on their flight back to the *Hook's Revenge*, each reflecting on their own failures. Jocelyn flew ahead of Roger, wanting to be alone. It wasn't until they landed on the deck that she saw the blood that ran down his arm and dripped from his fingertips.

"Oh, Roger! You've been shot!" she cried.

Roger shook his head. "I have?"

The girl pointed at the blood, unable to speak through her worry and guilt. She should have protected him somehow—just as she should have been able to save her grandfather.

"Oh, I have." He sat on the deck. "I couldn't even feel it. . . ." He took in a sharp breath. "Until now."

Jocelyn tore his sleeve out at the shoulder, exposing his upper arm. Thankfully, the bullet had only grazed him. She ripped off another section of her hem and pressed it to the wound. Her men had gathered around when they landed, watching in silent shock, but now Smee stepped forward, armed with a needle and thread.

"Why don't I take you into the captain's chambers? I'll mend that tear in no time," he said.

"Can you do that?" Jocelyn asked.

Smee looked affronted. "An itty-bitty thing like that? Of course I can. I've mended worse splits in my sleep. Velvet jackets slashed ragged by a dull blade, silk waist-coats torn by the flick of a careless hook . . . those were hard mends, but a tiny flap of arm meat won't be a lick of trouble." He led Roger beside him. "Come along, you. I'll let you pick what color thread you like, and if you hold still, I'll even do some fancy needlework."

Jocelyn started to follow, but a question from Blind Bart held her back. "It was difficult to hear what was happening in all this fog, Captain. Where is your grandfather?"

She ground her teeth. "Krueger still has him. We have to get him back."

"How can we help, Cap'n?" Nubbins asked.

"You can't. I need to do this on my own," she said. *But how?*

An idea took form in Jocelyn's mind. She patted the journal in her pocket. "We know where he is going, and when he arrives, we will be waiting. This will be our final battle. It's Krueger or me this time."

The *Hook's Revenge* immediately set sail for Miss Eliza Crumb-Biddlecomb's Finishing School for Young Ladies. Jocelyn was banking on having at least two advantages over Krueger. Thanks to Starkey, she knew the location of the caves that held the treasure; she didn't need to work out any coordinates. And Jim McCraig had already translated the instructions written on the map. Krueger had surely not had it long enough to do so.

When he did finally make his way into the treasure chamber, she intended to be waiting for him.

They anchored the *Hook's Revenge* in a sheltered inlet bordered by sheer cliffs. There was a more convenient mooring place, closer to where they needed to be, but

Jocelyn hoped to remain undetected by Krueger to keep the element of surprise on her side. Knowing he would not set foot on the school grounds, she reluctantly left Starkey aboard, warily trusting that her ship would be there when she returned for it. She, Roger, and the rest of her crew piled into two dinghies and began rowing ashore.

Facing Krueger would be far more difficult than facing the crocodile. Though both were driven by a malicious will and an insatiable greed, Krueger possessed the will and greed of man—far stronger than any dark power on earth. The girl would need more than a belief in herself to prevail, though exactly what, she wasn't sure.

The group beached their boats on the shore, hiding them in tall sea grass. Far in the distance, Jocelyn could see small squares of light shining from the windows of her old school. She couldn't be absolutely certain, but one seemed to glow with a rosy tint. How long ago, it seemed, that she stood staring out the glass of her dreadfully pink room, looking toward the sea and adventure. Adventure had found her—both great and terrible—in ways she never could have imagined from the other side of the panes.

The crew followed their captain as she and Roger silently walked side by side up the path toward the carriage house. They hadn't spoken much since returning from their disastrous ransom attempt. Jocelyn's reticence was due to shame. She should have helped Roger free her grandfather somehow, or—even better—freed him on her own. Instead, her grandfather remained a prisoner, and Roger had nearly been killed. He claimed that his arm didn't pain him too badly, and the men made much over him for the scar he was likely to develop, but Jocelyn felt terrible just the same.

For the most part, the crew's mood was the polar opposite of Jocelyn's. Blind Bart listened eagerly, whispering a running commentary about the variety of insects and small mammals secreted in the vegetation nearby. "And that was the soft sigh of a red-tailed squirrel—quite distinctive, with a higher pitch and less forceful breath expulsion than its black-tailed cousins."

One-Armed Jack had "armed" himself with a cricket bat. He kept whacking it against tall grass and leafy branches to "break it in." Jocelyn was concerned he was going to break it off.

Nubbins planned their victory feast: "Salted cod with truffle oil. No—chipped beef on a rustic bread and a salad of young greens..."

Jim McCraig and his parrot chattered unintelligibly, but with great enthusiasm, to each other. Jim flanked Mr. Smee; they carried a box of supplies between them.

Even Meriwether darted about, softly jingling with excitement. As for Smee, his emotions were more erratic: thrilled at being so close to a place beloved to his dear

Captain Hook, yet despondent all over again at Hook's death. He bounced on the balls of his feet, exulting, "Just think, Johnny, this here was where the captain kept his treasures! I wonder if he ever walked past this very tree?" before being overcome with sudden sobs. "He was ever so indifferent to trees, the devil take his dear soul. What I'd give to have him here now and see him ignore that one."

Jocelyn did her best to offer solacing scolds, in an effort to keep him quiet. Presently they arrived at the carriage house.

"Allow me," Roger said, and stepped to the door.

"Don't forget, it sticks," Jocelyn said, standing back.

Roger put his uninjured shoulder into the door and pushed hard. The hinges grumbled in protest, but the door swung inward, admitting them into the dusty old carriage house. On the arm of the horsehair sofa, Roger's favorite book, *Impress Your Friends, Confound Your Enemies: 1001 Poisonous Jungle Plants and How to Use Them*, lay open, one page torn out. Other favorites, including *Gulliver's Travels*, *The Last Voyage of Ferdinand Magellan*, and *Man-Eating Beasts of the Amazonian Jungle*, lay about in piles. The marble bust of a forgotten dignitary wore a rather undignified and moth-eaten bonnet, unearthed from one of the old trunks. Broken pieces of the grandfather clock's face still lay scattered on the floor from the night Edgar delivered Captain Hook's letter and took Jocelyn away.

Nothing had changed. Nothing was the same.

Jocelyn could hardly believe how the room, once her favorite place on earth, could look both comfortingly familiar and absolutely foreign at the same time. Such is any true homecoming. Why, I remember arriving home for a visit the first time after I went to sea. Everything about the old place was exactly the same—except the front door locks.

Jocelyn shared a look with Roger—their first such since failing to rescue Sir Charles. The boy appeared as lost and bewildered as she felt, but in that moment, at least, they had each other. It didn't last. They both looked away.

Jocelyn pulled the logbook from her pocket and read, "'From the carriage-house door, take twelve paces in a southeasterly direction.'" She instructed the crew to remain outside and out of the way while she and Roger found the passageway. The carriage house was crowded enough without adding five grown men, a mischievous fairy, and a parrot to the mix.

Roger removed his compass from its special pocket and pointed them in the right direction.

"...nine, ten...Help me move the sofa, will you?... eleven, twelve," Jocelyn counted off. "Now it says to find a knothole in the floor that looks like the profile of a young Lady Jane Grey."

"There!" Roger said. "Aw, she looks sad."

"Can you blame her?" Jocelyn asked.

He grinned. "Not a bit. What's next?"

Jocelyn found it was easier to talk to Roger while they focused on the instructions. "'Count three floor planks to the east and find one stained a slightly darker color.' We need to pry it up." She handed Roger the book, worked the tip of her sword into a crack along the edge of the board, and succeeded in lifting it. A hollowed-out compartment lay beneath.

Roger looked down at the instructions. "Do you see a handle in there?"

"I do," she said, reaching for it.

"Wait—" but Roger spoke too late.

The girl tugged on the handle. Wooden doors slid out of the compartment, trapping her wrist.

"Arrrggghhh!" she yelled, trying to free her hand.

"Arrrr!" One-Armed Jack yelled from the doorway in response, before Mr. Smee shushed him. "She wasn't talking to you—were you, Cap'n?" He started forward, but Jocelyn stopped him.

"Wait, Smee. We don't know what other traps may be in here. Stay back, all of you."

"Are you hurt?" Roger asked.

She tugged again at her arm. It didn't budge. "No. Just stuck. Are there instructions?"

"Try rotating the handle three and one-quarter turns counterclockwise and pushing on it."

Jocelyn did so, and the doors slid away, freeing her wrist.

He scanned the next few lines of instruction. "Now give it a very gentle tug. Want me to do it?"

Jocelyn flexed her wrist. "No. I will."

She pulled, gently. An entire section of flooring lifted up in her hand. They had found the trapdoor!

"Begging your pardon," Smee called. "But can we come in now? Jim says the ache in his phantom leg is calling for rain any minute."

"Oh. Yes. Just be mindful you don't knock anything over."

Mr. Smee dug into the box of supplies, purchased with the gold Evie had pilfered from Krueger, and passed around brass oil lanterns. Jocelyn lit hers, but if anything the increased light made the passageway below look even darker.

"Follow me, men," she called out, with false bravery.

She stepped down into the dark.

CHAPTER THIRTY-FIVE

Blue-Bearded Bartleby Holds the Key

When the last man stepped through the trapdoor and closed it behind him, Jocelyn felt a moment of panic, as if the last shovelful of dirt had been cast on her own grave. The air was cold and damp, filling the girl's lungs with the taste of mildew. It was dark, so dark, even with the glow of their brass lanterns. Their tiny flames gave weak light to a set of rough steps, slick with moisture, that hugged a stone wall ringing a circular void. Jocelyn stayed close to the wall, unsure how far below them the bottom lay.

As a precaution, she coaxed Meri into coating the party with fairy dust, though she held doubts as to whether it would work on the grown members of her crew. She hoped this would not be the time to test it.

Jocelyn walked slowly, holding her light high for those who followed, but she felt an urgency building inside her. Had Krueger finished translating the map's instructions? Was he, at that very moment, on his way up the path to the carriage house? Would they be able to make it to the treasure chamber before him and have time to set up their attack?

Meriwether had no such concerns. He flew out over the abyss, playing a game of tag in the dark with Jim's parrot. The fairy's tiny blue light was a single shooting star in the darkness. If only Jocelyn could have wished on it and had her grandfather back, safe and sound.

So distracted was she by the fairy's flight, Jocelyn nearly led her men right into the abyss. She took her eyes from Meriwether just in time to see a section where there were no stairs at all. The gap yawned out over empty space. Several feet beyond, at the edge of her lantern light, the stairs continued as before, on and down.

"Everyone stop a moment," she called. Her words bounced around in the enclosed space, making her heart pound. Krueger could be above them in the carriage house even now. She had to get to the treasure undetected.

"Roger," she whispered, "are there instructions for how to move on? Should I fly to the other side?"

He held the book close to her lantern. "Just a minute. We need to . . ." He felt along on the wall until he found a stone engraved with the shape of crossed swords. "*X* marks the spot," he said with a grin.

The boy pressed it, and the sound of stone grinding upon stone filled the chamber. Jocelyn expected that a set of steps would pop out of the wall, filling the gap, but instead a door opened in the wall next to them. She hurried through, followed by her men.

The door hadn't been open more than a handful of seconds when it began to slide shut of its own accord. "Meriwether, this way," the girl called to her fairy. He shot through the opening, the parrot on his heels, in the nick of time. Indeed, the parrot lost the tip of her longest tail feather. Meriwether scolded her for her slowness. The bird squawked out a series of what were most likely swears. Meri replied with peals that most certainly were.

"My, but that was exciting, wasn't it, Johnny?" Mr. Smee said softly.

"I'm afraid the excitement is just beginning," Jocelyn said. She broke up the fight by asking Meri to sit on her shoulder and suggesting Jim McCraig request the same of his bird. The fairy began making a nest in the locks of her hair, but Jocelyn ignored him, holding out her lantern to get a better view of the space where they now stood.

It was a small chamber, guarded by the skeletal remains of five pirates, standing at attention in the middle of the room. Each had a key on a chain around its neck. Opposite from where they had entered, a heavy iron door was imbedded in the stone wall. There was no knob or handle, nothing but a keyhole cut in the door's center.

"So one of the keys must fit the door, right, Cap'n?" One-Armed Jack asked.

Jocelyn moved to the door and pushed. It didn't budge. "It appears that way," she replied.

Nubbins moved to inspect the skeletons. "But which one?" he wondered aloud.

"No one touch anything," Jocelyn commanded. "Roger, what do our instructions say?"

"I think it's a puzzle of some sort." He read from the book:

> This chamber is guarded by five of the fiercest pirates I ever had the honor to kill: Mo the Wild Spaniard, One-Eyed Walt, Red-Handed Hannah, Emmy Two-Buckle, and Blue-Bearded Bartleby.
>
> Blue-Bearded Bartleby would never stand next to someone wearing purple, in life or death.
>
> Brass is the poor man's gold. Mo the Wild Spaniard was a poor man.
>
> Both Emmy Two-Buckle and Blue-Bearded Bartleby loved their ships so much they had the timbers fashioned into parts of their bodies, to replace what they had lost.
>
> One-Eyed Walt had two eyes. He got his nickname because only one eye would look at you. The other was always roaming the room, watching for ladies.

After years of being chained in iron, Red-Handed
Hannah grew used to it and didn't feel quite right without
a bit of it on her.

Neither Blue-Bearded Bartleby nor Red-Handed
Hannah is wearing the color by which they are called.

Emmy Two-Buckle dyed her boot leather in kitten
blood.

Blue-Bearded Bartleby holds the key.

Jocelyn took a closer look at the line of pirates. On the
left stood a skeleton in a green velvet jacket and deep red
boots. The key round its neck was brass. Instead of bones,
its right forearm and hand were fashioned of leather and
steel.

One-Armed Jack patted the prosthetic longingly.
"Would you look at that, Cap'n?" he said. "Now that's
an arm."

"Leave it, Jack," Jocelyn commanded. "We're not here
for that." She went back to examining the remains, trying
to riddle out who Blue-Bearded Bartleby might be. Next
in line was a skeleton with a great yellow feather atop
its hat. It had no thumbs. Its key was of tarnished iron.

The third stood, balanced on one leg of bone and
another of wood, with a purple sash tied round what
was once its waist. Its key was also of iron.

The fourth skeleton wore woven pants, dyed sky blue.
It had a glass eye and carried a brass key.

The last grinned at them with splintery wooden teeth. It also wore red leather boots, these with razor-sharp buckles. Its key was of silver.

"Begging your pardon, miss, but maybe we should just gather up all the keys and try them, one by one," Mr. Smee said.

Roger shook his head. "The instructions say that there is a small glass vial filled with poison in the lock," he replied. "If the wrong key is inserted, the vial will break and the poison will atomize." He scrunched his eyebrows together. "What does *atomize* mean?"

Blind Bart adjusted his eye patches, seeming to take courage in his invisibility. "Turn to mist."

"All right, so the poison will turn to mist and . . ." He found his place in the book. "And fill the room. So . . ."

"Wrong key and we all die," Jocelyn said. "Could you read the puzzle again?"

While everyone else discussed the poisonous gas, Jim took part in a quiet conversation with his parrot. The man nodded his head, walked confidently to one of the skeletons, removed the key from around its neck, walked to the door, and slipped it in the lock.

"Jim, what are you doing?" Jocelyn demanded.

He said nothing, but turned the key.

Jocelyn's command of "Everyone hold your breath!" proved to be unnecessary. The door slid silently open on hinges that seemed as if they had just been oiled.

Jim removed the key from the lock and returned it to its place around the neck of the skeleton from which he'd taken it—they didn't want Krueger to suspect a trap when he came through. Krueger would have to puzzle it out himself in order to believe he was first. Jocelyn only hoped it took him longer than it had taken her man, to give them a bit more time to prepare an ambush.

Blind Bart held the door for everyone. Once they were all through, Jocelyn asked Jim, "How could you possibly know that?"

Mr. Smee interpreted his answer. "The parrot is right good at puzzles."

CHAPTER THIRTY-SIX

In Which Jocelyn Faces Her Fears

The iron door opened into a long, downward-sloping passageway lined with heaps of skeletal remains.

"I wonder who all these people were," Jocelyn said.

"Begging your pardon, miss, but I imagine I could take a guess. These 'uns here are likely the crew the dear captain hired to build the traps an' bring in his initial load of treasure. Can't have them leaving here and telling tales out of school, now, could he?" Smee gave one an amiable pat. "That captain, he thought of everything, didn't he, Johnny? I wouldn't be surprised if he paid them extra to haunt the place."

Jocelyn shuddered. "I certainly hope not." She picked up her pace. "What do we have to do next, Roger?"

He consulted the logbook. "It merely says 'Face your fear and claim your reward.'"

"'Face your fear . . .'" Jocelyn frowned. "I don't like the sound of that."

"But Cap'n," One-Armed Jack said, "the reward part is good, right? Doesn't that mean we are close?"

Jocelyn couldn't help being cheered by his enthusiasm, though only a little. "I believe it does, Jack. Thank you."

At the end of the corridor the cave split into five tunnels, too long for the lantern light to illuminate their endings. Next to each, trimmed in an ornate gold-leaf frame, hung a painting. Jocelyn brought her lamp close to examine the painting nearest her. The scene within was an empty graveyard, lonely and desolate. The artist had great skill. Looking at it sent a shiver down Jocelyn's spine. She took a small step back, trying not to think about Mr. Smee's talk of hauntings. "Which way, Roger?" she asked.

"There isn't anything else. That was the last of Jim's translation."

"I knew we were close!" Jack said, swinging his cricket bat arm in triumph and clunking Nubbins in the back of the head with it.

"Watch where you swing that thing, Jack, or I'll show you facing your fears!"

Jocelyn silenced the pair with a look. "Jim, was there more on the map? A part you may have forgotten to write down?"

He shook his head.

"All right then, Bart, do you hear anything down any of them?"

Bart stood in front of each passage in turn. "In one I heard the sound of a five-legged female spider doing an excellent job of overcoming her missing limbs. She had nearly finished quite an intricate web."

Jim McCraig beamed, patted his own "wooden" leg, and said something that was likely encouraging toward the spider.

Bart went on. "In another, I heard a soft patter made from the falling tears of a minuscule cave lizard. I was unable to discern the source of his distress—"

"This is all very interesting—" Jocelyn said.

"No, it isn't," Smee muttered.

"But," Jocelyn continued, "not very useful. Could you tell if one of the corridors leads anywhere?"

Blind Bart adjusted his eye patches. "I must sorrow-fully report that none of the various passageways appears to open into any chamber. Perhaps there is a closed door at the end of one. I would surmise the rest are what the French call a *cul-de-sac* and the English call a dead end, though I certainly hope we do not enter one and end up dead. However, with any dangerous undertaking that is a distinct poss—"

"Thank you, Bart," Jocelyn interrupted him again. "This must be another puzzle." She frowned, thinking.

"We are supposed to face our fear. Perhaps each of these paintings shows something to be frightened of. We should choose the one we fear most."

She looked over the rest of the paintings. There was one of a ship at sea about to be overtaken by a great storm, one of a school classroom lorded over by a stern-looking headmaster, one of a sad-looking old man sitting alone, and one of a dolphin.

Yes, a dolphin. You may find it easy to judge, sitting there reasonably safe and comfortable, far from the cave and those paintings, but it was a rather disturbing dolphin.

Jocelyn had no idea which corridor to pick. "All right, men, which do you feel is the most frightening?"

There was a chorus of responses, but none in agreement. After having the paintings described to him, Blind Bart said the ship represented the likelihood of drowning at sea. That was the most terrifying to him. Roger didn't like the looks of being cooped up with that headmaster. Mr. Smee was moved to tears by the frightful idea of growing old alone. Nubbins didn't like the graveyard.

No one liked the dolphin.

Before the argument got out of hand, Jocelyn grabbed a thighbone from a nearby skeleton and rapped it on the wall, demanding attention. The skeleton wobbled, its skull toppling from its neck bones and rolling into the center of the corridor where they stood.

"Men, focus! We can't lose our heads. We need to figure this out, and quickly. Krueger might be in the caves at this very moment!" She paced back and forth in front of the passages. "We could split up, trying each one, but I'm afraid of what would happen should we choose wrong. I could send Meri ahead to scout, but I don't know what it may take to trigger any traps. I nearly lost him once. I won't risk him."

Meriwether hugged her neck, crooning a soft tinkling. Jocelyn brushed him away and continued to pace, thinking. On her next turn, the girl nearly tripped over the skull. She kicked it away in frustration and it rolled down the passage marked by the painting of the headmaster. Before it had moved more than a few feet, a heavy stone fell from the ceiling, crushing the skull to dust beneath it. The stone slowly returned to the ceiling through some unseen rope-and-pulley system, resetting itself for the next person to attempt that passage.

"I'd like to change my vote," Roger said. "I no longer think we should go that way."

Jocelyn grinned, both at her accidental success and his comment. "No, but at least we've narrowed down our choices. Let's see if we can do it again."

They took turns bowling skulls down the remaining passages. Only one set off a trap. A series of long, tall spikes shot up from the ground in the corridor marked with the painting of the graveyard. One spike punched a hole in the skull before they all retracted and disappeared into the ground again. A person unlucky enough to walk that way would have been turned into a pincushion—and not the kind Miss Eliza used to insist Jocelyn embroider.

That left three corridors: the ship, the old man, and the dolphin. "Perhaps we should consider what Captain Hook might have feared," Roger said.

"What do you think, Smee?" Jocelyn asked.

Smee frowned. "He didn't fear a thing, so far as I know. At least, nothing besides the Neverland crocodile."

"I don't think that's it," Jocelyn mused. "The instructions say to face *your* fear, but I don't know which of these he expected everyone to fear. . . ." She trailed off, lost in thought. "I've got it!" she shouted, startling the parrot.

Jocelyn brought her lantern close to the ship painting again. "This isn't just any ship; it's the *Jolly Roger*! The only thing Hook would expect anyone to be afraid of is himself!" The girl looked closer and laughed, even as sudden tears filled her eyes.

"This is definitely the way," Jocelyn said as she wiped her eyes. "Let's go." She strolled confidently down the passage. Roger brought his own lantern close to see what she had discovered. There, behind the wheel of the ship, was painted a miniature Captain Hook. His fist was raised to the sky, and in it he held a tiny blue bottle, labeled COURAGE.

Evie had painted this, leaving a clue that Jocelyn and Roger would understand.

"Come on, men!" Roger called. "The treasure awaits!"

The corridor was rather short, though it twisted off to one side, making the end impossible to detect from the opening. By the time Roger and the crew rounded that corner, Jocelyn was already at a door set in the face of the rock.

The girl pushed, but it did not budge. She looked closely, trying to find a catch or keyhole, but nothing was there. "Spread out," she commanded her men. "Check the walls for anything out of the ordinary, like the *X* that Roger found earlier." Everyone began to search, holding their lanterns high and feeling along the walls. Jocelyn stooped to set hers down in order to use both hands—and there it was.

Near the ground, affixed to the rock wall next to the door, was a small oiled brass symbol. It looked like a hook lying on its side. Jocelyn reached for it, intending to turn it right side up, but at the last moment she changed her mind. She turned the symbol downward so it was not a hook, but a letter *J.* The door whispered a soft snick and swung open a few inches.

Jocelyn had unlocked the treasure chamber.

CHAPTER THIRTY-SEVEN

Hook's Finger

Jocelyn walked through that door and into another world. Or, at least, that was how it felt to her. She was in a chamber, easily ten times larger than the palatial estate she had grown up in. The cave held a subterranean lake—salt water, judging by the briny scent in the air. The lake gave off a faint green glow, helping to illuminate the space. At first glance above, the cavern seemed open to a sky strewn with thousands of stars, though none of the constellations were at all familiar to the girl. She rubbed her eyes and looked again. The stars were . . . moving.

Meriwether shot off her shoulder, flying up to get a closer look.

Roger came and stood beside her, his eyes reflecting the same starry light—and the same wonder.

"What is it?" Jocelyn whispered.

"I . . . I don't know," he responded, "but it may be the most beautiful thin—"

"Worms!" Mr. Smee called out. "Glowworms! They make their home in caves."

Glowworms are not normally found in English caves. I have it on special authority that Captain Hook had these specially imported.

He did love to make an impression, even if his methods were, shall we say, rather unusual.

"Those beautiful starry lights are . . . worms?" Jocelyn asked.

"Not the lights themselves, no," Smee said, cleaning his spectacles to give himself a better view. "It's their, ah, excretions that glow—ain't it, Johnny?"

"Ah, well, that's interesting . . ." Jocelyn said, looking at the cave's beauty in an altogether different light, so to speak. She pulled her eyes away from the glowworm leavings to take in the rest of the view. Clear quartz cave formations grew from the ground and hung from the ceiling like colossal icicles. The crystal caught the light from the lake and the ceiling and magnified it, making their lanterns quite unnecessary. The treasure chamber, to put it mildly, was absolutely stunning.

"But where is the gold, Captain?" Nubbins asked.

Good question.

"Look at that." Roger pointed to the back of the door

they had just come through. More code symbols—the same as on the map—were painted there.

"Jim, can you translate it?" Jocelyn asked. "And Smee, can you translate Jim?"

Jim nodded and went to work. In a moment he said something that Smee interpreted as "The treasure is balanced on Hook's finger."

"What does that mean, some kind of ring?" Roger asked.

"If there was a jewel of some variety on one of his digits, he took it with him inside the crocodile," said Blind Bart, "and, unfortunately for us, it never found its way back out."

"Hook gave us the finger," One-Armed Jack said, flinging his cricket bat around again.

Mr. Smee patted his flesh arm. "Aye. It certainly seems so, Jack. It certainly seems so."

"No, I mean, he has left the finger here for us, with the treasure atop. Look!" He motioned again with his bat, out to the lake.

The largest crystal formation of all grew from the center of the lake. Balanced atop it was a platform of a sort, piled high with something. It was difficult to tell in the dim lighting and from such a distance, but Jocelyn knew it was the treasure. She could feel it.

When Krueger came to try to claim it, she would be waiting.

★ ★ ★

Jocelyn took a moment to gather her resolve. She closed her eyes and breathed in the damp, briny air. She listened to the *drip-drip-drip* of condensation (*oh, please let it be condensation*) falling from the glowing ceiling. She held close all the belief she had in herself, preparing for what she knew would be the final battle between her and Krueger. She hoped it would be enough. She hoped *she* would be enough.

Then she opened her eyes and called her crew around her. They stood at attention, ready to hear her commands. Even Meri looked prepared to fight. He had streaked his face with glowworm waste, making fierce designs and adding a green glow to his usual blue.

"Men," Jocelyn said, "I know you are likely feeling nervous. Twice you have clashed with Krueger's men. Twice you have failed."

"That's our cap'n," Nubbins said with pride. "She's always ready with a pep talk when we need it."

"Quiet, you codfish!" she thundered. "This is no pep talk! This is me commanding you, as your captain, not to fail again." Her voice grew softer. "You've gained experience, fighting Peter and the lost boys. You are trained. You are ready. This time, you will prevail. *We* will prevail."

Pep talk or no, the men stood taller, heartened. It appeared that if Jocelyn believed, they could believe too.

"And now, for my plan," she said. "It's quite simple, really. We will hide and wait for Krueger and his crew to get here. As soon as they come through that door, you attack his men, while I attack him, save my grandfather, and go after the treasure. We have the element of surprise. We won't lose."

The crew hurried to obey Jocelyn's command, hiding themselves within the cave and leaving Roger and Jocelyn alone for the first time since he'd been injured. Alone—save for Meriwether, that is. The fairy settled on Jocelyn's head and stuck out his tongue, also painted glowworm green, at the boy.

Roger ignored Meri and rubbed at his stitches. "I feel awful that I couldn't free your grandfather, but we will get him back. I promise."

Jocelyn was taken aback. "*You* feel awful? I feel awful that I didn't help. I left you to try and get the gibbet open on your own. And because of me, you were nearly killed. Again. First the crocodile, then Krueger. I'm afraid our friendship may be hazardous to your health." She nudged him, gently, with her elbow. "I'm sorry I tried to force you to be unkind to Evie. I should have listened to you all along. I'd much rather be your friend than your captain."

Meri clanged a rude *ding-dong* and Jocelyn shooed him away. He settled onto a small rock ledge and turned his back on the girl, affronted.

"I see no reason why you can't be both, as long as the friend part is the most important." Roger grinned. "And I forgive you. Will you forgive me?"

"For what?"

Roger quickly leaned over and kissed her on the cheek. "For that." He reached up and rumpled her hair, snarling it into an unruly rat's nest atop her head. "And for that." He winked at her.

A flush crept up her cheeks and she smiled. But before she could finish saying, "I'll think about it," Meri had launched himself off the ledge and was flying for Roger's eyes, a trail of white-hot jealousy in his wake. Jocelyn intercepted him, plucking him out of the air and cradling him in her hand. He fought and struggled, but Jocelyn brought him to her mouth and gave him a light kiss on the top of the head—and this time the little man was conscious and able to enjoy it.

He collapsed on her palm in an embarrassed, yet delighted, stupor. Jocelyn and Roger both laughed at poor Meriwether's state. He had come completely undone. She placed him in her pocket and he pulled the flap down over him. Who would have thought he could be bashful?

"Jocelyn," Roger said, going back to their earlier conversation, "did you mean what you said about listening to me?"

She wrinkled her forehead. "Of course I did."

"Well then," he said, "I don't think your plan will work."

She opened her mouth to argue, then closed it again.

It wouldn't hurt to at least hear what he had to say. "Go on," she said.

"If we all rush Krueger and his men, your grandfather could get hurt. I think we need to wait until they separate." He pointed to the edge of the lake. "Look over there."

Jocelyn's eyes fell upon a small dinghy. So that was how Hook intended for the treasure to be reached. "I see it," she said.

"That boat is too small for Krueger and his entire crew. Knowing Krueger, he will want to see the gold before anyone. He'll go out there alone, and that's when you'll attack. The crew can take his men, and if you trust me to do it, I'll save your grandfather."

The only flaw she could see in his plan was that she hadn't thought of it herself, but perhaps that was all right. If she could be a pirate captain who didn't sack ships, perhaps she could also be one who listened to the good advice of her friends.

"I do trust you," she said, feeling the truth of her words. "More than anyone."

"Good." He flashed his just-for-her smile. "I won't let you down, Jocelyn. I'll get Sir Charles. You get Krueger."

Jocelyn nodded. "Tell the men," she said. The girl gave Roger a playful nudge, then lifted off. When Krueger arrived at the gold, he'd find more than he bargained for.

CHAPTER THIRTY-EIGHT

Captain Krueger Is Unbalanced

Jocelyn flew low, marveling over the lake beneath her. She hoped the water's glow was from a less disgusting source than the ceiling's. Yet even if it wasn't, such luminescence was beautiful to behold. The lake appeared to be very deep but was clear all the way to the bottom. She could see more of the crystal formations shining brightly on its floor. The treasure chamber was truly a wondrous sight.

She flew a circuit around the giant crystal "finger" growing out of the lake's center, inspecting it carefully. Given the puzzles and traps her father had set thus far, she felt it unlikely the treasure itself would be free of hazards. The column was thick at the base and tapered to a narrow point, from which a long rope ladder dangled. On the finger's pointed tip, a great wooden platform was precariously balanced. The treasure was even more precariously balanced atop it.

And what a treasure it was! Gold coins, bars, nuggets, and bullion; jewels raw and uncut as well as highly polished gems set into necklaces, rings, crowns, and scepters; statues, fine art, and other antiquities from throughout history; crates bearing such labels as PROPERTY OF THE ALEXANDRIA PUBLIC LIBRARY and IF FOUND, PLEASE RETURN TO ATLANTIS—and those were simply the things Jocelyn could see. There were treasures untold buried within the pile.

All of it was arranged with precision on the platform, the only space free of treasure being near the center. That area was several feet in diameter and surrounded an open hatch in the platform's floor through which the ladder could be accessed. It was in that bare space that Jocelyn landed.

The platform tilted ever so slightly under her feet, and Jocelyn recognized genius in the design. If the weight atop it were to shift dramatically, the entire platform would tip, dumping the treasure into the lake. As a result, only small, carefully chosen amounts could be removed at once. Stealing the treasure would take weeks of painstaking effort.

She heard splashing from below. Krueger had arrived. She could see him, illuminated by the water, though she was certain he would be unable to see her in the dimmer light at the top of the platform. A second man pulled awkwardly on the oars. Jocelyn pulled her spyglass and brought it to her eye. It was her grandfather!

Jocelyn waited, impatiently. She tried to pass the time by thinking of what she would say when she met Krueger for what she hoped would be the last time. It seemed to take forever for Sir Charles to pilot the little boat, and longer still for Captain Krueger to scale the rope ladder. He was less than halfway up when she was suddenly overcome with doubts. What if she failed again?

A shadow crossed over the platform, interrupting her thoughts; then Roger was floating quietly beside her. He stooped, running his fingers gently through a pile of coins. The platform swayed a fraction of an inch. "Amazing," he whispered. "Good thing you can fly." He winked, then grew serious. "As soon as Krueger reaches the top, I'll row your grandfather to safety."

Jocelyn's hands felt clammy. "He will never stop coming after us. Not unless I defeat him."

"You will," Roger said.

"I wish you had another bottle of courage on you. I could use a little extra belief in myself."

He winked at her. "You can borrow some of mine. I believe in you."

Jocelyn was about to reply in kind, when she saw Krueger's hands grip the edge of the hatch. He had made it up the ladder. Silent as an owl, Roger dove toward the little boat, but Jocelyn did not watch. She kept her eyes trained on Krueger.

His head poked up through the hole, his ruined nose whistling with his exerted breathing. Though she stood mere feet from him, he did not notice the girl. He only had eyes for those mountains of gold. Jocelyn had never seen such a look of naked greed. He pulled himself through the hatch and gingerly approached the treasure, careful not to upset the balance of the platform. Krueger stooped and grabbed a coin, caressing it, before placing it in his pocket.

"Thief!" Jocelyn pointed her sword and took a tentative step toward him, the floor shifting slightly beneath their feet.

If Krueger was startled by her, he made no sign of it. He drew his sword and sneered.

Jocelyn gave her prepared speech. "The crocodile stole my father from me. You know what its reward was. You have stolen my grandfather and have attempted to steal this treasure, which is rightfully mine. Would you care to experience the same fate?"

"You silly, stupid child. Pirates are thieves! That's what we do. You cannot fault me for that any more than you can fault a fish for swimming. Do you expect to punish every one of them?" He lunged with his sword, causing the platform to tip. He quickly stepped back to balance it.

"No," Jocelyn said. "Just you. And not all pirates turn thief. I have not." Jocelyn leaped toward him, but instead of retreating, or parrying the blow, Krueger stepped into it, clearly more concerned with keeping the platform balanced than with his own life. Jocelyn's sword grazed his cheek, adding a new cut to his already disfigured face.

He wiped the blood with the back of his hand. "Then you are no pirate! Refusing to steal goes against the Code."

"I get to decide what I will be! I make my own code. Now throw down your weapons or I will dump this treasure to the bottom of the lake, where it will live, forever in sight of anyone who comes to this chamber, yet impossible to recover." She took a step away from the man, the floor tilting in her direction.

Krueger took a hurried step back as well, balancing the platform once more. "You miserable brat. If only I had killed you when I had the chance!" He pulled his flintlock pistol and leveled it at her.

"I wouldn't do that if I were you," Jocelyn chided.

He didn't answer, but neither did he fire.

"What's the matter? You're not curious as to why?" Jocelyn took another step backward, forcing him to do the same. "You don't have to ask. I'll tell you anyway. First, firearms are inelegant. Any pirate worth his salt depends on blade over bullet. Second, if you shoot me, I could fall off the platform. Do you think you can make it back to the center in time?"

"How about we try and see?" He cocked the pistol.

"All right then, if you want to be stranded up here. You see, I might not fall off the platform. I might fall where I stand. If I do that, your only options are to stay where you are and hope one of your men will be smart enough to figure out how to rescue you, or run for the hatch and lose all the gold."

The pistol shook in his trembling hand. He gnashed his foul, pointy teeth so hard he injured his gums. Blood ran from his mouth, mingling with what still flowed from his cheek, before dripping off his chin. He did not notice. "This gold is mine!" he raged. "Mine!"

Jocelyn chanced a glance toward the shore. It was too far for her to see her crew. She hoped they had been able to subdue Krueger's men. She was able to make out the dark silhouette of a small boat rowing rapidly away from the finger. Her grandfather was safe. It was time to end this. "Never mind. As I can see that Sir Charles is no longer your captive, I think you shan't have the gold after all."

Jocelyn did not know how unwise it was to taunt a man who had just discovered he had nothing to lose. He pulled the trigger. The ball raced toward the girl, but Krueger's aim was off by a fraction of an inch. The bullet crashed into a golden statue of a young satyr that stood near her. The figure fell as if killed by the pirate's gun, upsetting the balance of the platform again.

Krueger shuffled backward, all the way to the edge of the platform, but it still tilted in Jocelyn's direction. The treasure shifted, and a delicate balance was held, but one small move by either Krueger or Jocelyn would send the entire hoard plummeting. The pair locked eyes. Krueger's were filled with rage and defeat.

"Jocelyn!" Roger flew toward them. "I heard a shot. Are you all right?"

Krueger aimed again, this time at Roger. No treasure was worth the lives of those she cared for. Jocelyn lifted from the platform in flight. It tilted sharply in Krueger's direction; he had no time to balance it again. The pirate dropped his flintlock and fell, barely catching the edge of the platform as he went over. A waterfall of treasure cascaded past him, slowly at first, then faster, plummeting to the lake below.

Jocelyn took pity on him. "Roger, help me!" she shouted.

They hovered above the man, reaching for him. "Give me your hand," she said. "We'll fly you to the shore!"

Krueger locked his dark, soulless eyes on Jocelyn. They were filled with inhuman rage. Jocelyn recoiled. The man turned his head toward the shower of gold running past

him. A strangled howl burst from his throat. He gave the girl one last hateful look, then simply let go.

Even as he fell, Captain Krueger reached for the gold, snatching a handful of coins from midair and clutching them to his chest. A look of peace came over him just before he hit the water.

Captain Krueger would lie forevermore in a watery tomb, buried under the greatest treasure ever amassed.

CHAPTER THIRTY-NINE

Coming Home

It occasionally takes losing something important to help you realize what kind of person you are. For example, if I were to take your little finger, you might be sad, but if you were a person of any quality you would dwell on the nine you had left—and how you might use them to seek your revenge.

The last coin rolled from the platform, which was now nearly vertical, yet still attached by some unseen means to the stone finger. Once the water settled, Jocelyn could see the mountain of gold and jewels far, far beneath its surface—too deep for her to ever recover. So Krueger had the gold after all, and would keep it forever, though what happiness it would bring his corpse, she couldn't guess.

The treasure mattered far less than she had thought it might. Jocelyn had her grandfather, her crew, and her best friend. She felt rich.

Those warm feelings didn't last. They were replaced by fear.

The tilted platform had set off Hook's last trap, insuring that any thieves in his treasure chamber would stay there forever. The walls rumbled, casting glowworms from the sky like stars hurtling from heaven. A giant boulder dropped, sealing off the doorway from which they had entered the chamber.

Jocelyn flew through the air, her eyes darting to and fro, searching for an alternate way out. The sound of grinding stone filled her ears, and more boulders dropped, these opening at least a dozen conduits around the edges of the chamber, each spewing a great rushing force of water into the lake. It quickly began to rise. Her crew and her grandfather—along with Krueger's men, stripped of their weapons—stood scattered near the shore of the rising lake. Panic etched their faces.

"Roger!" the girl cried. "Gather everyone together and have them prepared to move. I'll find us a way out!"

But no way presented itself. It appeared that after all they had been through, their adventure would end here. They would drown.

Who puts a lake inside a cave anyway! Her mind caught

on that idea. How *did* the water get inside the cave? There had to be an underground spring of some sort. And if water could get in through it, maybe they could get out the same way. She flew back and shouted her hunch over the rushing water.

She pointed at what she hoped was their escape. Near the far edge, under the water, along the rock wall, was a place that was darker than the rest. It was a long shot, but it was their only one. The girl made sure Meriwether was still firmly tucked away in her pocket, and told him to hold his breath. Jocelyn grabbed her grandfather's hand, wishing she had time for a proper reunion, and dove into the rapidly rising lake. Roger, her crew, and Krueger's defeated pirates followed. Even Blind Bart, with his lifelong terror of the water, did not hesitate to dive in. He would apparently rather drown attempting to save himself than drown without hope.

Jocelyn dove deep, then deeper, kicking for where the water was darkest. Sir Charles proved to be a surprisingly adept swimmer and helped to propel them along. They found the entrance to an underwater tunnel and fought against the current to enter. Jocelyn hoped the passage would not be longer than their air supply.

Just as she felt all was lost, the tunnel widened and they were out. The pair kicked toward the surface. They broke through, and Jocelyn took a shuddery breath. The first thing she noticed was the starry sky—real stars, not worm excretions. The second thing she noticed was the bright smile under Sir Charles's drooping mustache. She had rescued him. She was home.

They climbed, dripping wet from the waves, onto the beach. Both her crew and Krueger's followed. Jocelyn had a moment of wild panic when she didn't see Blind Bart, but presently he came along, joining them on the sand.

"Sorry, Captain. After years of being held back by a fear of the sea, I felt I was overdue for a victory lap! The briny deep had me in her clutches, but she could not claim me!"

Jocelyn laughed in relief. Her men were all accounted for, Krueger was no longer a threat, she and Roger had made up, and she had her grandfather back. The girl threw her arms around him.

Sir Charles pulled back and looked at her. "I can't believe what I saw in there. I don't know what to say about this. A young lady such as yourself, leading a band of . . . of . . ." He looked around at her crew. "Thieves and miscreants . . ."

Nubbins tipped his hat. "Thank you!"

Sir Charles spoke over him. "And fighting. I saw you up there. I'm sure you didn't learn swordplay at the school I sent you to."

Jocelyn scowled. She hadn't dared hope her grandfather would be proud of her, but she *had* rescued him. Shouldn't that have gotten her out of a scolding?

He went on. "I'm speechless, really." (For a speechless person, he certainly had a lot to say.) "I can't help but wonder what your mother would think." Jocelyn lifted her chin, defiance preparing to spill from her lips, but she bit it back when she heard, "I imagine, knowing her, she would be quite as proud as I am."

"What?" Jocelyn wasn't sure she had heard correctly.

"Your actions were unconventional, to say the least, but you did what needed to be done and you did it beautifully." He turned to Roger. "You are not the friend I would have chosen for my granddaughter. However, it appears that she knows better than I." He stuck out his hand. "You will be a fine man one day. I hope you will allow me the honor of knowing you."

Roger took his hand and shook it, looking the man in the eye. "Yes, sir. If you will do the same."

Mr. Smee pointed out the lights of a ship on the sea. "*Calypso's Nightmare* is moored out there, with no captain to care for her." He dabbed at his eyes with his wet shirttail. "I do hate to see a ship abandoned."

Roger grinned at Jocelyn. "How would you feel about changing your title from captain to admiral? You could have two ships in your fleet."

She sadly shook her head. "I wish I could, but I'm afraid my adventuring days may be over. I could never sack an innocent ship, but without some gold, I can't outfit and supply one ship, let alone two." The girl turned her head back toward the sea. "The treasure chamber is surely flooded now. My father's gold is lost. If only I had grabbed some when I had the chance."

"Yeah. But trying to carry a bunch of gold would have made it impossible to swim. Unless"—he winked—"you happened to have pockets."

Roger started turning out the many pockets of his pants, emptying their contents in the sand. Gold pieces, pearl necklaces, jewels, even a diamond the size of a goose egg. He had smuggled a small fortune out in his wonderful pockets.

"I'm turning out to be quite a good thief," he said. "I happened to snag a bit even before Krueger made it to the platform. Now, I'm no expert on treasure, but I'm sure there is enough here for us to sail off on at least a few more adventures. We could explore new lands, just like Magellan"—he saluted—"Admiral Hook."

Jocelyn threw her arms around Roger and kissed him on the cheek. "That sounds splendid, Roger!"

Sir Charles cleared his throat. Jocelyn had forgotten he was there. Her face burned, but she did not bother to hide her grin.

"Young lady," her grandfather said, "I have one request."

"Yes, Grandfather?"

"Before you go off on all this adventuring, please sail me home. I have had enough adventure and am ready for my fire and slippers, hot tea, and a nice bowl of porridge."

Jocelyn grinned, remembering the porridge fight she had had with Roger and Evie. Roger must have been thinking the same thing, for he said, "Porridge, sir? Ah, so you must be as skilled in exotic weaponry as your progeny."

The old man looked on in bemused consternation as the pair of children collapsed together in hysterical giggles on the beach.

Mr. Smee shook his head. "Beggin' your pardon, sir, but I don't understand it neither. Then again, not everyone can be as sound of mind as you, me, and Johnny Corkscrew." He gave his sword a loving pat. "Isn't that right?"

Sir Charles shook his head. "Quite so, I imagine, quite so."

And that is the tale of how Jocelyn became best friends with her mother when the woman was yet a girl, defeated an evil foe, rescued her grandfather, fought and made up with her other best friend, and found, then lost, the greatest treasure known to man (but did not mind it so much after all). Good-bye.

★ ★ ★

Of course, Jocelyn's story doesn't end here. It's not so much that her tale has come to an end as that my patience has. Her life and adventures went on and on and on, but this is as good a place as any to stop.

Get Out

CHAPTER FORTY

In Which This Tale Draws to a Close

You are harder to get rid of than lice in my sister's mustache. More verminous, too.

All right, all right, I will tell a bit more. But you must know that when I am finished with the tale, I will also be finished with you—by any means necessary.

Certainly there was a celebration once they all made it back to the *Hook's Revenge*. I think everyone was a bit surprised to find that Gentleman Starkey had not taken the opportunity to simply make off with the ship, though no one was more surprised than Starkey himself. In gratitude, Jocelyn offered him captainship of the *Calypso's Nightmare* under her command as admiral. He agreed, and signed on the now-unemployed crew of the late Captain Krueger under his leadership.

As for Starkey, that moment reversed in him a lifelong-held belief that *all* children were terrible. No, from that day on, he knew the truth. Though most were noisy, sticky, whiny little blighters, Jocelyn was . . . less so.

Truth be told, she had already offered the captainship to Roger but had been turned down. It seemed the boy preferred to stay close to her. And he didn't mind being under the girl's direct command, so long as she agreed to listen his ideas, at least a portion of the time.

Roger returned her father's logbook and Jocelyn flipped to a new page. She titled it *Admiral Hook's Pirate Code*. The entry was this: *There is more than one way to be a real pirate.*

She slipped the book back into her pocket and shouted, "As commanding officer, I demand one thing of you all tonight!" The men awaited her instructions. "Enjoy yourselves!"

Nubbins crafted an amazing meal from the galley stores—even without a crepe pan. The party enjoyed their feast to the sounds of Jim McCraig and his parrot singing a completely comprehensible duet. Jocelyn had never gotten over how easy it was to understand the man while he sang. She now marveled that the parrot had the same quality.

One-Armed Jack surprised everyone by withdrawing yet another prosthetic from under his shirt. No, not another piece of kitchen gear or sporting equipment, but a proper arm of leather and steel. "I just couldn't help myself," he said, "when I saw it in the cave. It spoke to me. Besides, that skeleton in the puzzle room wasn't getting much use out of it."

Jocelyn merely laughed and helped him tie it on.

Jack waved it around as menacingly as he was able. (Not very.) Having had the original bitten off by the Neverland crocodile was impressive enough on its own, but to then be the bearer of a new claw hand, stolen off the remains of a pirate who had been killed by the great Captain Hook himself? It was almost too much. Truly, Jack was in danger of becoming a living legend, at least to himself.

Not everyone could have even a fraction of that luck. Jim McCraig's fortunes took a turn for the worse when, during a break from their singing, his parrot plucked the sliver from Jim's big toe, effectively removing his wooden leg. His complaints were long, loud, and, as to be expected, unintelligible.

Sir Charles spent the evening discussing matters of import, and port wine, with both Mr. Smee and Gentleman Starkey, thrilled to find that both men were, like himself, aficionados of the finer things in life.

In a night filled with surprise and amazement, perhaps the most dramatic moment came when Blind Bart stood and declared, "After all the aquatic exercise tonight, I have triumphed over my intense phobia of the water. Indeed, I feel I need no longer rely on my eye patches for protection."

For the first time since any of them had known the man, he uncovered his eyes and blinked upon the world. At that very moment, however, poor Meriwether—who seemed to have contracted a cold from becoming too damp—broke forth with a mighty sneeze. A shower of fairy dust sprayed Bart in his tender, wondering eyes. To hear him scream, the pain must have been something like looking into the heart of a thousand blazing suns. He firmly clapped his patches back over both eyes and never could be prevailed on to remove them again.

Jocelyn took Meriwether to her cabin and fed him a thimbleful of Nubbins's best cold-cure soup. He drank it up and made a nest in her hair. The girl sat quietly on the bed, her fingers playing over her locket, thinking of her mother. She missed her.

Jocelyn pulled the logbook from her pocket again and opened to the first page. She ran her fingers over the note Evie had scrawled just before leaving the Neverland. It had all happened so fast, Jocelyn felt that she hadn't gotten to say a proper good-bye. But even if there had been more time, it would have been impossible.

Some good-byes are altogether improper—indecent, even.

The girl's musings were interrupted by another sneeze from Meriwether, and a shower of fairy dust that coated the book. Jocelyn went to wipe it on her sleeve but pulled back, wide-eyed. Glowing words appeared, floating to the surface of the page.

> Dear Jocelyn,
>
> Oh, how I wish you were here to talk to in person. I'd love to tell you all about the things that are happening in my life, and hear about what is happening in yours. Who else can I speak to of all this? Instead, I'll talk to this diary, which I know you will one day find. (I had it embossed with J. H., for Jocelyn Hook.)
>
> I saw him tonight, Jocelyn: Captain Hook—James. He was talking to Gentleman Starkey in the gardens, but I pretended not to notice. Instead, I let drop the fact that my father has bought a new ship and intends to send me on a pleasure cruise. It is my hope that we will meet at last, for how could a pirate resist a new ship?

The girl turned the page, plucked Meri from her head, and shook him over the diary. More entries appeared, detailing the very exciting adventures of a young woman experiencing first love. Jocelyn read them all—only slightly disgusted at the mushy parts. She missed her mother all over again, but felt grateful for another chance to hear her voice.

The final entry was short. It read:

> Dear Jocelyn,
> My adventures are drawing to a close. Yours are about to begin. I have no regrets.
> Love, Mother

Jocelyn thought back on their adventure together. She had made mistakes, to be sure, but things had worked out as they were meant to. And who knew, perhaps she would see Evie again, somewhere, somewhen. The Neverland was filled with impossible things, after all. It was conceivable that other places were as well.

The girl snuggled down into her bed and drifted off to sleep, rocked by ocean waves in uncharted seas. Roger had suggested that once they returned Sir Charles to his home, they should set a course for someplace altogether new, in neither England nor the Neverland, and Jocelyn had agreed. They would let the wind decide.

The girl was excited for what the next day might bring—and the day after that. Her whole life was ahead of her, thrilling experiences waiting just over the horizon. She would meet them as they came. Growing up would be a grand adventure.

The End

ANSWER TO THE SKELETON RIDDLE

ACKNOWLEDGMENTS

I am extremely grateful to the many people who have helped me continue Jocelyn's adventures. Raising my mug of grog (or rather, root-grog) to each and every one of you.

Especial gratitude to:

Keith and Chenowa Egawa for reading and advice on my Tiger Lily chapters. I also owe a debt of gratitude to Gary Dawes and Loretta Three Irons in the Crow Tribe Education Department. I very much wanted to write Tiger Lily and her people sensitively and with respect. If I have made any errors, the fault is mine.

My fearless editor, Rotem "Mo the Wild Spaniard" Moscovich. It is a joy to be edited by you. Additional thanks to Mary Ann Zissimos, Julie Moody, Karen Sherman, Tyler Nevins, and the rest of the black-hearted rogues at Disney • Hyperion.

John Hendrix, a most talented rapscallion, who surely mixed his ink with blood and sweat (most likely his own) in creating this book's beautiful artwork and cover.

Emma "Emmy Two-Buckle" Trevayne, Claire "Silver-tongue" Legrand, Black Becky Albertali the Oreo Plunderer, and Annie "Big-Fat-Ugly-Bug-Face-Baby-Eating" (and fan of *Muppet Treasure Island*) Cechini for the sanity-saving calls, texts, FaceTimes, and Gchats. I'd sail with you swashbucklingly fierce ladies anywhere.

Brooks "Blue-Bearded Bartleby" Sherman, a true scoundrel and blaggard. Thank you for always believing I can, and reminding me when I forget.

One-Eyed Walt for making me better at everything I do. Is it too corny to say I'm thrilled to have you as both my co-captain and first mate? It is? Don't care. I love you.

Red-Handed Hannah. It's such a privilege to be both your mother and your friend. Thank you for teaching me and inspiring me every day. Sorry about the giant hair-bows. (Not sorry.)

All the indie booksellers who have championed *Hook's Revenge*, particularly those that have hosted me and my shenanigans: The Book Bin in Salem, Oregon; Powell's Books, A Children's Place Bookstore, and Green Bean Books in Portland, Oregon; Rediscovered Books in Boise, Idaho; Tattered Cover in Denver, Colorado; Mockingbird Books in Seattle, Washington; and The King's English in Salt Lake City, Utah.

Additional gratitude to the Salem Public Library—

which is both my childhood and current library—for lending books and support, and for so often providing me a quiet place to write.

And to you, dear reader. Thank you for joining me here again.

ARRRRRR!

THE KEY TO THE CODE